Four White Roses

by

Judy Ann Davis

Four White Roses

Cover Art by *Kim Mendoza*

The Wild Rose Press, Inc.
PO Box 708
Adams Basin, NY 14410-0708
Visit us at www.thewildrosepress.com

Publishing History
First Fantasy Rose Edition, 2017
Print ISBN 978-1-5092-1456-3
Digital ISBN 978-1-5092-1457-0

Published in the United States of America

He looked toward the porch in the dying light and sighed. "I don't know what to do with this monstrosity. No one seems interested in buying it. No one wants to live in it. It's like a giant worthless gift. Maintenance costs exceed its usefulness. The heating bill is enormous. I have to pay to get the grass mowed in the summer and the snow shoveled in the winter." He shrugged his shoulders in resignation and stared down the street where the street lights had come on. Their globes looked like Japanese lanterns floating in the air. His gaze found hers again. His expression was miserable and grim.

Torrie tipped her ball cap up and gave a cursory glance at the house. She pursed her lips and fell silent. Should she tell him the truth? Or should she wait until he and Estella were settled in? The knowledge twisted and turned inside her. As much as she hated rumors, she hated lies even more. There were enough of both of them flying around town...and some were about her. What to do? Finally, she flung her hands up in despair.

"Of course no one wants to buy it, Richard Lee," she uttered with unmistakable candor. "I have it through reliable sources your grandmother's house is haunted."

Praise for Judy Ann Davis

"*FOUR WHITE ROSES* is full of wonderfully enchanting characters who stay with you long after you finish reading the book."

~Nicole Fitton, author of All Tomorrow's Parties

~*~

"The writing is beautifully descriptive with a touch of wry humor. In the first paragraph, we meet quite a character, and each succeeding 'actor' to take the stage is as lifelike and well-developed. The characters make any novel, and the author has characterization down to an art."

~Linda Nightingale, author of
Morgan D'Arcy: A Vampyre Rhapsody

Dedication

Producing a novel requires a collaborative effort.
I am most grateful to some talented people
who have helped me along the way.
~*~
Many thanks to Suzanne Webster,
a long-time friend, who is my final draft reader and
who suggests corrections and changes;
and Kinan Werdski,
editor at the Wild Rose Press, Inc.
who never ceases to amaze me
with her outstanding editorial talents.
~*~
I am also blessed to have the support of
my husband, family, neighbors, friends,
community members, and fans.
~*~
To you all—I give you my heartfelt thanks.
You keep my passion for writing alive.

Chapter One

Hands crossed at his chest, Richard Lee Redman leaned against the fender of his recently purchased SUV and peered through the fading daylight at the road sign along the berm where he had stopped. No, not where he had stopped. Where the piece of worthless junk he was driving had died.

"Stupid, stupid, stupid." He berated himself aloud and raked his hand through his already disheveled hair. Why had he thought his trip from Dallas, Texas, to Hickory Valley, Pennsylvania, would be easy? Before he even turned the key in the blasted vehicle, the gods of rusty nuts and bolts had already determined it needed to go straight to the great junkyard in the sky. Unfortunately, they hadn't sent him the message.

Good condition. Reliable—with many more miles left in her, the car salesman had spewed as Rich scribbled his name on the purchase agreement. Too bad those many more miles didn't include the last ten to his destination, as the road sign so aptly indicated.

Rich gave the vehicle a hostile glare and kicked the front tire with the toe of his Italian leather driving mocs. How could he have been so naïve? He was thirty-seven years old. And a lawyer, to boot. Old enough to know when he was being taken by a sweet-talking, over-zealous car salesman. He should have never rushed through a decision. He knew better. But it had the room he needed, the price had sure been right, and the salesman had promised to push the paperwork through in record time.

He turned and glanced through the back seat window where his eight-year-old daughter, Estella, was sleeping. The trip had been tiring, and she needed the rest. And she was one of the reasons he decided to purchase a larger vehicle. He didn't want her to agonize over which of her favorite toys or clothes she could take for the month-long stay. Being a single dad wasn't an easy job. It had taken him days to gather up and pack all Estella's can't-live-without items and necessities— like the garbage bag full of stuffed animals riding shotgun in the passenger's seat.

Removing his cellphone from his pocket, he dialed his real estate agent and family friend, Marlene Hess, who lived in Hickory Valley and had agreed to open up his grandmother's house and get it ready for his arrival. The homestead, dating back to the early 1900s, had a barn, some sheds, and over a hundred acres of land in meadows and forests.

He had requested she arrange to have the electricity and cable turned on and to stock the house with only a few provisions, like breakfast food, coffee, and clean sheets and towels, just enough to get them through the night and morning until he could grocery shop and get his bearings. Two years ago, when Rich had learned of his Grandmother Gertrude's death, he had flown to Pennsylvania for the funeral and had locked up the house, handing the keys over to Marlene to rent, to offer it as a lease-to-buy, or to concoct any kind of deal to keep it occupied, heated, and off his long list of problems to solve.

Marlene answered on the first ring.

"This vintage piece of scrap iron I'm driving just broke down ten miles outside town along Route 6," he said brusquely. "And the dang mosquitoes are starting to bite."

"Well, hello to you, too, Richard Lee Junior," Marlene said. "I warned you. That's what happens when you buy a used car from those unscrupulous Texans. Bet he was wearing a big, shiny belt buckle and one of those fancy white Stetsons while he spieled, 'Such a deal I have for you!' How's Estella?"

"Sleeping. Thankfully, I don't have to hear for the one-thousand-sixty-fifth time, 'Are we there yet?'" And yes, he thought to himself, the salesman *was* wearing a white hat and a rather large belt buckle while crowing about the stupendous deal he had to offer.

Marlene laughed. "Good to see your humor hasn't been destroyed by a little setback. Here, let me get you the number for the local towing company. It's Henry's Garage off Main Street. Same garage and towing service that was around when you were a kid. Only Henry's much older now."

"Ancient, you mean."

"That too." She spouted off a series of numbers. "Call me back if you hit a snag, and I'll see what I can do."

"Thanks, Marlene. Sorry for bothering you."

"No bother. It's why you hired me. Dinner and milk are in the refrigerator. Bread is in the bread box. I'll stop over in an hour or so and drop off a can of coffee and see what else you might need. I'll bring the unopened letter from your grandmother we talked about." She paused. "Try to have a nice evening,

Richard."

"Yeah, easy for you to say," he muttered under his breath as she clicked off. "You aren't the one stranded in the middle of nowhere." Around him, tiny frogs argued in the nearby wetlands before darkness fell. Somewhere far off, a lone hawk emitted a series of hoarse screams as it began its nightly hunt.

Hoping the garage hadn't closed for the day, Rich punched in the local number on his cellphone.

A cheery female voice answered on the first ring, "Hello, Henry's Garage and Towing Center. We tow, so you can go. How can I help you?"

"I need a tow truck out on east Route 6, about ten miles from town, right at the sign at the head of the valley," Rich said curtly. "My old SUV just gave up its last breath and what it really needs is last rites."

"I'm sorry, sir, but Henry and his crew are off for the day at a fishing tournament in the next town. If you lock your car and leave your keys in the drop box beside the garage door with a note, they'll pick it up in the morning."

Lock it and leave the keys in town? Rich laughed cynically as he simultaneously squeezed the phone in his hand and swallowed to keep his irritation under control. He forced himself to take a deep, cleansing breath and bite back the smart remark materializing in his head. *Stay calm. Be nice,* he told himself. *Remember, you are stranded.*

He swatted at a persistent mosquito hovering above his head and asked, "And please tell me, how do I get to the garage with a trunk full of suitcases and a sleeping kid?"

"Well, Mike's Taxi Service is not available either

since Big Mike is at the fishing tournament, too." The woman paused and hummed a merry tune under her breath. She had a soft, melodic voice. "I could pick you up and drive you to your destination as long as it's in Hickory Valley. It'll take a few minutes since I have to lock up the shop here." She paused again. "You said ten miles east? And the name is…?"

"Richard Lee Redman."

"Oh, brother." She heaved a long audible sigh. "My lucky day. The prodigal grandson returns." Before Rich could ask her what she meant by the remark, she hung up.

Minutes later, he was even more surprised to see a ragged-looking pickup come chugging up the road. It looked worse than the SUV. It was dirty gray and had dented, mismatched fenders, one painted a dark green and the other sprayed with an ugly brown primer. It coughed and sputtered like it had just smoked a pack of cigarettes as it pulled up behind his vehicle.

The driver cut the engine, shoved a shoulder against the dented, sticky door and jiggled the handle before it flew open and she jumped down. She was a lithe woman of average height and wore paint-splattered coveralls swamping her thin frame. Both the sleeves and pant legs had been rolled up several times. Long slim fingers with blue nail polish peeked out from the sleeves, and chunky, brown, steel-toed work boots poked out from each leg opening. Her blonde hair, closer to white than yellow, was scraped back from her face in a ponytail and trailed out from the back of a frayed red ball cap with the logo: *Henry's Garage—We Tow, So You Can Go.*

"You're very fortunate, Richard Lee Redman. I

was just about to close up Henry's shop and head home." She approached the car and stood, hands on her hips, as she openly surveyed him from head to toe, smirking as her gaze traveled from his Ray-Ban sunglasses flipped up on his head to his blue silk dress shirt to his alligator belt and then on down to his designer slacks and Italian leather driving mocs.

"What…what are you doing?" she asked, her delicate forehead wrinkled. "A photo shoot for GQ in Hickory Valley?" Not bothering to hide her cynical tone, she added, "You do know you're in rural Pennsylvania?"

"Very funny. Don't remind me." Rich stared at her. She was incredibly beautiful despite the baggy coveralls and scuffed work boots. Her heart-shaped face, dotted with a light sprinkling of freckles across her cheeks, and her pale hair reminded him of someone he should know—someone from the past. Her voice was familiar, and he was certain if he had the time to do a memory search, he'd come up with her name. But it was her eyes that drew him in like magnets. They were neither green nor blue, but a stunning and irresistible aquamarine, and as he gazed into those eyes, a sharp sense of attraction caught him by surprise. He searched his brain again. "Should I know you?" he asked. "You obviously have me at a disadvantage from the simpering look on your face."

She laughed, those devastating eyes twinkling. "Torrine Larson. I'm Elsa Larson's younger sister. I was five years behind you in school."

"Little Torrie Larson?" He studied her, baffled. "The wily kid who used to sucker us into playing any game involving a ball and then beat the pants off us?"

"Yep, that's me. My dad said he almost went broke buying sports equipment for my three brothers and me." She paused, then sighed. "But eventually, we all must grow up, Richard Lee. So you won't be surprised when I tell you I recently took up golf instead of competitive team sports. Now I push around a clumsy bag of clubs. We all have our burdens to bear, don't we?" A smile softened her face, and she pointed to the rear of his vehicle. "Well, let's get all your paraphernalia and suitcases loaded and haul you off to your grandmother's house." With grace and determination, she moved to the SUV, popped the back hatch, and started dragging the suitcases out.

"Wait, I can help." Rich jumped forward. "And please, call me Rich." They reached for the same suitcase and their hands collided. His gray eyes met her aquamarine ones, and his skin tingled where they had touched. She yanked her hand away.

"I doubt all of these will fit in the cab. Are we using the truck bed?"

"That's the plan." She started toward the pickup with a suitcase and duffle bag.

"But your truck looks like it was hauling"—he paused and tried to resist saying junk, but it flew past this lips anyway—"junk. No offense, but everything is going to get dusty on the drive in."

"It's not my truck. It's Henry's. And it was hauling junk. It's made to haul junk." Torrie stopped, set the luggage on the road, and held up a hand. "The way I see it, you have two choices." She stabbed the air with her index finger. "One—take what you need for the night and anything else that will fit in the cab with you and your daughter and lock the rest up. Or, two"—another

7

finger pointed skyward—"we take it all, and you don't have to worry about getting it later tomorrow at the garage. Your call. If you're worried your designer luggage will get dirty or scratched, let me point out commercial flying leaves a lot to be desired in this day and age, at least where dents, scuff marks, and scratches on luggage are concerned. I promise I'll drive slow. No bouncing. No quick turns. No dirt roads. I promise."

"I don't think this piece of crap could go fast or make a quick turn," Rich muttered under his breath.

"Says the man who needs a ride because his piece of crap died." Torrie peered around at the SUV side window and tilted her head toward it. "It looks like your daughter's awake. You'd better see to her while I transfer this load. Looks like you brought enough to stay until Christmas."

He glanced at her and thought he heard a slight hint of sarcasm in her voice, but her face was impassive, focused on expertly transferring his belongings. "Well, I wasn't quite sure what clothes or toys Estella might need, so I dumped in as much as would fit," he admitted sheepishly. He turned and jogged toward his vehicle, calling over his shoulder, "Will you please make sure my computer is stowed in the cab?"

****

Torrie looked at the luggage and boxes piled high to the SUV's ceiling and shook her head in disbelief. "No wonder this poor thing died," she mumbled. "It's a miracle the suspension held under the weight." She pushed aside two boxes to grab another bag, realized he was hauling water, and smirked. *Three cases of bottled water? What was he thinking? We drink from a creek? We don't have grocery stores?* She chuckled, but within minutes she had efficiently loaded the pickup bed. She waited by the driver's door while Rich scooped up his daughter, a stuffed purple giraffe, and a pink backpack, and carried them to the passenger side.

"Hi," Torrie said, hopping in and smiling at the little girl as Rich positioned her between them on the front seat, shut his door, and fastened their seatbelts. "My name is Torrie. What's yours?"

"Estella," the little girl said through a yawn. Her silky, ink-black hair was pulled away from her little delicate face with a striped pink headband matching her cotton sundress. In her hands, she clutched a Ramona Quimby book. She looked over at her father with big brown eyes framed in long dark lashes. "Are we there yet? I'm getting hungry."

Rich winced. "Almost. Just a few more miles. Our car broke down while you were sleeping, and Ms. Larson was kind enough to give us a ride to town."

Estella nodded and rubbed her eyes, then ran a hand over the seat and peered at it. "You have a dog, don't you?" she asked. "It has light brown hair. What's his name?"

Eyes trained on the road, Torrie nodded. The child was observant. "Yes. Henry of Henry's Garage has a golden retriever named Ratchet. Actually, three of us take care of him. During the day, he stays at the garage, but goes home with Henry at night. My brother and I take turns making sure he's fed, has water, and sees the vet."

"I always wanted a dog," the little girl admitted, "but Daddy said dogs are hard to take care of in the city. They need room to run and play."

When Torrie glanced at Rich, he gave her a

withered look that begged, *Please don't go there. This topic has been sorely overworked.*

"Do you work at the garage?" Estella asked, oblivious to the silent discourse between the grown-ups.

"I sometimes help out, but not with fixing the cars or trucks. I help with the paperwork. But today, I took a day off from my full-time job because I promised the owner I'd cover for him while he and his employees went fishing. It's an annual tournament with prizes."

"But you're in work clothes."

"My coveralls? Yes, I decided it would be a good time to work on my van while I was answering the garage phone. The back cargo space needs new carpeting." She glanced down at Estella's book. "I see you like Ramona Quimby books. They were a favorite of mine."

"I have a lot of Ramona books. Some of them are in Spanish."

"And you can read them?"

The little girl nodded. "My mommy spoke Spanish."

"Ah-ha," Torrie said, nodding again. She remembered Rich's grandmother telling her Rich's late wife was from Barcelona. She had also heard she'd been a model and costume designer who used to jet-set around the world working on movie shoots.

Rich cleared his throat and interrupted. "She also takes Spanish in school."

Torrie looked over at him in time to see a flash of anguish in his eyes. She patted the little girl gently on her knee. "So tell me, Estella, how did you like the trip from Texas?"

Estella giggled. "It was fun. Especially when we

camped out and it rained. Daddy said it rained cats and dogs, but not really. There was a lot of water, and a river ran through our tent. Daddy said some words he wasn't supposed to."

"Estella," Rich said in a low voice. "*Ahora no*. Not now."

But the little girl ignored him, grinned, and forged onward. "Anyway, we moved the tent onto a hill and put the rest of our stuff in it, and we slept in the back of the car. That was fun."

"I'll bet," Torrie agreed, smiling. "So how long are you Texans planning to stay in Pennsylvania?"

It was no secret around Hickory Valley that Richard Redman owned his grandmother's house since her death two years ago. Had Rich's father not passed away from a heart attack five years ago, he would have been the logical heir as Gertrude's only son. Rich's mother, Joyce, would have never had a chance to inherit any part of the Redman estate since Gertrude always considered her a gold digger and haughty fashion diva whose integrity and parenting skills were less than stellar. Gertrude had once revealed to Torrie that she had danced a little jig around the kitchen when Richard Senior announced he finally parted company with Joyce, just after Rich headed off to college.

It was also no secret that Marlene had tried to rent Gertrude Redman's house out to anyone at a rock bottom price just to keep it occupied and to keep the heat paid through the winters, but she hadn't been very successful. A family would no sooner move into the house than they'd move out again in less than a month, often leaving behind their deposit. No one would even bite on a rent-to-buy option either. At first, everyone surmised the three-story house was too large for most people, and the utilities were too costly. It was also located at the edge of town, away from the business district. But as time wore on, people gave up on any reasonable explanations. The house was a huge white elephant.

Torrie recalled the rumor circulating around the local area. Marlene Hess had recently found a letter addressed to him and dated just days before Gertrude died. It had been sealed, stamped, but never sent. Although Torrie detested the rumor mill about town, she suspected Marlene was the main reason Rich was here in Hickory Valley. She had been on the payroll of the Redman family since she was a teenager, helping the family in various capacities over the last thirty-some years. She now ran her own lucrative real estate agency inherited from her father, but she managed to forge a long-time, genuine friendship with Gertrude Redman. Marlene had indicated to Torrie it was time for Rich to make some decisions about the homestead. She was tired of trying to keep the gigantic structure occupied.

"I don't know exactly how long we're staying," Rich admitted. "I planned for a month to be safe. I need to check things out and see what my options might be. Now with school finished, we have the whole summer to decide. Luckily, I can work from my grandmother's house with a phone and computer."

Torrie smiled, eyes trained on the road. "Well, you picked a good month. June is perfect with its warm, sunny weather." Torrie loved June of all the months in the year. June was the month of roses, her favorite flower. And summer in Pennsylvania was spectacular, with its luscious shades of green and skies with varying blue hues that could outshine the colors of the sea.

Minutes later, she pulled into the large circular drive and stopped in front of the house, an arresting white structure with dormered second-floor windows looking over the front yard like two giant eyes. A wide porch with a gingerbread railing encircled both the front and two sides of the house.

Hopping out, Torrie walked to the back of the truck and dropped the tailgate. Together with Rich, she paused to watch Estella race up the front walk and onto the wraparound porch where she headed to a wooden swing in the right corner. Turning to Rich, Torrie suggested, "Why don't you unlock the house and show Estella around while I bring the luggage in and set it inside the door in the foyer?"

"Oh, no. I can't let you do it by yourself."

Torrie waved him away. "I can handle this. It's late and you need to feed Estella before you both settle in for the night."

"How much do I owe you?" Rich handed her the key to the SUV and withdrew his wallet.

She waved him away again. On her right hand, a delicate gold ring covered with clusters of expensive stones twinkled in the fading light. There was no wedding ring on her left hand.

"Just consider it a favor." She smiled. "Gertie and I were friends and belonged to the local garden club and the Garden Club Federation of Pennsylvania. There are some flowerbeds in the backyard where we raised wildflowers, some gladiolas, and roses. I would like to talk to you about maintaining the flowerbeds and rose gardens when you have a few minutes. Once you're settled, I'll stop by. A cup of coffee should make us even."

Nodding, Rich put a hand gently on her shoulder. "Thanks, Torrie. Really. Thanks so much for your help. I can't wait to see your brothers, especially Lars."

He looked toward the porch in the dying light and sighed. "I don't know what to do with this monstrosity. No one seems interested in buying it. No one wants to live in it. It's like a giant worthless gift. Maintenance costs exceed its usefulness. The heating bill is enormous. I have to pay to get the grass mowed in the summer and the snow shoveled in the winter." He shrugged his shoulders in resignation and stared down the street where the street lights had come on. Their globes looked like Japanese lanterns floating in the air. His gaze found hers again. His expression was miserable and grim.

Torrie tipped her ball cap up and gave a cursory glance at the house. She pursed her lips and fell silent. Should she tell him the truth? Or should she wait until he and Estella were settled in? The knowledge twisted and turned inside her. As much as she hated rumors, she hated lies even more. There were enough of both of them flying around town…and some were about her. What to do? Finally, she flung her hands up in despair.

"Of course no one wants to buy it, Richard Lee," she uttered with unmistakable candor. "I have it through reliable sources your grandmother's house is haunted."

Chapter Two

With Estella clinging to his hand, Rich stood in the foyer of his grandmother's house and was assaulted with so many childhood memories it was almost unbearable. This was the refuge where he came every summer to escape the sweltering city and the troubled marriage of his parents, and to get tender loving care from his paternal grandparents, who doted on their only grandchild.

Grandmother Gertie's house was a solid old structure, dating from the time when his great grandmother, Hilda, came from Austria before the First World War and fell in love with a humble but highly-skilled carpenter who built her a stately, impressive mansion with two fireplaces and five bedrooms on the southern end of the town's main thoroughfare.

The house now needed a bit of work, Rich realized, but most of it was reasonable and cosmetic. New paint and wallpaper would brighten and chase away the gloom. The cherry floors under his feet needed a good buffing and polishing—or maybe sanding and sealing—to look almost new again. And the scratches on the ornate cherry woodwork only needed to be touched up by someone with a skillful eye and a careful hand.

Estella tugged on his fingers. "You promised we'd see everything and then eat. I want to find my bedroom. You said I could choose. You promised, Daddy."

"Okay. Let's finish the downstairs first." They peered into the massive front living room where little change had occurred over the years. A brown leather couch and gold velvet wingback chairs faced the marble fireplace and beside them sat matching, spindled end tables. A glass-encased bookcase along one far wall held treasures from a hundred years ago when his great grandmother arrived—1916 German coins, a wind-up tin car, and other odds and ends. In the dining room on the opposite side of the house, an antique, inlaid dining table surrounded by eight chairs looked as if it were purchased only yesterday. Just like Great Grandmother Hilda, Grandmother Gertie preferred to eat in the kitchen except for special occasions. A matching corner china cabinet held delicate bone china tea sets, a porcelain tea strainer, hand-painted vases, Bavarian fruit plates, and many more delicate knick-knacks from long ago.

"Everything here is sooo old," Estella remarked, her voice a soft whine. She trudged behind him as he bypassed the study with its heavy, paneled door that had been locked when the house was rented, but was now open. Inside he could see his grandfather's handmade, floor-to-ceiling glass cabinets flaunting even more paraphernalia and a huge collection of teddy bears.

"I know, Estella." He nodded. He would have to find someone to help unload, inventory, and box up all the contents in every cabinet in the house. It was obvious why no one wanted to rent the place. The rooms looked depressing and outdated, stuffed with vintage items meaning nothing to families in a modern world. The place was tired and worn. But haunted?

Ghosts? He shook his head. No, not possible. It was just a silly rumor, probably started by kids.

He headed straight to the recently redone kitchen, bypassing the downstairs bedroom. It was light and airy with new white cabinets, light gray granite countertops, and all new appliances. Two sets of French doors, the farthest one opening to a functional family room and the other leading to a back porch, stone walk, patio and backyard, now allowed the afternoon sun to flood the once dimly lit back of the house.

Rich peered out onto the porch where two white wooden rocking chairs invited guests to linger outside and enjoy the panoramic beauty of the stone-walled fields and forestland extending to the horizon. The same towering oak tree that once held an old-fashioned rope swing when he was young still shaded a corner of the backyard. Beyond it, the huge, colorful flowerbeds Torrie had mentioned stretched out, and beside them was a timeworn gazebo his grandfather had built. Up a path to the right, a carriage house stood among a stand of pine like a lone sentry on duty.

Estella ran to the front foyer and picked up her backpack, then raced back and shouted, "Come on. Let's go, Daddy. I want to find a room where I'm going to sleep tonight. And I'm hungry."

Together, they climbed the stairs to a landing where four spacious bedrooms filled the upstairs along with a walk-in closet, central bathroom, and steps leading to the third floor attic. Rich stopped at the first corner room, which used to be his bedroom when he lived with his grandparents. Colors of oyster and blue now accented the walls. On the shelves beside the long mirrored dresser, his grandmother had positioned his graduation photo along with pictures of his various high school sports. A stab of longing and nostalgia washed over him as he stared at them. His own parents had never made any effort to display any of his accomplishments when he was growing up. His grandmother, however, collected and proudly pinned every newspaper clipping mentioning his name on the front of her refrigerator.

From across the hall, Estella's high-pitched squeal interrupted his reminiscing. "Hey, Daddy, look at this! It's a room for a fairy princess! I'm choosing this one. Pleeease?"

Rich crossed the hallway. The room glowed a soft rosy color in the fading sunlight. Delicate striped wallpaper in shades of rose, pink, and white covered two walls while the opposite ones were adorned with a small cabbage rose design. A white eyelet comforter covered a full-sized canopy bed. A porcelain doll with dark hair, dressed in white silk and lace and wearing an intricately fashioned bonnet, sat on the window seat across from the bed. A battered toy chest had been placed against the wall below the dormered window, and Estella knelt and opened it, pulling out games and toys from Rich's childhood in Hickory Valley.

Marlene, he said to himself. This must have been Marlene's doing. He never recalled a time when the room was pink, even when he came for the funeral two years ago.

As if he had conjured up the woman, the doorbell rang. Before he could reach the bottom steps, Marlene opened the door and met him at the bottom of the steps, her siren-red, four-inch heels clicking on the wooden floor. Her short hair, almost as red as the shoes, was fashioned into a spiked, trendy hairstyle. A pair of stone-washed jeans hugged her tall thin frame like a second skin.

"How'd you get in?" he asked.

"I'm your real estate agent, remember?" She dangled a key in front of him. "Maybe you ought to keep this spare in case you get locked out. I brought the coffee and some good Jameson Irish whiskey, eighteen-year variety, not twelve. For later." She wiggled her eyebrows at Estella and dropped the key in his hands, then held up a plastic grocery bag and headed to the kitchen in the back. "Please tell me you have the oven turned on, Richard Lee Junior, and the pan of lasagna pulled out of the refrigerator."

He trailed behind her. "Not yet."

She shook her head, snapped the oven on, opened the refrigerator, and took out the pan. From the bread box, she retrieved a loaf of bread. "The child should have eaten by now."

"Estella and I were exploring." Rich leaned against the doorjamb and watched her work. Marlene had been a dedicated friend and employee of Gertrude's family for as many years as he could remember. Growing up in Hickory Valley, Marlene had worked with her father in real estate since she was sixteen. Twenty-three years later, when Howard Hess announced he was retiring and headed to Florida and life in a condo at the beach, it had seemed natural for Marlene to take over the business. Unmarried and a few years shy of fifty, she could give the thirty-year-olds a run for their money with her high-energy personality. The business hadn't floundered in the least. Marlene had to hire more agents to keep up with the new clients and demands on her time. When Gertrude was alive, Marlene often popped in to see the old woman and have a cup of blueberry tea.

But what he recalled most about the woman was her efficient, assertive temperament and good business sense. Through the years, she was more like a big sister to him. When he was in grade school, she used to babysit on those summer nights when his grandmother went to play bridge or needed an evening out. She never let him beat her at any board game they played. Marlene was a tough cookie. Strict, but fair. In some ways, she taught him to be competitive and tough, too.

Through the screen from the opened French doors, a gentle breeze picked up the smell of new mown grass, phlox, and pine. It had been a long time since he had experienced such clean, inviting outdoor smells. "I've been meaning to ask you whether you might have a lead on someone who would be able to do some light housekeeping, cooking, and babysitting while Estella and I are here," he said.

Marlene turned. "I was waiting for you to ask that question." She sliced some bread and put it in a basket. She pointed to the cupboard. "Get three glasses out. Yes, I have someone in mind. Her name is Lucille Smith. Everyone calls her Lulu. She lost her husband last year and needs something to do to refocus her life. She knew your grandmother well. They played in the same card club and were best friends."

"And just how old is this woman?"

"Seventy-five."

"You're kidding, Marlene. I need someone to keep up with Estella." He set the glasses on the table.

"This ol' gal can run circles around you, Estella,

and me. She's from a farm on the other side of town, and there's nothing she can't do. She raised five kids and has won numerous blue ribbons for her canned and baked goods at the county fair. I'll have her stop over tomorrow morning, and you can decide." Marlene set the kitchen table with three place settings. "Now go call Estella for dinner. The poor child must be starved."

Later, while Marlene cleaned the kitchen, Rich tucked Estella into bed and showered before he rejoined her in the living room. In her lap, Marlene had the mysterious envelope, the unsent letter she had mentioned to him over the phone. It was the main reason he was returning to Hickory Valley. He was annoyed she refused to deal with it, but she said she felt uncomfortable opening it or sending it in the mail. "If it truly is important, and if it contains your grandmother's last words to you…or requests of you," she had told him, "you need to read it at the homestead."

Beside her, on the end table, she had two glasses with amber liquid emitting the smell of rich smooth whiskey. When he took a seat in one of the wingback chairs, she handed one to him. "To a pleasant, prosperous visit to Hickory Valley," she said, raising her glass and touching his with a soft clink.

Rich stretched out his legs and took a sip. "I was so pleased to see Grandmother Gertie had the kitchen remodeled and the bedrooms repainted and refurnished. It makes it so much easier for us to stay here."

Marlene swirled the whiskey in her glass. "She started the renovations six months before she died and left me strict instructions to have them finished if something happened to her. The only thing I had to do was to get the front bedroom papered and painted pink, and have the canopy installed over the bed. I suspect Estella is delighted?"

"Estella is ecstatic over the room. Thank you. I wish my grandmother could see her now. She's older and funnier and witty." Rich took another sip of whiskey. "The old toy chest brings back a ton of memories. I'm going to check out some of those old games we used to play. Remember how you used to clobber me in chess?"

Marlene laughed. "Yes, but you beat me in *Memory*. I never could get those crazy tiles to match each other."

He paused a moment to stare into his drink and reminisce before looking at Marlene. "The porcelain doll was really a nice touch. Estella loved it, since it has dark hair like hers."

"What porcelain doll?"

"On the window seat."

Marlene raised an eyebrow and a momentary look of discomfort crossed her face. "I never left a porcelain doll in the pink bedroom."

Their eyes met, each clouded with uneasiness. Rich was the first to break contact and shrugged. "Well, someone did. Maybe someone from the cleaning service rearranged things. You don't believe in ghosts, do you, Marlene?" He frowned and watched her expression change to one of faint caution.

"Well, Richard Junior, I've certainly not been able to get a house this grand to sell. And in Hickory Valley and the surrounding area, the housing market is getting stronger every month." She handed him the sealed letter. "Let's get this over with and find out what your grandmother had to say. We're lucky we have this. If it hadn't been for Ivan Winters, your grandmother's accountant and loan officer down at the First National Bank, who suggested I check the house one more time for unopened mail and bills, I might not have found it. It was shoved into a pigeon hole on her desk in the study where she did paperwork."

With steady hands, Rich took the envelope and tapped it on his knee. There was a faint smile on his lips. "The sweet old lady can reach me from the grave. Last wishes of the deceased are always the hardest ones to carry out." Silence descended as he opened the envelope and read the one-page letter. Finally he looked up, his lips thinned in irritation. He handed it to Marlene. "Looks like she got me."

Marlene took the letter. "You sure you want me to read this?"

He nodded.

She settled back into the chair and kicked off her shoes. Taking her time, she read the letter. When she was finished, she dropped it in her lap and sighed. "Well, I didn't see this coming." She looked down at it one more time, forehead wrinkled. "So, there's hidden jewels, supposedly brought over from Austria before the war by your Great Grandmother Hilda, that never came to light in the last one hundred years. And you have a half-sister somewhere whom Gertie wants you to find for a trust she had set up for both of you." Marlene shook her head. "Looks like your dad got you, too. A half-sister? Aren't you shocked?"

Rich heaved a weary sigh and ran his hand through his still-damp, sandy-colored hair. "If you understood the pitiful marriage my mom and dad had, then no, it's no surprise. They both cheated, I'm guessing." He looked at her with a disheartened gaze. "I wonder why Ivan Winters never said anything about a half-sister when I was clearing some of Gertie's accounts at the bank. He told me the trust would become available in three years when I was thirty-eight, but he never told me there was a stipulation to include a half-sister."

"Was she mentioned in Gertie's will?"

"No, of course not. This is all news to me."

"Then, I'd guess he figured you already knew or perhaps were on a need-to-know basis. Since the trust didn't directly involve you yet, but rather an individual whom no one could locate, it wasn't critical to transacting business."

"Wasn't critical? Marlene, I've been handling my grandmother's investments for the last ten years. The least that doofus Ivan could have done was to give me a heads up."

"It wasn't Ivan's place to tell you about a half-sister, Richard Lee. It was only the bank's responsibility to manage the trust."

"I suppose you're right." Rich rose and paced the room, stopping at the fireplace. "Good grief, what a mess!"

Marlene chuckled a dry, heckling sound. "It looks like you might be extending your stay a little while longer than a month to sort out this tangled web."

"You think this is amusing?"

Marlene yawned and rose. "No, I think I need to go home, take a shower, and go to bed. Things always look better in the morning."

Rich walked her to the door. "Can you tell me, what's the story with Torrine Larson? I see she's back in town."

"She has been for a few years. After she graduated from Duquesne in Pittsburgh with a degree in art, Torrie headed to New York City. Supposedly, she was engaged." Marlene shrugged. "About six years ago, she returned. No diamond. No marriage. No reasons for her return. There was gossip, of course, but I'm not spreading any. I'm guessing there are more than a few scars, but it's Torrie's story to tell, not mine. Her parents and family are very supportive of her. Torr and Regina Larson have always been exemplary parents to all their children. Rumor has it Ivan Winters at the bank is very interested in her along with a dozen others, but she doesn't return the attention."

Marlene opened the door. "She started a business here with her older brother, Finn, and sometimes she helps Henry when he needs someone to man the phone. I believe she also does his bookkeeping. Her younger brother, Gus, is a mechanic and works for him, too."

"Where does she live?"

"In a small apartment across the street from Henry's main garage above a warehouse he owns." Marlene leaned in and bussed Rich lightly on his cheek. "Welcome home. It's so good to see you again. Don't forget, if you need anything, just give a jingle. I'm on the payroll to help with whatever you might need."

She slipped out the door before Rich could ask her what kind of business Torrie Larson had started.

Chapter Three

After checking to see if Estella was still asleep, Rich refilled his glass and strolled out onto the back porch. He had always loved nighttime in Pennsylvania. Rural life in the evening was so different from the commotion, noise, and bright lights of the big city. The branches on a stand of pine near the carriage house sighed in the warm breeze like they were settling into a comfortable bed for a much-needed rest. Fireflies winked and danced out on the lawn to the harmony of caroling crickets and cicadas.

He leaned against a post and reread the letter, then stared off to the distant hills fading away as gray dusk turned to darkness. One more thing to add to his long list of things to do. Renovate the outdated monstrosity of a house. Find a buyer at a worthy price. Go on a wild goose chase to locate a half-sister he didn't even know existed. And last, unearth century-old jewels from Austria—rubies to be exact—that no one else in over a hundred years could locate. Rich sighed. What a fine cactus patch he fell into! Now his plan to blow into town, sell the house, and make a quick exit within the month was shot to hell.

"Did I throw you for a loop, Richard Lee Junior?" a scratchy voice asked.

Rich jumped and looked around. From the farthest corner of the porch, a rocking chair moved slowly back and forth. Back and forth. But there was no one sitting on it. The night had become still and tranquil without a hint of a breeze.

Rich set the glass and letter on the railing and rubbed his tired face with his hands. "It's been a long day," he muttered to himself, "and now I'm hallucinating. I swear I'm hearing a voice sounding like Grandmother Gertie's." His gaze traveled to the moving rocker, and he gave it a quizzical look.

"You *are* hearing me, young man," the voice said. "Hallucinating, my foot."

Rich continued to peer at the rocker, now rocking at a faster pace.

"Grandmother? Gertie? Aren't you supposed to be dead?"

"I am dead."

"Then aren't you supposed to be somewhere else? Like in another dimension? In heaven or riding a cloud somewhere?" He pointed upward. "Or am I drunk and I don't know it?"

"Phfftt, you're hardly drunk. And I'm not going anywhere while I have unfinished business here on earth."

"Didn't anyone tell you to go toward the Light?" His voice rose an octave now.

"Of course." The voice was getting as annoyed as he was. "But not when I know things you don't. Not when I need you to finish a few unresolved issues for me."

Rich moved a little closer to the moving rocking chair and blinked, still trying to process everything. "Can you do that?"

"Do what?"

"Just waltz around willy-nilly on earth after you die?"

The rocker slowed.

Rich dropped his head in his hands and mumbled, "Please, please, please. Let this be a dream...or the effects of good eighteen-year aged Irish whiskey. I'm losing my marbles."

The voice interrupted, "Buck up, Richard Lee. You aren't losing your marbles, although you may have a hole in your bag. You are my last hope. You need to find your half-sister, who needs your help, and you need to find those Austrian rubies I've searched for my entire life. If not for me, for Estella. It's my great-granddaughter's heritage and inheritance. Did you read the letter and understand it?"

"Yes, but for the record, how can I tell you're really the ghost of my grandmother? Tell me something most people don't know about me."

"For goodness sake! What is this? *Jeopardy*? I see you still can be a pain in the backside with your endless quest for the truth. How about this? The kids used to tease you and call you Richie Rich. And every time you got yourself tied in a sanctimonious knot over it, I used to tell you they could have chosen worse names like Dumbo or Dimwit."

Rich's eyes widened as he stared at the rocker. "It really is you. Grandmother Gertie. Why me?"

"Because you're the only direct surviving relative, Dimwit."

"But I really don't know where to start."

There was a long whoosh of air, like a disgruntled sigh. "Just how did you pass the bar with such a dull, negative attitude? How about some creative thinking?

How about your grandfather's study for starters?"

"Where in the study?" he asked, but he instantly knew he wouldn't get an answer. The rocking chair now stood motionless.

"Holy moly, let this be the effects of alcohol or a bad dream," he muttered before turning and trudging inside, locking the door, and heading straight to his room to sleep.

Chapter Four

Rich slept like a stone. If it wasn't for Estella standing beside his bed and speaking in a cheerful chirpy voice about needing breakfast and wanting to go outside to explore as he promised her at bedtime yesterday, he would have crawled back under the covers for another seven hours. Then, when he remembered Lucille Smith was planning to stop by in the morning, he dragged himself out of bed, pulled on a pair of jeans, and hurried barefoot and shirtless to the kitchen to put the coffee on. He was helping Estella with a bowl of cereal when the elderly woman arrived, using the back entrance, knocking on the first set of French doors opening into the kitchen.

With a basket on her arm, Lucille Smith took in Rich's bare chest and feet in one sweeping glance and shook her head, then his hand, and murmured a curt hello. Like a bee zoning in on a flower, she headed straight to the kitchen. She was a little woman with a face wrinkled like a raisin, and her gray hair was braided and wound on top of her head. She wore a turquoise blouse, a red skirt, and a clean, pressed, bright yellow apron over the outfit. Well, at least they wouldn't lose her, Rich decided, as she set her basket on the counter and pulled out a plate full of freshly baked blueberry muffins. She had both Estella's and his attention immediately.

The little girl rose from the table. "I'm Estella," she politely said.

"And I'm Lulu Smith," Lucille said. "Pleased to meet you." She looked around the kitchen and let out an appreciative grunt. "A person could do some good cooking in a kitchen this fancy."

"What we need," Rich said and waved a hand in the air, "is someone for a few hours each day. Someone to help keep us tidy, fix a lunch, and possibly make a dinner I could re-warm. We'd even work around any hours you might have for appointments or personal matters." He bit his lip. "You see, I'm planning to do legal work for my Dallas office in the mornings. I have research to do, and I need to get this house renovated and ready to sell. It could use some sprucing up. It's no wonder Marlene can't sell it. Also, I need someone to help with Estella while I work."

"And you aren't exactly Emeril Lagasse, I understand," Lulu said, her little wizened eyes sizing him up.

"Bam!" he replied with a devilish smile.

"I'm guessing you had a housekeeper when you were in Texas?"

"Yes, ma'am. And a cleaning service which Marlene hired for this house as well. You'll need to instruct them on what you want done."

The little woman rose to her full four-feet-ten-inch height, but this time surveyed him with a motherly stare. "Well, when do you want me to start?" Her gaze dropped to his bare feet. "It looks like you've already run out of shirts and socks and need clothes laundered."

"Don't you want to discuss an hourly rate?" Red-faced, he glanced at his sockless feet. "I wasn't expecting you to arrive this early or I would have been dressed and presentable."

"Whatever you think is fair." She shrugged.

"What do you think, Estella?" Rich asked.

The little girl took a step forward. "Can you iron, Mrs. Smith? My daddy can iron wrinkles *into* any piece of clothing. It's a real talent of his."

"Estella."

"But it's true," the little girl said. "And can you do a French braid? My daddy doesn't know anything about fixing hair."

"Estella!"

"I can do both." Lulu chuckled. "But you must call me Lulu." She pulled out Estella's chair, motioned for her to sit, and placed a muffin on her plate. "We need to make a list of what foods you both like. Then you and I can go grocery shopping later today." She waved Rich into a seat opposite his daughter, handed him a muffin, and refilled his coffee cup.

Rich took a bite, swallowed, and felt like he was going to swoon. The muffin had just the right amount of sweetness, and the cinnamon and sugar topping was outrageously delicious. It sure beat cold cereal. It was going to be a fine day. He was sure of it.

****

Torrie took a deep breath and strode up the walk to Gertrude Redman's residence with the purple toy giraffe in her hand. It was as good an excuse as any to stop in and get acquainted with Rich and Estella. She would be seeing a lot of them when she came to tend the flower gardens out back, and she needed to tell him about his SUV, which her brother and Henry had towed to the garage.

She looked at the purple giraffe and thought of another child a short distance away who also adored stuffed animals. She had no idea how the giraffe had been forgotten amid the luggage last evening. Then she thought of all the many boxes, bags, and suitcases she had unloaded. It was like hauling a traveling circus. Estella should be lucky only one toy had been left behind. But Torrie knew how attached little girls could be to their fuzzy critters.

Rich answered the door with a muffin in one hand and wearing only a pair of black designer jeans. Torrie's eyes widened when he opened the door. He was a magnificent, handsome specimen of a man, tall and fit. He reminded her of a cheetah with his tawny hair, sleek physique, and penetrating charcoal eyes fading now to a soft dusty gray. She remembered her sister telling her that Richard Redman's patience was his virtue, but once angered, he could take down the devil with his sharp eloquent tongue.

"Torrie," he said, "what brings you around so early in the morning?"

She held up the giraffe. "I thought Estella might be missing this. And Henry said your SUV isn't limping along. It's going to need a lot of work, including a new transmission. He wants to know whether you want to put more money in it or whether you're planning to replace it."

"Come in, come in," he urged. He finished the last bite of muffin. "You have to taste Lucille Smith's blueberry muffins."

"Gosh, I don't know," she said. "This is my day off, and I have loads of things to do. I don't usually do breakfast."

From the back of the kitchen a voice called out, "Torrine Jane Larson, get in the kitchen and have a muffin and something to drink. You don't eat breakfast? You know better. Get in here. Right now. Don't make me come out there and grab you by the back of your neck."

Torrie grinned. "Lulu Smith is here?"

"Yes, I hired her this morning to help with the house and Estella."

Minutes later, seated at the table beside Estella, a purple giraffe, a half-clad man, and eating a muffin, Torrie said, "If you need a ride to see about a rental, I can drop you off."

"No, I want a ride to a car dealership, preferably your brother's. I need to buy a new vehicle with a warranty that assures me it will not take its last breath with me in it." Rich rose from the table and took his plate and cup to the sink.

"Why don't you use your grandmother's vehicle in the garage?" Lulu suggested.

"Does it even run?" He glanced at the little woman leaning against the counter like a colorful elf with a dish towel already in her hands.

Lulu grunted.

Torrie laughed. "Run? Does it run? It purrs like a kitten. It's a '67 GTO convertible."

"You're kidding." A devilish glint flashed in his eyes and a slow smile morphed into a wide grin. "My grandmother actually had it overhauled?"

Torrie rose and walked to the side door at the far end of the kitchen leading to the garage. Like a game show hostess, she opened the door and swept her hand through the air at the sparkling red GTO. "Black leather seats, black convertible top, the works. Runs like a charm." Joy bubbled in her voice as she explained, "Gertie always left the keys in it. She even had shoulder harnesses installed in front and back. If you're only making short trips to the grocery store or downtown, it'd be perfect. I'm guessing it's a gas hog."

"I thought she sold it."

Lulu spoke up. "No, she put it in storage after your Grandfather Matthew died. She only brought it out a few years ago and had it tuned up. Our bridge club used to cruise around town with her. On Sundays, she and I would take it to the lake and drive around listening to the young motor heads whistle and hoot at us. Nothing like a spiffy, vintage car to get a little attention from a man, regardless of his age."

Rich leaned on the door jam and studied the two women. "Since you ladies obviously know more about the house and property than me, can you tell me whether my grandmother ever installed Internet service? Marlene had the phones and television cable turned on, but she never mentioned the Internet."

Torrie stared at his well-muscled chest and could feel her face grow hot. She was sure her heart skipped a beat. She cleared her throat and stuttered, "There's a…there's a connection in the study. I can help to get you online. Where's your shir—laptop?"

He smiled, a warm, almost too intimate smile assuring her he caught the blunder. "In the hallway. I'll run up and get dressed and be right back down for a lesson on connectivity."

"Connectivity?" Torrie raised an eyebrow.

"Sure, Internet connectivity." He looked her over seductively. "Were you thinking of something else?"

"Yes…no. Yes! I mean, yes, I'll meet you in a few minutes to help with the Internet," she stammered. She brushed past him heading for the study. What was she thinking? She remembered the promise she had made to herself six years ago. She would make no space in her life for men. She was finished with this thing called love and all its fickle disappointments. She wasn't going to risk her heart again, especially to someone as good-looking as Rich Redman.

"And while you two fool around with wires, innuendos, and eye signals, Estella and I are going to the grocery store," Lulu announced. "We're going to get dressed, get our hair combed, and make a list of our favorite foods, aren't we darlin'? Maybe Estella can tell me some favorite foods you might like, Richard." She looked at the little girl and winked.

"Can we get ice cream?" Estella asked. "Daddy likes beer and peanuts."

"Any flavor you want," Lulu replied. "But I think we'll skip the beer today. I'll give some serious thought to the peanuts."

Rich sighed. "You're a gem, Lulu. And I use Rich now, not Richard Lee Junior any longer."

"Goodness sakes," Lulu said. "But you'll always be Richard Lee to me."

Minutes later, as she waited in the study with the laptop booted up, Torrie looked up as Rich strode into the study. He was incredibly suave. His expensive gray slacks flaunted his well-built physique. Wearing a crisp white shirt rolled up to his elbows, he looked like he could really be a GQ model. The Ferragamo loafers on his feet must have cost more than a week of her wages. He had shaved and he smelled heavenly. She'd bet his aftershave cost a bundle of bills, too. His no nonsense, in-charge demeanor only added to his sexual appeal.

"You're connected," Torrie said. She pointed to a corner of the desk. "I took the liberty of piling some of the papers and books into stacks so we could have room to work. The password is *rosa alba*."

He shrugged like he didn't care how she had rearranged the desk. "How did you figure out the password?" He leaned over her shoulder, so near she got a better whiff of his to-die-for aftershave lotion. His breath ruffled the hair at her ear when he asked, "Rosa alba? White rose?"

"Yes, your Latin is good."

"Not good enough if Gertie is using Latin for all her online passwords. Is there a notebook my grandmother kept with all this information?"

He was too close for her to shake her head. Much too close. "No, but Gertie and I used to post pictures of our roses and other flowers on our Garden Club's Facebook site so I'm quite familiar with her computer and her line of reasoning."

"My grandmother was on Facebook?"

When he eased away, she quickly slid out from the chair and skidded a few feet away. This was a man she could not get involved with. He was a big city lawyer who was headed back to Dallas as soon as his legal obligations to his deceased grandmother were completed. And he had a child to raise. He certainly didn't need another one.

She spoke, "Yes, and I really have to leave. If the modem needs to be reset, the password is on the box on the shelf underneath it. All numbers."

"But you wanted to show me the gardens and

flowerbeds." He moved closer, his smoke gray eyes so compelling they made her pulse skitter.

"Okay." She checked her watch. "I guess I can spare a few minutes." Unnerved by his nearness, she whirled and headed toward the French doors at the back of the house. Outside, she led him to the edge of the patio and onto a walk ending at the gardens in the corner of the yard. Beside them a ramshackle chicken coop had been beefed up and converted into a potting shed, but farther up, the old gazebo looked like it was crumbling before their eyes.

Torrie hoped with all her heart what she was about to explain about the flowers would not cause problems in selling the house. She wondered whether she should tell him that she and Gertie had started all the many flowerbeds so she could do floral arranging using homegrown perennial flowers during the spring, summer, and fall. She had started adding them last year into her floral bouquets and arrangements, and already she had a healthy local clientele. Growing her own flowers helped keep the costs down, and her buyers liked the idea of using seasonal flowers they could recognize. It also enhanced business for the landscape center where she designed them.

Unfortunately, she was in debt. She and her oldest brother, Finn, had taken out a loan to start the partnership. But she had her own set of problems neither Finn nor her family knew about. She owed Ivan Winters, president of the downtown bank, money for a personal loan he'd given her to pay off the remainder she owed for land acquired in New York. She and Daniel Forrester, her long-time boyfriend, had purchased it seven years ago with the intent to build a house and settle there. The loan was hanging around her neck like a poisonous snake, ready to strike at a moment's notice whenever Ivan grew weary of her stonewalling his amorous advances.

****

Rich followed Torrie out into the bright sunlight. What looked like one gigantic flowerbed yesterday in the dark was actually a series of beds, each exactly the same size, but separated with paths between them for easy access to the flowers for weeding, watering, or picking the blooms. Torrie motioned for him to follow her until they reached a midway point among a row of beds.

"Do all these flowers and plants have something to do with how you make your living?" Rich watched her wander over to what looked like a bed of roses and bend to check the stalk on one of the plants. Her slim fingers touched it lightly, almost caressing it. Clad only in a pair of khaki cargo shorts, tank top, and sturdy hiking shoes, she appeared oblivious of her natural beauty. Her pale yellow hair was twisted up on the top of her head in some sort of fancy knot, but tendrils had already dislodged themselves and fanned her face in a halo.

Another wave of attraction, verging on lust, rushed over him, and he backed up a step, forcing himself to concentrate on their conversation.

She squinted up at him from her squatting position and shaded her eyes against the sun, unaware her sunglasses were perched on her head. "Yes, my brother, Finn, and I started a landscape and nursery two years ago. It's called Larson's Landscaping."

"A novel name."

"And for a purpose. It's our family name, and the double letter *L* lends itself to a keen-looking logo and allows our advertising to be in the upper half of the alphabet for listings on the Internet and in the Yellow Pages. We're just getting off the ground this year, and I have to admit, we're mowing a lot of lawns until we can get some better revenue with landscaping contracts and sales from the nursery. But the summer is just beginning here."

She stood, slapping her hands together to brush off the dirt. She waved at the plants in the bed beside her. "Your grandmother and I were trying our hand at grafting and saving this particular type of rose. This original white vintage rose is from the last and only surviving bush from the clippings your Great Grandmother Hilda carried out of Austria before the First World War, sometime in the early 1900s. It's beside the potting shed. We're trying to get healthy rose stock started here so we can graft them. We've also taken clippings to root."

She pursed her lips and looked up at him with those mesmerizing aquamarine eyes. "You realize these roses are over a hundred years old? They're one of a kind, and if we don't save the line, they'll be lost forever. Gertie was an amateur gardener and she was— and I still am—a member of the American Rose Society headquartered in Shreveport, Louisiana. It's one of many organizations in the World Federation of Rose Societies. These roses aren't just old. They are rare. They are fragile. I'd like to be able to continue working with the beds here, if possible. I know you want to sell the house."

Rich shook his head and surveyed the sky. It was

going to be a perfect day with mild temperatures. Cotton-like clouds floated along a sea of blue. He lowered his gaze. "I don't know what to say. Let me think about this. My grandmother sure left me a lot of headaches and a lot of things to consider. I don't suppose the flowers in these beds could be removed and replanted somewhere else?"

Torrie let out a long audible sigh. She shook her head. "I'm afraid we'd lose too much. What you see here is over five years of work. I doubt some of the roses would hold up well to replanting." From her pocket, she pulled out a ring with a key. "Before I forget, this is the key to the sheds and the garage door. I'd like to be able to come over, water, weed, fertilize, monitor, and work the flower beds until you decide what you're going to do with the house and land."

She followed his gaze across the beds to the gazebo. "Your grandmother loved that ragged old gazebo your grandfather built. We used to take a break in it and have a glass of lemonade after we weeded the flowerbeds. It has a romantic touch and nostalgic aura."

"It looks like it needs to be firewood."

"Oh, no. Maybe some paint and new screening would help?" Torrie offered him a hopeful expression. "You grandmother told me she used to carry dinner out there on Sunday evenings, and Matthew and she would eat by candlelight."

From behind them, in a bed of Shasta daisies, a whirligig started up in the light breeze. It was a whimsical cat, the yellow scarf around its neck flying out behind it. It was riding in a vintage, red convertible car. But instead of the sign saying Route 66, someone had blackened out one of the sixes to make it Route 6 in an attempt to replicate the road into Hickory Valley. Torrie looked at it and laughed. The sound of her voice was like the tinkling of tiny bells—light and joyful. "It was a present from her bridge club on her eighty-fifth birthday," she told him.

"Don't you think it's a bit audacious?"

"For Gertie? Heavens, no. But if you ever want to get rid of it, I'll take it off your hands. It makes me smile." Torrie chuckled. "By the way, have you seen her cat?"

"A cat? A real cat? Like a domestic feline? Here on the grounds?" Rich's voice rose in disbelief.

"Yes, her name is Sheba. She's white. I'm not sure she's exactly domestic. She was a stray your grandmother took in a few years ago. She stays outside and takes shelter in the front shed where there's a hole in the back. Marlene and I take turns feeding her, which is another reason I have the key. We keep the cat food against the far wall in the garage." She paused. "It might be a good chore for Estella while she's here."

He stared at her with a confused, sour gaze. "Just what I need! Estella getting hooked on a cat. She's been hounding me for a pet for the last two years." The corner of his mouth twisted with exasperation. "Keep the key."

He looked around the backyard, which had become overgrown with rhododendron and other bushes he didn't recognize. Even the trees needed trimming. "Did Gertie ever talk about family? Did she ever mention anything about another grandchild or me having a half-sister?"

Now it was Torrie's turn to be confused. "You mean your mother had another child?"

"No, I think my father might have been less than a steadfast spouse. But then, my mother left a lot to be desired as both a mother and wife." Rich sighed, a half-weary, half-disgusted sigh. "I have no idea how I'm supposed to find this long-lost sister. Then there's the continuing tale from the past about jewels brought from Austria in the early 1900s, hidden, but never found."

Torrie bit her lip. "There are old journals in the study, written by your Great Grandmother Hilda. Your problem will be her English. Gertie said she spoke it flawlessly, but sometimes when she wrote it, she threw in a few German words and phrases. If she gave any hints about the jewels, you might find them there. You'll have to look up some words and phrases. I have an excellent German/English dictionary you can use."

His eyes widened and he stared at her. Complete surprise and adoration washed over his face. "You know German?"

Torrie's raised her arms, palms facing. "No. Don't get any ideas. I took German in high school and college. Two years each." She stepped backward. "I can read it a little, write it even less, speak it hardly at all. I'm no expert."

"Well, you're light years ahead of me. All I know is passable Spanish." His gaze circled the yard again before they came to rest on her. "Are you free for dinner some night?"

"No," she said and backed away even farther. A look of panic crossed her face. "Sorry. My week is usually full. I have Sunday and Wednesday off, but I do Henry's payroll on Wednesday morning. I'm headed there next to pick up invoices I need to look over." She chewed on her lower lip and looked toward the circular walk leading to the front of the house like she might escape given the chance.

"It's not a date, Torrie," he said quietly. "I just want to have a nice dinner somewhere and talk. Just as friends. Maybe there's something you can tell me about my grandmother that might be helpful in getting to the bottom of all these questions. How about Sunday?"

She shook her head. "I have plans for Sunday, sorry. On weekdays, Finn and I take turns working late to accommodate customers who stop in after work to pick up shrubs for evening or weekend do-it-yourself landscaping."

His gray eyes darkened as he held her gaze. "Come on, you're making this difficult. How about a late dinner this Friday?"

She looked at the ground and sighed. "I guess. If we go out of town."

"Afraid to be seen with me?"

She rubbed the back of her neck, then stared at the whirligig for a minute before speaking. "No, let's just say I have a reputation for not dating, not getting involved, so I don't want to run into anyone I might know and put myself in the gossip pipeline."

"Okay." He nodded, a thoughtful smile curving his mouth. "Fair enough. But promise me you'll wear something that'll knock my socks off. We're not going on a trek out of town in a red muscle car just to eat at a burger joint."

Her sweet melodious laugh rippled out as together they watched a breeze stir the propellers on the whirligig and send the car and cat bouncing up and down like they were racing on a highway.

"Deal," she finally said.

Chapter Five

Larson's Landscaping sat on the edge of town and welcomed visitors with its rustic split rail fence winding around a flagstone patio dotted with cement benches and large vats of colorful flowers and bushes. A wide, blue front door sat under a huge green, white, and blue striped awning covering the entire front of the long low building and offering customers shade from the sun and protection from the rain.

When Torrie pulled into the parking lot, she spotted Joe Bradley under the awning, assembling a garden cart with pneumatic tires and two shelves. A high school classmate of her older brother Finn, Joe had started working for them on opening day. When he didn't have small carpentry or construction jobs, he often filled in for Torrie on her Wednesdays off, performing all the needed mechanical chores. A solid man of medium height, he had a square face, bronzed by the wind and sun, and large callused hands.

"I see the new cart finally came in." Torrie walked up to where he was working. Joe looked up and smiled. "Yes, this one's a beauty. It can be easily pulled or towed around the nursery. The two shelves give us extra storage and should save us some time when moving stock around. So how's my favorite girl?"

Torrie laughed. "Fine, as usual." Joe Bradley had called her his favorite girl since she was little Torrie

Larson, tagging behind every one of her older brothers and her only sister, Elsa. Finn and Joe were nine years older than she was and they had a tendency to spoil her rotten. When she was in first grade, she convinced them to build her a treehouse in the backyard. Joe was a natural with tools, and his carpentry and mechanical skills were top-notch even as a teenager. The treehouse in an old elm boasted a small porch, windows covered with plastic so she could play in it in bad weather, and a small cabinet inside to hold her bat, balls, and toys.

Joe was one of her brother's best friends, one of her favorite people, and her closest friend. He was a dependable bachelor and was always available to help her when a drain backed up in her apartment or when a door lock broke and needed to be replaced. He had never once been part of the rumor mill when she returned from New York with an infant and no husband, nor did he ever have any disparaging words about her plans to raise Iris, her six-year-old daughter, alone. In fact, Joe had a soft spot for the little girl who adoringly trailed behind him at the landscape center asking endless questions, which he patiently answered.

"I need to find Finn," Torrie said. "He promised to watch Iris on Friday night."

Joe looked up under craggy eyebrows and studied her for a moment. He frowned. "I can babysit for you if you need help. I've told you that a million times now."

"Thanks, Joe. You're a peach, and you've come to my rescue a million times. I appreciate it. But Finn was planning to go to Elsa's after work. He can easily bring Iris back and keep her for a few hours so I don't have to get up early on Saturday morning to pick her up for the weekend."

He nodded. "All right. Let me know if it doesn't work out with Finn. I can always leave here a little early on Friday and get her." He picked up a screwdriver and some screws and washers and started assembling the rack for the cart.

"Is there anything I can help with? What needs to be done?" Her gaze circled the premises from the patio to the fenced in lot overflowing with hearty shrubs, trees, and potted flowers.

"Just those two flats of purple petunias over there. They need to be taken out to the loading dock. Lulu Smith ordered them and said we could drop them off at Gertie Redman's house. I see Rich is back in town. This time with his daughter. Your brother said you gave them a lift into town the other night."

"Yes, I did." So the rumor mill had started. Torrie picked up a flat of flowers and trotted to the parking lot where her van was parked beside the loading dock, then repeated the trip one more time. She wiped her forehead with the back of her hand and stood before Joe with her hands on her hips. "I'm headed back to town and can drop them off. I just put new indoor-outdoor carpet in the van the other day and covered it with a big piece of plastic to keep it from getting soiled. I just have to remember to use the plastic."

"You're trying to keep a delivery van's carpet clean?" He chuckled, studying her face with an amused expression.

"What's so funny?"

He shook his head. "I don't know how you do it, Torrie, but you've somehow managed to get dirt on your face in the short time you shuttled two flats to the loading dock. Maybe we need to wrap your head in plastic."

"For Pete's sake, not again!" Torrie swiped at her cheek and then her forehead. It was an ongoing joke at the landscape center how Torrie could attract dirt without much effort.

There was laughter in Joe's eyes as he resumed his work attaching the wheels to the cart's frame. "And a word of caution," he said without looking up, his voice growing serious, "Ivan Winters is inside with the boss man."

"Oh, brother," she groaned. "What does he need from Finn? He never buys anything." She dusted the palms of her hands together to dislodge the dirt and eyed the front door as if it was blistering hot and a dragon might jump out of it. "What's he doing here?"

"What he always does," Joe said in a calm voice. "Looking for you."

"Well, I wish he'd save himself a lot of aggravation and give up. I have no plans to go to dinner with him, or go out for a ride, or meet his endless mind-numbing clients for drinks."

"How many times are you going to turn the man down?"

"As many times as is needed to get the message across."

They exchanged a knowing glance.

"For heaven's sake, Joe, he makes me *want* to drink."

His low, raspy chuckle followed her all the way to the front door. But her hand barely touched the doorknob when it swung open and Ivan Winters stepped out.

Torrie eyed him cautiously. He was a banking

cliché. His whole appearance screamed financial guru from his dark suits right down to his meticulously shined, black loafers. She was certain his ingratiating demeanor and fake air of authority had been honed from schmoozing wealthy customers, handling their money, and securing low interest loans for them. Lately, he seemed to pop up every place she went, and she half-heartedly reminded herself to check her van to see if it was bugged with a tracking device.

Ivan's father, Dr. James Winters, had been the town's only doctor for over forty years before retiring a few years ago. He was loved and respected among the town's population. Everyone knew he had been disappointed when Ivan chose the First National Bank and a swanky corner office over a career in medicine.

"So there you are," Ivan said. "My, my, looking as beautiful as ever." He moved closer to her. Too close.

Torrie took a step backward. "Ivan, nice to see you. What can we help you with today? Maybe some annuals or perennials or a new summer bush? We just received a shipment of flowering almonds and the marigolds and pansies are spectacular this year. Everyone's buying petunias. Better grab them while there's a selection to choose from." She heard Joe snort from behind her.

Ivan dismissed her spiel with a curt shake of his head. "Nothing, nothing. I actually stopped by to see you. Do you know you have dirt on your face?" He squinted through his wire rims at her.

"So I've heard." She swiped at her forehead with the back of her hand, transferring some of the dirt onto it. She looked at it, frowned, and wiped her hand on the side of her shorts.

Ivan looked at her with hopeful, expectant eyes. "I'm getting a few banking associates from out of town together at a local restaurant on Friday, and I was wondering whether you'd like to be my date for the evening."

Over my dead body. Torrie cleared her throat. "Sorry, Ivan, but I made plans to have dinner with a friend on Friday night." It was the truth. It was exactly what Rich had called them. Friends. It had been a long time since she had dinner at a nice restaurant. She was looking forward to an evening where there was no pressure, no romantic implications, but a lot of good food and adult conversation.

A look of disappointment crossed Ivan's face. "Well, maybe next time," he said. "There will be a next time. Right, Torrie?"

Torrie hesitated. She dug her fingernails into the palms of her hands, "We'll see. No promises, Ivan."

"You'll *see*?" There was a sharp edge to his voice. "Can you be a bit more specific?"

"Not really," she replied meekly. She could feel him frowning without having to look at him. "The landscape center is always busy at the beginning of summer, Ivan."

"Don't you think you owe me a favor once in a while?"

This time she heard more than mild irritation in his tone. The last thing she needed was for Ivan to get upset and go off the rails on her in front of everyone. She was never happier to hear her phone ring than at that very moment.

"Excuse me." She stepped backward a few paces and held up a hand. "I have to take this." She turned around, glanced at the cellphone, and saw the caller ID pop up as her own name. Suddenly she realized the phone she was holding hadn't played her usual tune, but rather an unrecognizable pop tune. Brows wrinkled, she said, "Hello, Torrine Larson."

"Torrie, this is Rich. I need to talk to you. Am I interrupting you?"

"Actually, this is the perfect time." She shifted to her warm, customer-friendly sing-song voice. "And don't be silly, of course you're not interrupting me. What kind of shrubs were you interested in buying?"

There was dead silence for a moment. "You do know you're talking on your brother's phone?"

"No, I didn't, but it's okay. He'll understand. Our customers come first. Did you say you needed to order some flowers instead?" Torrie cast an uneasy glance over her shoulder at Ivan while she frantically searched her brain trying to discern why Rich Redman had her phone. She pulled the phone from her ear and looked at the home screen with a picture of a motorcycle behind the icons. Gus! She had her youngest brother's phone.

"Let me guess," Rich's soft sexy voice purred. "You're trying to avoid someone around you, aren't you?" A deep, rich chuckle rumbled through the phone's speaker.

"Yes, absolutely." She silently pleaded for him to play along so she could make a clean escape from Ivan Winters before he caused a scene. "Did you have a particular arrangement in mind? Local flowers, perhaps?"

And he did. "Well, yes. I have an absolutely fabulous idea swirling around in my head at the moment. Unfortunately, the arrangement has nothing to do with flowers."

"So sorry to hear that." Torrie felt her face grow hot. She looked over her shoulder again. Ivan Winters inched closer, obviously hoping to catch a part of the conversation.

There was a long, audible sigh from Rich. "You wound me, Torrie Larson. Listen, Gus stopped by and dropped off your phone, hoping to catch you here. The phones were switched when you left them in the pickup. You grabbed his after you rescued Estella and me."

"Ah ha, now I'm on the same page."

"Well, now. Since we're on the same page," Rich's deep voice bounced back, "I've taken seven calls on this blasted phone. Two from your mother—who, by the way, was very warm and cordial—and five from people who want to place orders for floral arrangements. I have no clue whether they want local homegrown, imported, or exotic flowers. But if I have to hear 'I Love the Flower Girl' one more time, I'm going to pitch the phone in the rose beds out back."

"Hey, let's not make any rash decisions. I'll be right there to help you." Delighted to avoid a confrontation with Ivan, Torrie gave Joe and him a quick wave and trotted to the parking lot with the phone still plastered to her ear.

"Wait, wait," Ivan sputtered. "I need to talk to—"

Ignoring him, she shouted, "Sorry, guys, I *have* to take care of this."

She climbed into the van and breathed a sigh of relief. Dumb luck, she decided, was definitely better than none at all. Again, she had dodged another bullet with Ivan. How much longer could she thwart his advances? Yet, she wasn't sure dealing with Rich Redman would be any easier than handling the blustering banker.

****

The sun was casting long afternoon shadows when Torrie drove to her sister's house later in the afternoon, after dropping off Gus's phone at the garage. Overhead, a gentle breeze slowly pushed fleecy clouds eastward. The half-hour drive gave her time to mull over what had happened back at Gertie's house when she returned the second time with the flowers for Lulu.

Rich had been waiting for her and had answered the door with a pained grimace on his face, his hand gripping the cellphone. "This may cost you yet another dinner date," he groused. "Or…maybe some other type of compensation for taking all these confounded intricate messages." He waved a pile of notes under her nose. "I know what baby's breath is, but I don't have a clue what bouvardia and trachelium are. I can't even spell the darn words. And delphinium just sounds too racy to put in anyone's bouquet."

"Here's Lulu's flower delivery," she said, trying to keep a straight face. She pointed to the two flats she had deposited on the front porch beside the door. "First of all, it's not a date on Friday. It's more like an outing. Second, I don't need your notes, genius, if you left the callers' numbers on my phone."

"Outing?" His grimace morphed into a bewildered expression that made him look like a kid who just had his candy stolen. Except he was no kid. He was a man who exuded sensual masculinity. "Hey, you owe me for that ridiculous conversation. Who were you trying to avoid?"

"No one important."

When she stepped up to grab the notes, he scooped her into his arms and, without warning, planted a light kiss squarely in the center of her forehead, oblivious to the dirt. Before she could react, he shoved the notes and phone in her hand, spun her around, and nudged her toward the steps. "Now go pluck the local flowers and bamboozle all those poor unsuspecting customers. I have work to do." He smiled an arresting smile.

"Bamboozle?" She turned toward him and gave him a perplexed look. "Seriously? Isn't that a word to better describe *your* occupation?" Forcing herself to suppress a grin, she clambered down the steps and called over her shoulder, "Don't forget to feed Sheba. Have Lulu teach you."

She slid into the driver's seat and tossed the phone and notes onto the passenger seat. But before she could pull away from Gertie's house, her phone rang. This time it wasn't her usual ringtone. Rich Redman had changed her tune from *I Love the Flower Girl* to the *Yellow Rose of Texas*.

"The audacity of that man! What a blockhead," she sputtered aloud. How dare he toy with her ringtone? Her mother had suggested the 60's song when she first started floral arranging at the landscape center. She reached for the phone and answered more sharply than she normally would, "What? What do you want now, Richard Lee Redman? I'm driving. I can't talk."

There was a pause on the other end of the phone, and Torrie hoped he wasn't going to say *you*—or his Friday outing with her was going down the drain.

Instead, he merely said in his low and sensual voice, "You know you have dirt on your face, don't you?"

Torrie hung up on him.

****

A half hour later, Torrie pulled into her sister's driveway, just outside Hickory Valley. Elsa lived with her husband, Neil, in a renovated farmhouse with enough land for a few alpacas for producing yarn.

Torrie spied Iris flying high into the air on a swing set along with Elsa's two boys. The little girl came tearing across the yard to meet her, and Torrie was barely able to get out of the van before Iris flew into her arms.

Many nights Torrie lay awake and wondered how she could ever repay her sister, who had taken in the little girl as an infant and made her part of her family, so Torrie could work and not worry about babysitters— another cost she could hardly afford. Torrie considered herself fortunate she could see Iris every Wednesday on her day off, and then pick her up for the weekend. Adaptable for a child her age, but quiet and demure, Iris had settled nicely into a schedule of being beside her when she worked on Saturdays at the landscape center. All day Sunday was strictly theirs to enjoy before she drove her back to Elsa's in the evening. Only close family members knew how hard Torrie was working to scrape together enough money to get a bigger apartment so Iris could stay with her in town and start first grade in the fall.

Iris slipped out of her mother's arm. She was a small girl and had the same aquamarine eyes and white-blonde hair as her mother. "Mommy, Aunt Elsa said she'd bake cookies with me later this afternoon. Swedish angels crisps. It's an old, old recipe of Great

Grandmother Larson's."

Torrie stomach churned with guilt and frustration. She should be the one making cookies with her child. She pasted on one of her false smiles she had perfected over the last few years. "Wonderful, honey. Aunt Elsa is a terrific baker. Her cookies are the best."

The little girl nodded. With her tiny hand in Torrie's, Iris pulled her across the yard to the house with the boys tagging behind. When they entered the kitchen, Elsa turned from mixing ingredients in a bowl at the counter. "I was wondering when you would arrive. I just baked a coconut cake with pineapple filling and toasted coconut frosting. Let me finish this cookie batter and put it in the refrigerator. It'll keep." She turned to the children looking at her expectantly. "We're having grapes for our snack this afternoon and you can take them outside to eat while I talk to Aunt Torrie for a few minutes." Obediently, all three waited as she handed them each a small plastic bag of grapes and a juice box. Amid a noisy discussion of who had the most, they headed out to the picnic table on the lawn to count and eat the contents in their bags.

"I don't know how you do it," Torrie said. "All these kids and still you find time to bake and sew, raise alpacas, weave, and keep everyone happy as well."

Elsa laughed. "I bake and sew and keep house. Keep everyone happy? Not my job! Wait five minutes until they all start quibbling, and you'll see how happiness flows through this house." She tapped the spoon on the bowl, covered it, and put it in the refrigerator. "Finn stopped by earlier today. He says the landscape center is doing so much better for early summer than it did last year."

"It is. And we are mowing more lawns and selling twice the shrubs and flowers as last summer."

"How's the floral arranging?"

"It's starting to surge." Torrie frowned. She thought of the five notes lying on her passenger seat. Five orders in one day were encouraging. Word of mouth was beginning to bolster sales along with her website. "But it looks like Rich Redman is here to sell Gertie Redman's house and all my fresh local flowers will have to be uprooted and replanted, unless I can convince him to let me rent the portion of land where they're growing. I could lose a lot of healthy stock, and the vintage roses are in a precarious position with new grafts on some of them."

Elsa set two plates on the table. "That's not good. You and Gertie spent a tremendous amount of time working with those roses." She proceeded to cut them each a slice of cake. "Have you talked to him about it?"

Torrie's mind flitted back to their conversation on the porch and the innocent kiss he planted on her forehead. The man was an enigma. She couldn't quite read him. In control, was all she could think, and how glorious he smelled. How gorgeous and sexy he always appeared.

"Just briefly." Torrie picked at the cake with her fork. "And that's another problem. I tried to explain why I don't date, but he wants to take me out to dinner Friday night as friends."

"How wonderful!" Elsa gave her a soft sisterly pat on her arm. "I hope he takes you dancing, too. In high school, all the girls swooned over his ability to dance. You know, Torrie, it's time to get back in the groove."

"What groove? There never was a groove. Just a

huge ditch I fell into six years ago."

"Because you won't let anyone get close." Elsa stated the obvious. "You know Ivan Winters down at First National has persistently asked you out."

"And I persistently refuse." Torrie wrinkled her nose. "I'd rather snuggle up to an adding machine than date him. He never stops talking about numbers or boring interest rates and the stock market." *And he continually throws subtle hints at me about the money I owe him…and maybe some other special favors.*

But my, how good it felt to be wrapped in Rich Redman's arms, she thought. The man was solidly built, all muscle without an inch of fat on his body. Why, oh why, had she ever agreed to have dinner with him? They were complete opposites. This was a high profile man, a well-known lawyer. A man who could find out the truth about her, about Iris, and about the debt she owed to Ivan Winters.

"Of course he likes to talk about money. He's a banker, after all." Elsa's words jerked her wandering mind back to reality.

"Yes, I guess, you're right." She fidgeted in her chair. "I need a favor. I need to borrow a dress for tomorrow night and a pair of your heels. I asked Rich to take me out of town so no one would see us, and he said to wear a knock-out dress if we're going to eat fancy and use his grandmother's '67 Goat."

"Good luck with sneaking out of town in a red muscle car." Elsa snickered. "And do I have the perfect dress for you." Grinning, she rose from the table, disappeared into her bedroom, and returned with a crimson dress with the tags on it. It was a flirty-looking, short mini-sheath dress. Strappy, four-inch gold shoes dangled from her other hand. "This dress will fit you perfectly and will make your hair shine like moon beams, and these shoes will make you look like you're all legs, but not slutty. There are advantages to looking irresistible when you spring on him your desire to keep those flowerbeds intact."

"Elsa, I'm not trying to get the man aroused or gain advantage by using any kind of sexual ploys. This is strictly a dinner between friends."

"Sure it is," Elsa said in a knowing voice.

Chapter Six

The night was still young when Rich walked out on the porch with a glass of Lucille's homemade lemonade. He shoved a hand into his back pocket, leaned against a porch post, and looked at the distant field glowing like a golden blanket in the light from the huge full moon above. The frogs and insects in the grass sang their ongoing soft, comforting chorus of music. He realized he had missed it, having lived so long in the city. He decided it had to be the whiskey the last time he heard his grandmother's voice. He'd be more careful and would only occasionally imbibe. He had to keep his wits and sanity intact. Right now, he needed a clear head to think.

"Pretty sight, isn't it?" a scratchy voice from the opposite end of porch said.

Startled, Rich jumped and looked over at the rocker. It started to move even though the night was windless and quiet.

"Sheesh, I thought I was hallucinating the other night or having a bad dream," Rich said. "Then I decided I was only having a bout of insanity brought on by exhaustion, or maybe top-shelf whiskey overload. I convinced myself you didn't really exist, Grandmother Gertrude." He heard a cackle and watched the rocker move slowly then pick up speed to a rhythmic cadence.

"Sorry, no hallucinations, no dreams. Now your

sanity, I can't vouch for that, my boy."

He turned and looked back out over the yard. "Tell me, why did you and Torrie Larson start all those flowerbeds beside the shed?"

"We wanted to save the last surviving white rose bush your Great Grandmother Hilda planted from clippings she brought to America from Austria. Torrie loves roses. She's trying to make a go of it with the landscaping business and her floral arranging. You should stop in and see all the beautiful bouquets and planters Larson's Landscaping offers. The girl has talent."

"I just might do that," Rich admitted.

"So you're taking her to dinner on Friday night?"

"Yes." He couldn't believe he was having a conversation about dating with a ghost. And the ghost of his grandmother to boot.

The rocker slowed a little. "Go easy on her, Richard Lee, she's very fragile, despite her seemingly confident attitude. The girl has a heap of troubles for someone so young."

Rich turned and stared at the flower beds, a colorful whirl of color underneath the rays of the moon. "I checked with the lawyer's office and the bank, and I see you set up a trust fund for me and this lost, nameless half-sister of mine. How do I give half the proceeds from a trust to someone I don't know—or can't even be sure exists? Where do I find this person?"

"You'll figure it out. Don't you want to meet her?"

"And what if I don't?" He sighed.

"Don't want to meet her?"

"No, what if I don't figure it out? What if I can't or don't get the money to her?'

Gertie laughed. "Then I'll have to come back and haunt you."

Rich looked heavenward. His expression was one of pained tolerance. "I thought that's what you're doing now."

"Phfftt. Don't be impertinent, Richard Lee Junior. It doesn't fit with your moral integrity, nor with your kind but too often noble nature."

He looked over at the rocker, which had come to a dead stop. Suddenly a cool breeze swirled around him and disappeared.

Gertie was irritated and was obviously finished talking.

Chapter Seven

Rich stood in his bedroom before a floor length wardrobe mirror with four pairs of eyes watching him. It was fifteen minutes before he was supposed to meet Torrie at her apartment for their dinner date. On the bed, Estella sat cross-legged, two pigtails jutting out from the sides of her head and tied with pink ribbons. Beside her, the purple giraffe gazed silently at him as well. Dressed in three different shades of pink with a green apron, Lulu sat in a wingchair by the window with her lips pursed. Marlene in her signature four-inch high but now electric blue heels, stood at the corner of the bed shaking her head in exasperation. Across the foot of the bed at least a dozen ties were laid out and lined up like tin soldiers. When he had solicited the females to help him select one, he had no idea what fashion horrors he was about to endure.

"Okay, the blue shirt with the gray slacks doesn't make you look as stiff and lawyerly-looking as the white shirt does," Marlene said. "Too bad you don't have any softer-colored shirts." She dangled three other ties in her hand she had brought along with her.

Rich glowered at her. "Lawyerly-looking? Softer-colored? Are they even words? All I want to do is *not* look like an affluent stuffy lawyer with a stick up—" He stopped and looked over at Estella, then continued in an irritated voice. "I want to look dressy, but not straitlaced or smug. You know what I mean."

"But you are a stuffy lawyer, and it's no secret your bank accounts won't bounce, you dolt," Lulu said with a huff. "I thought you and Torrie were going out as friends."

"We are. But I don't want her to feel uncomfortable, and I want to feel casual, but well-dressed." He picked up a blue and white striped tie and held it to his chest. All three females groaned. He chose a darker blue one and the groans grew louder. He glared at them. "I'll have you know some of these ties are pure Italian silk and cost a fortune. To some people, neckties are a symbol of success and authority."

"Then send them back to Rome and let the Pope bury the lifeless-looking things." Lulu rose. "They look like they *should* be on a corpse."

Rich looked at Marlene. "Can you believe I'm paying her to insult me?"

Lulu snorted. "No, Perry Mason, you're paying me to feed you, do your laundry, and oversee the household. The advice is free." She headed for the door. "I'm going home, kids. See you in the morning."

"I can't wait," Rich muttered and followed it with a dismal shake of his head.

Lulu paused and offered him a don't-you-dare-tangle-with-me stare, then looked at Estella with a tender, warm, grandmotherly smile. "Your daddy doesn't realize the only reason I take his grief is because I love to be with you, doll face. You have a good night with Marlene. Tomorrow we're making brownies and Perry Mason is getting zip, zero, none, nichts, nada." She headed out the door.

"Stop calling me Perry Mason!" Rich shouted at

her retreating back. He heard her cackling laugh as she hustled toward the stairs.

"Okay, Sunshine," was the only response that filtered up to him.

Laughing, Marlene said, "Well, I can see Lulu fits in perfectly with this household. She can hold her own with you, Richard Lee Junior."

When Rich gave her a scathing glance, she held out the ties in her hand and sighed. "Pick one. They all go well with the shirt, and they aren't as severe or boring as yours. Hurry up, or you're going to be late."

"Those? It looks like someone scribbled on them." Rich eyed the ties suspiciously.

"The designer would be thrilled by your compliment."

"I have an idea, Daddy," Estella scampered off the bed with her giraffe under her arm. "Take them with you and ask Torrie which one she likes the best."

Rich let out a long audible breath of relief and scooped up his daughter in his arms. "Estella, My-Bella! Yours is the first good idea I've heard all day." He kissed her on both cheeks and twirled her around. "Don't give Marlene a hard time, now," he instructed. "I'll see you in the morning." He grabbed his sport coat and the ties and tore out of the bedroom.

Torrie's apartment was only ten minutes away and Rich arrived with just minutes to spare. Scooping up the neck ties and four white roses from the passenger seat, he took the stairs two at a time to her second-floor apartment. It was a drab little place of brown wood siding with unpainted wooden steps, but Rich suspected she chose it because of the cheap rent.

With sweaty palms, he stopped on the landing

before pushing the doorbell and blew out a breath of air to calm himself. He was out of his comfort zone. He was not used to dating. In fact, he had rarely gone out since his wife died two years ago. Often the guys in the office had tried to fix him up with someone, but most times he had declined—declined even meeting new women for drinks after work when friends were present to break the ice. He hated the whole idea of hanging out in bars and local clubs and hooking up. He just didn't feel ready to move on until he'd met Torrie Larson. She was literally a down-to-earth kind of girl. And she looked sexy whether she was wearing oversized coveralls or cargo shorts splattered with mud.

But nothing prepared him for the Torrie Larson who answered the door. She was wearing a simply sumptuous, strapless, satin dress in vibrant red. The dress made her aquamarine eyes glow like rich jewels and exposed her flawless, creamy neck and back, so smooth he wanted to reach out and caress every inch of her bare skin. And it was so short, it was every man's dream of what a real dress should be. Her killer gold heels were designed to get a man's attention and drive him crazy when his eyes locked onto those shapely legs disappearing under the dress. She had her hair tied into a fancy twist at the back of her head, but already errant tendrils escaped to frame her face.

"Wow, you look stunning," he said and handed her the four white roses.

"Then this qualifies for knocking your socks off?" She took the roses and laughed. It was a pleasant, musical laugh, soothing to a poor, sex-starved soul.

Rich followed her inside the tiny apartment. Of the matchbox variety, it had a small eat-in kitchen and a pass-through counter as well. The cupboards, obviously old, had been repainted in a creamy white and new tan countertops had been installed along with new black appliances. Pictures of animals, drawn and colored by a child of elementary age, were splattered all over the front of her refrigerator. Through the pass-through window, he could see a tiny living room full of mismatched furniture, but pulled together with an assortment of colorful pillows. In a corner, a round willow basket was filled with toys and stuffed animals. He surmised a postage-stamp-sized bedroom and bath were in the back.

"Four roses? Not a dozen? Not one? But four?" Torrie smiled.

"For four days of knowing you."

"Ah, so sweet. Thank you." She poured water into a bud vase, trimmed the lower leaves, and arranged the blossoms.

He leaned against the counter watching her. "I have a problem."

She studied his downcast face. "Can I help?"

"I was trying to decide which necktie to wear and couldn't." He held up the three ties Marlene had purchased for him.

She dried her hands on a dish towel. "I'm assuming the sport coat is navy blue."

"Yes, it's in the car. "How'd you know?"

"You seem like a classic kind of guy who likes navy." Brows wrinkled in concentration, she fingered each one, then selected the dark blue tie that looked like someone had scribbled on it in colors of lighter blues and gold.

He set the other two ties on the counter, flipped up

the collar of his shirt, and wound the tie around his neck. "Do you have a mirror?" he asked, fumbling with the ends.

"Here, I can do this." Torrie stepped up to him and took the two ends of the tie lying on his chest. "With three brothers, I'm a pro."

She was standing so near his lips brushed the hair at her forehead, and she was wearing a heady perfume all over her luscious body. It smelled like a mixture of citrus and flowers and could drive a man absolutely insane. If they didn't get out of this small apartment, he was going to grab her right on the spot and kiss her senseless.

Within seconds, she had the tie in place. She lightly patted his chest. "There. You look perfect." When their eyes met, Rich swore she could read his mind. She nervously stepped back, spun, and dashed to the living room where she grabbed her purse and a lacy wrap from the back of a recliner and hurried to the front door.

"Who's the famous artist on the refrigerator?" he asked as he passed it.

"Kids," she said evasively. "Did you know Elsa has two boys?"

****

Torrie settled into the passenger seat of the GTO and decided she would cast aside her worries for a few hours and just enjoy an evening out. The ride to Gibson Lake was heavenly. Rich had thoughtfully put the convertible's top up and had barely interrupted her reverie as she watched the countryside fly by. She had forgotten how silence between two individual needn't be painful, but peaceful and comfortable. It had been ages since she had been at a restaurant that wasn't fast

68

food and cost over a few dollars for a meal. It wasn't in her budget. These days there wasn't much in her budget except hotdogs and cheap food, rent, and utilities. Sometimes Henry even let her rent slide a month when unexpected bills popped up. She was also paying Ivan a little each month on her personal loan, but he was getting bolder each month, pressuring her to date him even though she had no inclination to become involved.

When they finally stopped at a German restaurant on the wharf beside the lake, Rich broke the silence. "I hope you like German food. But if not, I heard they have fabulous seafood and steaks."

Torrie tilted her head and chuckled. "Most of the time I'm eating on the run, grabbing a sandwich or hamburger from a fast food place. This will be delightful. Honestly."

The hostess led them through the dimly lit restaurant to a small, secluded table overlooking the water. Flickering blue candles accented the crisp white of the table linens. Night was drawing near. Outside, miniature lights in the potted greenery lining the wharf twinkled like a swarm of fireflies. It was a fairyland sight inside and out. When she opened the menu, Torrie noticed it was in both German and English. She also noticed the prices were extraordinarily high. She sucked in a breath of air.

"Something wrong?" He leaned forward and looked at her with concern. "If you don't like what's on the menu, I'm sure we can get you a special order. I never thought to ask whether you had diet restrictions or food allergies."

She shook her head. "No, I was just thinking my German needs some work," she lied. She was glad when they were interrupted by a waitress who brought out a bottle of wine, a well-aged German Riesling, obviously called in by Rich earlier in the day. She smiled a warm, welcoming smile at Torrie, then poured some wine for Rich to approve. He nodded, and she filled both wine glasses before moving toward another table.

"Please, Rich, tell me our wine didn't cost over twenty-five dollars a bottle."

He looked at her with a gentle, bemused gaze. "Relax, Torrie. Let's just enjoy the night. What's a German meal without a good imported wine? Please allow me the honor of paying you back for rescuing Estella and me." He raised his glass to hers. "To renewing old friendships."

A flash of humor crossed her face. "And finding misplaced jewels and relatives."

He set his glass aside and leaned back in his seat. "You know, I have a proposition for you."

Torrie choked on her wine. "What kind?" She brought her napkin to her sputtering lips.

"Not what you're thinking, but I am open to all kinds of possibilities." His voice was warm, soft, and husky. "You said you're off on Wednesdays, and I need someone to examine the journals and help me with the German."

"No, I couldn't." Torrie dropped her gaze and knew his sharp eyes were scrutinizing her. Wednesday was the only day she had during the week to see Iris. It was the day she cut Henry's payroll, although it didn't take more than an hour using the software and a computer since all his employees used direct deposit. "I'm pretty busy. I have Henry's payroll."

"We can work around his payroll. How about afternoons?"

"I usually go visit my sister or my family." Torrie hated to lie, hated not telling him about her daughter. She was a single, unwed mom. Not even a widow. Rumors around town were already unpleasant. A man of his caliber would never entertain the thought of being around someone like her. Especially if he found out what her ex-in-laws thought about her.

He frowned. "Give me four weeks of Wednesday afternoons and I'll double the amount Henry pays you an hour to do his payroll. You can do the payroll in the morning, and afterward come over to the house. I'll have Lulu make us some lunch so we can start working immediately, if you need to leave early."

Torrie shook her head. "I'm sorry. It just won't work."

"I'll triple it." He threw out the offer with a half-smile this time. "You're killing me here, Torrine Larson. I need your help with the German." There was a hopeful glint in his smoky eyes.

"Triple it? You're serious?" Torrie stared at him awestruck. Triple her pay for four Wednesday afternoons? Good heavens, that was a lot of money. And my, what it could buy. She could always see Iris later in the evening. The nighttime drive would be taxing after a long day, but it would only be for a month. It was certainly worth the inconvenience and sacrifice. The money would buy her daughter new school clothes. She was about to speak when a figure towered over her.

"Well, well, well, this is a surprise," the voice said. "Imagine seeing you here." The man turned and nodded a greeting at Rich. "I see you're back in town, Redman."

Icy dread ripped through Torrie's stomach. Ivan Winters. The very last person she hoped to see this far from Hickory Valley. She felt her face grow hot and was angry at herself for being embarrassed. She had as much right to be there as he did. She forced out a tight smile. "Hello, Ivan, how are you?"

He glared at her, his lips thinned with irritation. "Rather lavish place for eating with just a friend, don't you think?" His eyes took time to sweep around the room before settling on her again. "But you do look elegant tonight, my dear. Too bad you couldn't have joined us. If you have a few moments I'd like to introduce you to some of my associates. We have a table in the back of the restaurant."

Torrie nervously twisted the ring on her hand. "Maybe some other time, Ivan. We haven't been served our meal yet." She adjusted her smile and prayed he would leave them alone. It was well-known around town that Ivan harbored an aggressive demeanor, especially if he was drinking. "Rich and I are trying to get caught up on old times, and I've some business to discuss with him."

"It will only take a minute."

"The lady says no," Rich spoke up. His earlier warm smoky eyes turned to cold dark marble. "I promised her dinner and an enjoyable night for rescuing me and my daughter when we arrived in Hickory Valley. I am not in the mood to share her at the moment, and especially since we've only had a sip of this well-aged German wine." Like he was dismissing a bothersome gnat, he added, "Have a nice evening, Ivan.

Your guests are waiting for you." He signaled to the waitress who earlier poured their wine.

Ivan glared at Torrie, then spun on his heel, and disappeared into the crowded restaurant.

When the waitress arrived, Rich spoke with icy disdain. "Please send a couple bottles of your very best white wine over to the table of bankers in the back of the room. Put it on my tab and make it as dry as they are."

The young girl smirked, covering her mouth with her hand to suppress a giggle. "Yes, sir. Will there be anything else?"

"Yes, we'll have the house special, if it's all right with you?" He looked at Torrie, who nodded. Rich stared at the waitress. She had dark brown hair and an easy smile. "Didn't I just see you at Webster's Burgers and Fries Restaurant in Hickory Valley?"

The girl nodded in agreement. "Yes, I work there days, and here a couple nights. I'm Denise." She waved across the room to another young woman with light brown hair who was filling a tray with water glasses. "You can make better tips here. Danielle, my sister, works here, too. Anything else?"

"No, not now. Thank you." When she left, Rich's lips turned up into a comical smile. "Well, that should keep the good ol' banking boys off our backs for a little while."

"You didn't have to do that," Torrie said. She hung her head. How could Ivan Winters do this to her? He acted like he owned her. And he was hardly cordial to Rich. "This night is going to cost a fortune."

"Torrie." She felt his hand cover hers on the table. "Will you please just forget about the cost of everything for the next three hours? Can you try?" His voice had a warm, but authoritative tone. "Just take a deep breath and relax."

She forced a tentative smile. "Ivan gets into his banker's role and seems a bit snobbish at times. He meant well. I never thought I'd run into anyone I know here. I feel like the kid caught with her hand in the cookie jar."

Rich looked across the table and his face split into an infectious grin. "Well, if the restaurant is the cookie jar, then I must be the cookie! I haven't had this much fun for a long time."

Suddenly Torrie had the urge to laugh, her mood suddenly turning buoyant. "You know this will be all over town tomorrow."

"It's headed straight for the gossip pipeline, I imagine."

She ran her finger down the handle of her silverware, toying with them. "Ivan was the one I was avoiding on the phone the other day when Gus and I had our phones switched. So tell me, how is Estella doing with Lulu?"

He chuckled. "They're ganging up on me. Another reason I could use you. There's security in numbers. Estella has spied the pots on the porch and wants to plant flowers in them, and she's been eying the flowers in your beds out back. Her mother must be rolling over in her grave. She never would have gotten her hands dirty."

"Tell me about her."

"Margaretta?" He shrugged. "She was beautiful. Bilingual in Spanish and English. She loved her job, which was jet-setting all over the globe following movie stars and their shoots. She designed costumes and always had to be on the set to be sure everything was perfect. To be honest, we disagreed a lot. I wanted her to stay home and spend more time in Texas once Estella was born." He looked out the window, his gaze distant and forlorn. "I told her not to hop that small plane to Mexico after I checked the weather forecast. She wouldn't listen. She said I was an overly cautious worrier. She and the crew flew into a wicked storm and the plane went down."

This time Torrie placed a hand on his and studied him. "I'm sorry for bringing up bad memories."

"No, it's all right." He squeezed her fingers and met her gaze calmly. "She's been dead for two years, and I'm over the hard parts. I just can't seem to get back into going out. I'm so glad you agreed to have dinner with me. If I have to talk to crazy Lulu and all the dolls and stuffed animals magically appearing with Estella as dinner companions, I'm going to need a psychoanalyst."

In the background, a small Bavarian band had started playing a soft waltz. Rich stood. "Come on, let's give those bankers an eyeful and some juicy gossip for tomorrow's pipeline. I want my lady in red to dance with me. We've already blown your cover. You look gorgeous tonight, and I say we work up an appetite while waiting for our food."

"Oh, no, we shouldn't."

"Oh, yes, we should. Let's both of us be daring tonight." He pulled her to her feet and with hands linked, urged her toward the dance floor where he grasped her firmly and pulled her close. Too close. When she tried to resist, he said, "Easy, Torrie, time for you to be the fearless one. Let's give Ivan Winters a spectacular reason to be ticked off."

"This is so wrong and so deceitful!" Her laugh rippled, low and smooth. But she let him pull her so tightly against him she could smell his spectacular spicy cologne. With her cheek resting next to his jaw, she gave in and snuggled close, following his lead. He was an excellent dancer, just like Elsa said, and Torrie found herself getting swept up in the lyrics and beat and enjoying the warmth and heat of his body. She knew she needed to talk to him about her flowerbeds and renting the land. Maybe if she agreed to help him with his great grandmother's journals, it would give her time to convince him the plants needed to stay intact. But for this moment, she was going to forget all her troubles and just enjoy the music and the dance. In her life there were few things that felt this good. And she was going to savor it.

****

It was late when Rich and Torrie headed back to Hickory Valley. Both of them were content to just listen to the low, soft music from the radio and enjoy the peaceful feeling of being beside each other. Half-way there, Torrie broke the silence. "When I talked with Henry the other day, he told me Gertie's husband had a brother named Walter. Henry indicated he was an old bachelor, more like the black sheep of the family."

"Interesting." Rich turned the radio even lower. "My dad never mentioned he had an uncle. Did he say whether this brother of my grandfather was still alive or where he lived?"

"No," Torrie admitted. She leaned her head exhaustedly against the seat. "But it's a start. Maybe he knows something about the jewels. Maybe Gertie even told him something about your father and his little diversion from his marriage."

"Little diversion?" Rich snorted. "Is that what you call cheating in a marriage?"

Torrie winced. "It's called adultery. I was trying to be kind." She sat up straighter in her seat. "Listen, if we're going to turn over rocks looking for this half-sister, you need to be able to accept there might be other unsavory secrets that come to light."

"Then you'll help me?" His exuberance was visible in his voice. He pulled into a parking space beneath her apartment, slid out, and rounded the car to open her door.

Torrie stood beside the car. "Let me think on it over the weekend and get back to you?" She patted him gently on the chest. "No need to walk me to the door, Rich. I know the way. It's been a heavenly evening and fabulous dinner. Thank you for everything."

"But I want to walk you," he said softly and nudged her on her back. They climbed the stairs ending on the landing. He held out his hand and she searched her purse for the key.

"I'd invite you in for coffee, but it's late, and I have to work the landscape center early tomorrow morning," she said. "I promised Finn. We're moving perennial stock around."

"I understand." His voice was low and husky as he unlocked the door, dropped the key in her hand, and pulled her close, enveloping her in a snug embrace.

Torrie melted into his arms. It felt so good and so right. Too bad he was only here for a few weeks. Even a summer fling might not be a bad idea, she thought.

Then she remembered she was keeping secrets that could surface and hurt everyone if he found out.

"I had a wonderful time tonight, too, Torrie," she heard him say into her hair. She looked at him. His gaze traveled over her face and searched her eyes. A second later his lips descended to meet hers. The kiss was slow and gentle. Nothing like she expected. She felt a slow flame begin to burn all the way down to her toes in her strappy heels. When she lightly nudged him away, he pulled back and placed another soft kiss next to her ear, whispering, "Goodnight, Torrie Larson. Sweet dreams."

Then, like the gentleman he was, he turned and walked down the stairs without looking back.

Chapter Eight

Rich Redman was sure he was going to strangle Lulu if he had enough energy to get out of bed and walk downstairs. It was Saturday morning, and even though the sun wasn't up, Estella was. She leaned over his bed, giraffe under one arm, shook the bed, and whispered near his ear, "Are you asleep, Daddy?"

"Yes," he mumbled, eyes still closed. "If you are a little girl in pink pajamas, you're supposed to go back to bed."

Estella giggled. "No. Get up," she urged. "We have to go to Larson's Landscape Center. Lulu said if we bought some flowers, she would help me plant the empty pots on the back porch. I want to do it. I want some of those purple flowers like Lulu bought, but in pink. Can you pleeease get up and take me?"

Rich opened one eye. "Petunias. They're called petunias. We have all afternoon to get *petunias*, Estella."

"We do not." She set the giraffe on his chest and planted her hands on her hips. "We need to get Sheba a flea collar, too, and I need clothes like everyone else wears to work outside."

"You have jeans to wear. Why does Sheba need a flea collar?" He yawned.

"No, you don't understand. I want the kind with hooks. Not those girly pink ones. I want old ones."

With a weary groan, he forced both eyes open and squinted at her. While her voice held a tinge of exasperation, her little face was puckered in a downright serious frown. "And Sheba needs a flea collar…" Rich searched his half-alert brain for a logical reason. "…why? For a necklace?"

"No! Oh, Daddy, don't be silly. Lulu said we have to get Sheba a flea collar or else I can't bring her into the house."

Into the house? Rich rolled into a sitting position and scrubbed his hands over his face. "Ah, Estella, please, please, go downstairs and pour yourself some cereal. I'll be there any minute to pour the milk if you're having trouble. I promise. And I promise we'll figure this all out, okay? Daddy needs a minute or two to wake up."

Minutes later, when he walked into the kitchen, he could smell the coffee brewing. Lulu was scrubbing potatoes and peeling carrots at the sink. She had placed a clean cup and a quart of milk beside the coffee machine for him. "Good morning, Sunshine," she said cheerfully. She looked at him clad only in jeans and shook her braided head. "I did laundry, you know."

He groaned. "Lulu, don't you start, too. You lost two points for getting Estella worked up about the flea collar and planting flowers in the blasted pots on the back porch, but you won them back with the fresh coffee. You don't want to lose more points for wisecracks, do you? Did you know, Redman points work similar to frequent flyer miles but with a twist. You can turn them in for cash." He squinted at her. "I thought you wanted weekends off."

"I did, but then I remembered I needed Monday

morning off for a doctor's appointment. I figured if I started early this morning, I could whip up an all-in-one-pan dinner for tonight and another one for Sunday. You would only have to pop them in the oven and have a hot meal." She turned back to the sink. "Now tell me about these Redman points. How do they work and how much are they worth, Sunshine?"

"Lulu, you don't have enough willpower to keep your thoughts to yourself and earn them." He expelled an exhausted sigh, took a sip of coffee, and looked over at Estella, who was already dressed in a blue sundress and sneakers. Her chin was propped on her hand as she looked at a gardening magazine, obviously belonging to Lulu.

"Look, look," she squealed, pausing with a spoon in the air and holding up a picture for him to see. "I want these! Like this girl is wearing in this picture. Only I need ones for little kids, and I want old-looking ones. I don't want to look like a novice gardener."

Novice? Who taught her that word? "Bib overalls. They're bib overalls." He peered at Lulu's back. She was wearing a green and white polka dot blouse with a red skirt and an orange flowered apron. She was probably not the best person to ask about fashion, but he decided to give it a shot anyhow. "Lulu, where do I find bib overalls for little girls in this town?"

Lulu turned from the sink, holding a carrot in her hand. She shrugged. "It's been a long time since I've shopped for kids' clothes. Why don't you ask Torrie?"

"Ask Torrie? Why Torrie?" He looked at her with knitted brows. Elsa had two sons, Finn's kids were older than Elsa's, Gus was still single, and Lars, Elsa's twin, had just gotten engaged. "Why would Torrie know where to buy little girl's clothes?"

Frowning, Lulu started to speak, then thought better of it and turned back to her work at the sink. "Right," she said, "maybe not the best idea, come to think of it. Why don't you get Marlene on it?"

"But they have to be used and old-looking," Estella reminded him. "I don't want to look like I'm a gentleman farmer either. I want to dig in the dirt and get my hands muddy when we plant the flowers. Maybe I need a pair of work gloves, too? I can wear them when I go with Lulu to her farm. You can help, Daddy. It'll be fun."

"I'm sure it will be," Rich agreed, thinking he'd rather have a root canal than go hoeing in someone's farm lot. He didn't want to tell her he wasn't exactly a dirt, manure, and trowel man. "But you have to run upstairs and put jeans on to go to the landscape center, Estella."

Gentleman farmer? Now where did she learn such a rarely used description? He threw a sideways glance at Lulu, who had moved to the refrigerator and poked her head inside as if she were searching for lost gold.

****

Torrie Larson stood at the cash register of the Landscape Center and started to count the opening till for the second time. Her mind was not on her work, especially at six in the morning. She had gotten little sleep the night before and had lain awake trying to decipher what really happened between Rich and her. The gentle kiss they had shared last night was no friendship kiss.

Joe came up to the counter and leaned against it, jingling two screws in his hand. "So how's my favorite girl and how did dinner go last night?"

Torrie looked up. "Good morning, Joe. I'm fine, but tired. The evening was nice and the dinner was excellent. Have you ever had German *rumkugeln*?"

"No, but it sounds like one mean rash if you get it." He winked at her.

"Rum balls, Joe, not a rash." Torrie laughed. "And they were delicious."

"So I gather you and Rich hit it off?"

Torrie shrugged. "We had a good time, except for the sneak appearance by Ivan Winters. Of all the restaurants in the area, Ivan picked the same one Rich chose."

"Be careful around Redman," Joe warned in a low voice. "I'd hate to see you get hurt, Torrie. Be even more cautious with Ivan the Terrible."

Torrie looked at him and his face clouded with uneasiness. Or was it despondency?

"He's going to be headed back to Texas in a month," Joe added. "I'm doing a few renovations for Marlene Hess, and she asked me if I wanted to do some renovations for Redman. He thinks some updates might help sell Gertie's house. I heard it's haunted."

"Come on, Joe, you don't believe in ghosts, do you?" Torrie grinned as she straightened the last bills in the register and closed it.

Joe grinned back at her. "Well, it looks like I might find out. He wants to update the living room first." He tossed the screws in the air and caught them. "I need to run to the hardware store and get some more of these. I left Iris on the monkey bars at the side of the building. Can you handle things here? Finn's at the far back of the lot rearranging fruit trees."

"I got it," Torrie said. "Don't hurry. Grab yourself a donut and a cup of coffee."

But she realized she didn't have it, when she turned the "Open" sign on the door to face the outside and Rich Redman pulled into the nursery at exactly eight a.m. with Estella in tow. Heart thumping, she quickly looked through the side window at the monkey bars, but Iris had disappeared. She breathed a sigh of relief. If she wasn't on the bars, she was tagging after Finn, farther back in the shrub and tree section. Rich would never see Iris or get wind of the fact she was a single mom on a shoestring budget.

Early on, Iris had learned she couldn't be out of sight of Torrie, Finn, or Joe when she accompanied her mother to work. Torrie worried about strangers when the center was packed with customers and she couldn't keep track of everyone milling around. But this early in the morning, the only worry she had was Rich Redman. There were no other cars in the lot. Most families were just getting up at this time.

Minutes later, Rich sauntered into the store and looked around the interior from floor to ceiling with a serious, meticulous gaze. Dressed in a windowpane checked shirt rolled up at the sleeves and another pair of designer jeans that emphasized his handsomely toned body, he was one smooth specimen of a man. Definitely sleeker than the polished maple countertop Torrie was leaning on to ogle him. When his gaze finally landed on her, she smiled, and he ambled over.

"Estella wanted to look at the pink flowers at the side of the building, and I think she spied the monkey bars. It's a nice idea for customers with kids. Do you remember when you challenged your sister and her friends to see who could hang the longest upside down on the bars at your house? The prize was a Snickers candy bar."

Torrie nodded, grinning. "And you and I were the last ones left hanging."

"And I almost passed out from so much blood rushing to my brain. What were we thinking?"

What he didn't say, Torrie noted, was he finally gave up and let her win. And as a consolation prize, she had split half her candy bar with him—because as a silly eleven-year-old girl, she had a mad crush on the good-looking sixteen-year-old who was the only one of Elsa's male friends who had taken the time to notice her when she was hanging around. Most of the time, they ignored her or treated her like a silly child.

"What brings you here so early this morning?" She picked up a paper towel and wiped the counter down.

"You." He looked at her with his seductive gray eyes, then cleared his throat and added, "And my daughter. She wants pink petunias to plant in those huge pots sitting on the back porch. Lulu agreed to help her. If I'm not careful, I may have a country kid on my hands. She loves tearing around outside. She even wants a pair of worn-looking bib overalls to wear when she works. She saw them in some gardening magazine Lulu brought over to the house."

Torrie laughed. It was a familiar good-feeling laugh erupting from the very heart of her. "Bib overalls?"

"Yeah. Know where I can get a pair of those?"

"There's a consignment shop on Market Street and a Goodwill store around the corner from Henry's Garage."

"You can't get them new?"

"Well, yes…you can." Torrie felt her face turn red. She'd forgotten money was no object for him. He probably wouldn't want his daughter in second-hand clothes. "I suppose you can get stone-washed ones if you shop online."

He leaned across the counter and took her hand in his, caressing it softly. "So tell me, Fraulein Larson, did you decide whether you can be my interpreter and assistant on Wednesdays?"

"Rich, for Pete's sake, it hasn't been twelve hours since you asked." She pulled her hand away just as the front door opened and both Iris and Estella barreled into the store.

Torrie stiffened as fear rippled along her spine.

"Hey, Mommy," Iris said, racing up to the counter and breathing hard. "This is Estella. She's eight. She says she knows you. She wants some pink flowers like petunias, and I think she needs some white impatiens or something else to go with them."

Rich eyed the little girl with white-blonde hair and wearing, of all things, bib overalls. He glanced at Torrie. There was no mistaking their almost identical resemblance right down to the aquamarine eyes.

"Why, why—" Torrie stuttered. "Why don't—"

Rich interrupted, squatting down to their level. "Hi, I'm Rich. What's your name?"

"Iris," the little girl said.

"A beautiful name," Rich said and brushed away some straw clinging to the sleeve of her white shirt. "Why don't you take my daughter and show her *all* the flowers, Iris?" His tone was calm and gentle, and he smiled tenderly at both girls. "I'll be out in a minute to help. Don't wander too far." He stood.

The door hardly banged shut when he looked at Torrie, a shadow of confusion and annoyance crossing his face. Their gazes met and held.

"I can explain," she said, biting her lip and breaking contact first. She looked out the window before turning back to him. She set her chin in a stubborn line. "She's my daughter, Iris."

"Where do you keep her? Under a flower pot?" There was no mistaking the ire in his tone. "And why?"

"You wouldn't understand."

"Try me, Torrie."

"She's six. I'm not married," she said in a staccato voice. "I moved here to be next to family and raise Iris. My sister Elsa babysits her while I work. I see her on Wednesdays and on weekends. My apartment isn't in the best section of town so I prefer she stays outside town with Elsa and her boys during the rest of the week. Is there anything else you want or need to know?" She came around the counter, brushing past him, and headed for the door. "Now what kind of flowers were you looking for?" Her tone was so cold it could freeze water in a summer birdbath.

****

On Sunday afternoon, Rich sat at the desk in the library with a stack of journals laid out in front of him and rubbed his jaw. It would be a tough job going through all these entries by himself. He looked over to where Marlene was rummaging through cupboards and drawers below a set of library bookcases. She had stopped at the house to see if he needed anything. Estella was out back trying to find the elusive cat. Earlier she had given him a verbal synopsis about the threat of an escalating flea population among felines. They had stopped at a pet shop yesterday and purchased Sheba a collar and a bunch of squeaky toys that Estella was sure the darn cat would fall in love with.

He thought about the incident with Torrie at the landscape center. After they had gone outside and gathered the girls to pick out flats of flowers, Torrie had been more than kind to Estella, showing her all the possible varieties to plant in Gertie's pots on the back porch. But she was like an icicle toward him, barely speaking, and keeping a distance between them. And every time she addressed him, there was a hint of censure in her tone.

"Why didn't you or Lulu tell me Torrie had a little girl?" He looked up to see Marlene now running a finger down the long open rows of books above the drawers and cupboard and checking each title. Today she was wearing lime green heels with jeans. "Not my story to tell." She turned and looked at him. "I'm sure she'll tell you her whole life's story when she's ready."

"I doubt it."

"Why? What did you do now, Richard Lee Junior?" Marlene turned and leveled a cool, disapproving look his way.

The doorbell rang, and the sound of Estella's flip flops beating their way to the front door echoed through the house. He rose from the desk and headed after her. Torrie stood in the open doorway along with Iris, who was wearing a pink shirt with the ever famous bib overalls. He regarded Torrie quizzically for a moment before he came to his senses and said, "Come in. Come in." He pulled Estella against him to allow them room to enter.

"We can't stay, we were just dropping off a package for Estella." Torrie's lips parted in a stiff smile. There was a wary look in her eyes.

Estella came to his aid. "Just for a few minutes, pleeeease, Torrie? I want to show Iris my cat."

"Great Grandmother Gertie's cat," Rich corrected her. "Actually, the *outdoor* cat."

Estella shrugged, grabbed Iris by the hand, and pulled her inside. "Her name is Sheba. When my dad calls her the useless, flea-bitten, sorry ex-mouser, he doesn't mean it. She doesn't catch mice 'cause we feed her."

"Here," Iris said and shoved the package toward Estella.

The little girl's eyes widened in delight. She took the package and looked at it from all angles before she tore into it, sending paper flying as she pulled out a pair of used bib overalls. Her high-pitched squeal splitting the air made Rich want to cringe. He watched Estella embrace Iris, then scamper over to Torrie and slam into her, hugging her about the waist. "Thank you. They're exactly what I wanted, Torrie. And you found worn ones!" She pulled away. "Come on, Iris let's go to my room. I want to put these on and show your mom. Then we'll look for the cat." Amid an outburst of shrieks and giggles, the girls raced down the hall and stomped up the stairs.

Rich blew out a breath of air and scratched his head. "Wow. How did you do it? How did you get the right size?" he asked. "How thoughtful of you, Torrie."

"It's a girl thing," she said and smiled.

Behind them Marlene walked to the door with a slip of paper in her hands. She greeted Torrie warmly and turned to Rich. "Okay, I found the family Bible and left it on your desk. I don't know if it will be any help. Gertie's husband's younger brother was called Walt, and according to a newspaper obituary about Matthew's death, he lived in New York. I'll try to see if I can track down an address for him, but at his age, he could be in a nursing home or deceased." She patted Rich on the back. "Remember, the pot roast with vegetables in the refrigerator is ready to put in the oven for dinner. Directions are on the counter. Don't screw it up or you'll have Lulu to answer to."

"Don't leave because of me," Torrie said. "We just stopped to drop off the overalls."

"Trust me, I'm not leaving because of you, sweetie." Marlene patted Torrie softly on the arm. "I have a big night ahead of me at home. I'm painting my bathroom and a friend is helping me. I'm buying the wine. He's responsible for the paint and brushes." She wiggled her eyebrow and grinned. "I'll leave the rest to your imagination." She hurried down the front porch steps. Her lime green heels flashed in the sun as she slipped into her Lexus.

Holding the edge of the door, Rich said, "I want to apologize for my rude remark at the landscape center. It wasn't warranted. I was totally out of line. I have no right to question you about your daughter or your life."

He reached out to touch her, but she stepped back warily and waved away the apology. "It's all right. I'm used to it."

He raised a hand, palm out. "No, it isn't all right. I'm sorry. Okay? How about a truce? I want to show you the journals I found in the study." They looked up as the girls clomped down the steps and dashed toward the back door. "Wait," he yelled at Estella, "aren't you going to show Torrie how you look?"

Estella and Iris scampered back. The little girl had put a pink shirt under the overalls to match Iris's. Estella twirled in front of both of them. "See? A perfect fit!" The two girls raced off again toward the back yard. "We have to find Sheba," Estella shouted over her shoulder. "Lulu said we shouldn't rehabilitate her to indoor life. I'm not sure what rehabilitate means, but I'm going to try to coax her inside."

Rich rolled his eyes toward the ceiling and heard Torrie chortle.

"How much do I owe you for the bib overalls?" he asked and motioned Torrie to follow him to the library. He noticed she kept a safe, respectable distance between them.

"Nothing, they were only a couple of bucks. After our dinner last night, I think I owe you." Torrie laughed again, and Rich could feel the iceberg floating between them start to melt. He breathed a sigh of relief.

From a tall stack, Torrie pulled out one of the journals and started to leaf through it.

"The ring on your hand is striking," Rich said. He had noticed it when they first met and at the restaurant. The jewels, fashioned into what looked like a flower pattern, shone brilliantly and were obviously top quality.

"Thank you, I designed it myself," she said and shut the book. "I worked for a jeweler in New York after I finished art school. I'd love to get back into it, but it's costly to set up a business or even design as a hobby. Gold and silver are at sky high rates, and good quality stones are pricey—a reason why I like flower arranging instead."

She looked at him and gave a resigned shrug, setting the journal aside. "I want to clear the air here, Rich. I'm willing to help you on Wednesdays, but there is something you need to know. I am a single mom, and I'm proud of it. I was planning my wedding to Daniel Forrester when he was asked to assist with the horrific forest fires plaguing the West six summers ago. He was a helicopter pilot trained in firefighting, specifically urban high rise, but also wild land and forest."

Rich interrupted softly. "Torrie, you don't have to tell me if you don't want to."

She ignored his warning. "I found out I was pregnant just days after he left. I decided I wouldn't surprise or burden him with any unsettling information while he was in a dangerous situation, but I'd wait until he came home from what was supposed to be a four-week stint. Two weeks into the action, his helicopter went down and he was killed."

Rich closed his eyes, feeling utterly miserable. "Torrie. I'm so sorry," he said in a hushed voice. "It must have been tough on you and tough on his parents. At least Iris brings you all joy like Estella brings to me."

Torrie shook her head and dropped her lashes to hide her hurt. "His parents wanted nothing to do with the baby. His mother accused me of being a gold digger and sleeping with someone else." She bit her lip and her eyes teared up. "So, I gathered Iris up and came home to a real family. My family."

Before he knew what he was doing, Rich reached out and pulled her to him, enveloping her in his arms, tucking her head under his chin and rocking her gently like she was a child. He stroked the back of her head. "It's okay," he whispered as she broke out into heart-wrenching sobs. "I know what it feels like to have your heart suddenly ripped out and all your feelings shattered like a piece of fragile glass thrown against stone."

"But he died never knowing he had a daughter," she said in a choked, desperate voice against his chest.

Rich tightened his embrace. "It's all right, Torrie. He knows, he knows. Trust me. Wherever he is, he knows."

After a few minutes, Torrie pulled away, swiped at her eyes with the back of her hand, and composed herself. She took a deep breath. "I'm sorry. After six years you'd think I'd be over it."

"I don't think you ever get over it. You just learn to live with it."

Biting her lip, she sniffed and took the tissue he offered her. She gave him a forlorn nod before she said, "So, if you still want a Wednesday assistant, I could use the money." She looked at him with a tiny spark beginning to glow in her eye—eyes that Rich wished he could drown in. "And I want the triple rate you promised."

Chapter Nine

Torrie and Iris were long gone by the time Rich wandered out on the porch as a beautiful sunset disappeared and the graying night descended. Estella, ever the manipulator, had joined forces with Iris and together they had begged Rich to convince Torrie to stay for the pot roast supper Lulu had prepared. Torrie had reluctantly agreed, and Rich was careful to give her plenty of space, even when they spent some quiet time with a glass of wine on the back porch as the girls romped in the yard. Rich smiled. He had given Torrie the rocking chair his grandmother always used when she spoke to him out of the clear blue sky or from wherever she was hiding. He refused to sit in it since her first eerie appearance on the porch the day he arrived. The outrageous thought that Torrie might be sitting in his grandmother's lap gave him a bizarre feeling, even though it was downright laughable, the more he thought about it. He contemplated mentioning Gertie's ghostly appearances to Torrie, then decided against it. If word got out, people would think he was crazy. Maybe even Torrie would think he went off the deep end.

Later, he and Torrie had gone back to the study to look at some of the journals and papers Marlene had unearthed. Torrie suggested they start at the beginning and look at the very first journals Hilda Redman wrote when she arrived in America and married her husband. They each decided to take one and confer on Wednesday before they started to sift through old papers in the study's file cabinets. She also suggested they check out the local newspaper articles from the early 1900s.

A feeling of edginess washed over him as he gazed at the rose beds glowing like tiny luminescent bulbs. He needed to discuss the flowerbeds with Torrie. Maybe there was a way she could finish out the summer and fall before uprooting everything.

But Estella was going to be his real problem. Already she was getting attached to the house, her room, the town, and the land. She had even bonded with good-hearted, looney Lulu. Now since she had met Iris, and had a friend her age, it was going to be painful for her to leave.

He knew the feeling well. Each summer he had been dutifully shipped off to live with Grandmother Gertie and Grandfather Matt, and each August he was torn away from the fun-filled, healthy, and warm environment of Hickory Valley and sent back to Texas. Fond memories were often painful ones as well.

Then, in his sophomore year, when it was evident his parents' marriage was headed for the rocks, Gertie had insisted Rich be transferred to Hickory Valley to finish his last two years of high school in a stable environment. The fighting between his parents had escalated and had become unbearable. Harboring a bucketful of anger, he grudgingly agreed, and it later turned out to be the best thing that ever happened to him. His grandmother had redirected his anger, insisted he play soccer, and signed him up for a local church youth group. Because he always spent summers in Pennsylvania, he quickly realized it wasn't as difficult to fit in and be accepted as he had expected. Graduating at the top of his class was a gift he gave back to his grandmother alone for all her patience and hard work. She was more proud of his achievement than he was. She was more proud than even his own mother and father were.

"You know I begged your mother not to make me send you back to Texas after each summer you spent here with me," a voice said from the rocking chair behind him. "Joyce was adamant it would never happen. If your father hadn't insisted you come here each summer, she would have packed you up and sent you to some dude ranch or camp for rich kids instead. Luckily, once the divorce proceeding got underway, she was outvoted; and when high school rolled around, I finally got you for good—along with your stubborn Redman attitude."

Rich flinched and the hair at the back of his neck felt like bugs were crawling up it. "You know, Grandmother, you really have to give me some sort of signal when you want to start a chat with me. Popping up unannounced scares the hair right off my head. Don't they give specters some sort of warning bell to use?"

"Ding dong! Listen up, Richard Lee Junior. You think it's fun to fade in and out of your life like I'm a fuzzy radio signal?" The rocking chair began to move. "I see you and Torrie resolved your little differences."

Rich refused to take the bait. He wasn't going to talk about Torrie Larson with anyone. He needed time to figure her out. "What do you know about Great

96

Uncle Walt?"

"He went to New York to seek his fortune. He didn't keep in touch with the family." She snorted derisively.

"That's it?"

"That's it." The rocker creaked. "I see you're contemplating refinishing the floor in the living room and having the room repapered. Have Torrie help you pick out new furniture, or get those wingback chairs reupholstered. I'd stick with a gold color."

Rich's voice rose an octave. "You're serious? You're dead and you're worried about the color of upholstery *I'm* going to be sitting on?"

"Phfftt. There you go, Richard Lee, being impertinent again." The rocker rocked more vigorously. "Here's a tip. Look at any old ledgers and bills. There must be something I missed when I went looking for those jewels." The rocker slowed. "And get yourself a decent SUV to take those kids to the lake to fish and camp. You could use a pair of decent shoes like normal people wear, too."

"Camping? Surely you're jesting?" Rich pushed his fingers through his hair and glared at the rocking chair. He'd had enough of camping on the trip up with Estella when rains flooded their tent and all their belongings. There was no way he was subjecting himself to a repeat performance.

"What's wrong with my boots?" He looked down at his feet and inspected his alligator cowboy boots, then looked accusingly at the rocker.

But it had stopped. A warm breeze swirled around him, and he could swear a soft hand lightly caressed his cheek.

Chapter Ten

The house was silent and the kitchen was empty on Tuesday morning when Rich pulled on a pair of jeans and entered the kitchen. He poured himself a cup of coffee and found a batch of warm cinnamon rolls under a tea towel on the counter.

"God love you, Lulu," he said aloud and carried his coffee and roll onto the back porch. In the rose garden beside the shed he spotted Estella, still wearing her pajamas along with his grandmother's too-large rubber boots as she peered at a rose bush with Torrie, who looked like she was explaining something to the girl in very intricate detail. The child wore huge leather garden gloves on her little hands, held upward and bent at the elbows, to keep them from falling off. She inched closer, almost head to head with Torrie, and listened attentively, then nodded and smiled brightly. The sight brought a twinge of guilt and sadness. Estella needed a woman's touch. Estella needed a mother. As soon as the little girl spied him, she came tearing across the yard, hands still in the air with the oversized gloves flapping.

"I'm learning to graft roses." She skidded to a halt at the bottom of the steps and said in a breathless voice, "Torrie's here, but she didn't bring Iris." Her little lips bunched into a pout.

"So this is garden day?" Rich asked, leaning

against the post, as Torrie picked up a flat of flowers by the shed and carried it to the flower pots sitting below the porch steps on the walk.

She looked up at him. "Yes, I needed to check the beds, water the roses, and collect some different ornamental grasses to put in a summer bouquet for a customer."

From around the corner of the shed, Lulu appeared toting garden tools in a plastic tote. "Well, hello, Sunshine," Lulu said. "I see you found the rolls and coffee, but you still seem to have trouble locating shirts and shoes in the morning. It looks like you're beyond trainable."

Estella knelt down and fingered the colorful flower petals in the flats scattered on the walk. "Daddy always has trouble finding things when he just wakes up. He's grouchy sometimes, too." She poked at a pink petunia and scowled. "Torrie said she didn't bring Iris because it's not Lulu's job to watch her." She looked up at him, her lips now bowed into an exaggerated frown.

Rich spoke with staid calmness he hardly felt, "Is that so?" His eyes and Torrie's met, and he lazily appraised her, forcing spots of red to color her cheeks. Her olive green tank top over her camouflage cargo shorts made her fit perfectly in with the flora and fauna surrounding her—except for those exquisite aquamarine eyes framed by long dark eyelashes. "Well, I'm not opposed to having Iris come and play when Torrie checks the beds or helps me on Wednesdays. But it's entirely a decision for Torrie to make with Lulu and Iris."

Lulu peered up at Rich with her wizened face. "I'd be delighted to watch the girls. And I'm hoping there'd be some of those extra Redman points in it for me."

"You already earned some points for the cinnamon rolls." His mouth twitched with amusement.

"I did?" She grinned. "I need to start keeping track. I'm going to hold you to your word. I heard cowboys are men of their word." Lulu pulled out two trowels and set them on the pavement.

This time Rich threw back his head and laughed. "I'm not a cowboy, Lulu, but you are one plucky farm gal. Why is my daughter tearing around the backyard in her pajamas like a runaway waif?"

Lulu nudged Estella toward the steps. "Because she's a precocious child with a curious and stubborn streak like someone I know." She glared at him. "Estella was afraid she wouldn't see what Torrie was doing with the roses if she had to waste time getting dressed." She gave him another once-over glance and grunted. She nudged Estella again. "Let's get you dressed properly and fed before we tackle these pots and plants."

Estella clomped up the steps, the too-large rubber boots squeaking. "Daddy, can Iris come Wednesday and stay overnight? We could have a sleepover." She looked from Rich to Lulu to Torrie with hopeful eyes. Her gaze finally came to rest on Torrie. "Please?" she pleaded.

"I'd have to ask Iris first before we make any plans," Torrie said. "And your dad and I need to discuss it."

"I already called her yesterday at her Aunt Elsa's." Estella wiggled a hand in a glove and smiled. "I found Elsa Bergman's name in the phone book. Iris said yes."

Rich watched as Torrie's eyes widened in surprise

when she realized she had been undermined and flat out bested by an eight-year-old.

"You're going to have to get up even earlier to keep up with Estella," he said, enjoying her dumbfounded look. He ruffled the top of his daughter's messy head as she passed by. "Do as Lulu says. Torrie and I need to talk. *Ahora.* Now."

Estella's lip jutted out into a pout again and she crossed her arms at her chest still holding on to the sloppy gloves on her hands. "But I need to be here. I want to talk to Torrie and explain the sleepover and what we're going to do."

"I'll talk to Torrie."

"That's a conflict of interest!"

"Heaven help us," Lulu interrupted. "Come, child, let's go inside before you get yourself into more conflict than Dwight D. Eisenhower did in World War II."

"Who's he?" Estella asked, immediately distracted. She looked up at the elderly woman with a curious squint.

"A five-star general. A very important man. President of the United States. He was born in Texas and lived here in Pennsylvania. Come, I'll tell you all about him while I braid that mop of hair. In a way, he was something like you—a force to be reckoned with."

"Okay." Estella acquiesced begrudgingly. "But I want some blue nail polish like Iris and Torrie are wearing."

"Well, we can have a discussion about that, too," Lulu said in a placating tone, "but first you must get dressed and be presentable."

Rich held the door for them and mouthed *thank you*

as Lulu passed by, then said out loud, "When you get a moment, could you please get Torrie a cup of coffee and one of your cinnamon rolls? No, make it two, I could eat another one."

Torrie interrupted. "Thanks, but I can't stay." She placed a booted foot on the bottom step and peered up at him. Her aquamarine eyes now shone like sea-colored jewels in the bright sunlight.

"I insist you sit down while we discuss this sleepover or you're going to get a crick in your neck staring up at me." His smooth courtroom voice indicated there would be no dissent or further discussion.

****

Torrie took her usual place on the rocking chair and nodded her thanks to Lulu who brought out a tray with coffee cups and rolls. The one thing she could say for Rich Redman was that he was unaware of his charm and charisma, even when wearing tight jeans and nothing else. And his lead-colored gaze was unpredictable. His eyes could be dark and dangerous if angered, but sexy and calm when the storm blew over.

Rich slumped down into the rocking chair and blew out a breath of air. "Does it ever get easier? I swear, that child has perfected the ability to be quite annoying."

Torrie laughed. "Conflict of interest? Is she enrolled in a law class for eight-year-olds?" She picked up a cinnamon roll and took a bite. "No, it doesn't get easier. Remember what we were like as teenagers? I noticed she doesn't seem to give Lulu any trouble."

"Of course not, even I'm afraid of Lulu." Rich leaned his head back against the rocker. "Some days I can't figure out whether I'm Lulu Smith's employer or employee."

"She raised five kids just like my parents."

"How did they do it?'

"Lulu, like my mother, loves to create order out of chaos. They love to organize and keep others on track and in line. It's a real skill set." Torrie poured some milk into her coffee.

"Speaking of organization, can you come over tomorrow and help? And what do you think of this sleepover thing they have cooked up?" He looked at her, picked up a cinnamon roll, and took a bite.

"To be honest," Torrie said, "it would give Elsa a day off from babysitting Iris." And it would give her a chance to focus on her own two boys. "Iris needs a girl her age for a friend. I bet Estella does, too."

Rich held up his hands. "She does, but I know nothing about sleepovers. This is new uncharted territory. I'm going to need some help. Lulu leaves after dinner."

Torrie laughed. "I can stay and help them get ready for bed. You buy some microwave popcorn to make, and I'll rent a movie. Let's give Lulu a break from cooking and take them to Webster's Burgers and Fries for dinner. The milkshakes are fabulous. Come on, Rich, you remember what sleepovers were like." She looked at him and saw a pained silent sadness cross his face, and she realized he had never experienced one. She touched his arm gently. "Don't worry. I can take care of everything. I can teach you all you need to know about sleepovers."

"Now, there is something I can get excited about." He brightened and looked at her. His innuendo was obvious. "Can I book a private lesson?"

"In your dreams, cowboy," she said, rising. She tried to ignore the sexual sparks passing between them. "I have to go to work."

He rose with her.

"Don't bother showing me out. I still have work out back here. I want to check one more bed and spray the old rose bush by the shed with fungus spray to deter leaf mold." She moved to the steps and was certain his gaze was still fixed on her. She turned around. "Don't you have some important legal matters to take care of? Or some poor soul who needs your expert advice?" His seductive gaze made her stomach do a lazy somersault.

"I do, but I'd rather watch you." He smiled his charming Redman smile.

"Oh, brother." She walked down the steps, throwing an exit line over her shoulder. "You're hopeless, Rich Redman, you know that?"

****

The sun was high in the sky when Rich pulled Gertie's car into the parking lot of Henry's Garage at the other end of town, and a big caramel-colored dog trotted up to him looking for some affection. "You must be Ratchet," Rich said and scratched the dog behind his ears. Ratchet did a little dance, tail wagging, then followed him into a bay leading to the office.

Henry's Garage originally had started in a small red brick building before it outgrew its meager beginnings. To accommodate growth, Henry Jordan had merely added on more additions and bays until the building was now a series of mazes connected by arches and open doorways. Henry himself still preferred to stay in his tiny office in the old part, away from the noise of the engines and clanking of tools. He looked up and grunted when Rich entered with Ratchet. "I figured you'd be around sometime. Did you get the message my granddaughter, Denise, wants your SUV? She's working down at Webster's Burgers and Fries until she starts school. She's positive she knows someone who can get the parts and will fix it up so she and her sister can commute to the community college this fall."

Rich grinned. "I wonder who she enlisted as the crack mechanic to piece the blasted thing together?" He selected a stool next to the counter covered in red vinyl and patched with duct tape. Ratchet plopped down on the floor by his feet. "She can have it. Free and clear. I'm having the title sent up. I'm not throwing more money into a hunk of steel that abandoned me."

Henry laughed. A tall, thin man with steel gray hair, he always had a ready smile for everyone, but Rich noticed he now had a tired, almost gaunt look about him.

"I suppose you're going over to see Lars Larson at the dealership?" Henry shuffled a pile of papers on his overflowing desk to clear a spot on the corner.

"That's the plan." Rich picked up a pair of locking pliers lying on the counter and played with the adjustment on the bottom. "I need to pick your brain, Henry. Did you ever hear my Grandmother Gertie talk about Matthew's brother in New York?"

"Walt? Maybe once or twice, but not with any warmth."

"Do you know if he's still living?"

Henry shook his head. "Gosh, I really don't know."

"My father..." Rich paused and looked at the

ceiling, trying to find a way to ask a delicate, personal question. "My father, when he came to Hickory Valley in the summer, who did he spend time with?" Rich remembered back to the summers when his dad dropped him off at his grandmother's, but never left town until he made sure Rich was settled in for the summer vacation. Or at least it seemed to be his plausible excuse for staying longer. When he thought back on it, his dad's visits during his junior and senior years in Hickory Valley also involved a few extra days as well.

"To be honest, I don't know." Henry said. "He knew most of the people in town. He grew up here."

"Were there any lady friends?"

Henry's face flushed, and he looked at Rich with a quizzical expression. "If I think we're talking about the same subject, most men around Hickory Valley go out of town for that kind of business."

Rich hopped off the stool and Ratchet jumped up. He replaced the pliers on the counter and scratched Ratchet behind the ears again. "Well, I guess I'd better go buy a new SUV and see if Lars Larson remembers I can blackmail him if he doesn't give me a good deal. He pulled some outlandish stunts when we were in high school. I hear he's engaged and finally tying the knot this fall. Is Gus around?" Earlier when he talked with Lulu about finding someone to do some outside handy work for a few hours on weekends, she had told him Torrie's brother, Gus, often moonlighted doing both inside and outside handyman jobs in construction and landscaping.

Henry cleared his throat. A flicker of apprehensiveness crossed his weathered face. "I gave him a couple of days off. I hate to admit it, but I'm losing Gus come September. He got a new job offer to work as a mechanic at one of those big sports tracks in North Carolina. Things these days sure are different. It's not like it used to be. The big box stores with their own garages are now changing tires and oil, and doing inspections. There's no room for the mom and pop businesses any longer. There's just not enough work anymore."

Commiserating, Rich said, "It's the way of the world, I guess. Where's Kyle these days?" Rich knew Henry's son and his wife had moved somewhere up near the Great Lakes where he had a job in accounting.

"He just came back to Hickory Valley from Michigan when his company was downsized, and he's looking for a job in accounting or management. He doesn't want to disappoint his twin girls. Denise was planning to go to college for her nursing degree, and Danielle wanted to study to be an elementary teacher, so they came here and moved in with me. They're going to commute to the community college at Gibson Lake this fall. I sure wish this old garage could make more money, but honestly, it can only support one family. Gus sees the handwriting on the wall, so he's moving on."

"You aren't going to hire anyone?"

"Nah." The old man shook his head and heaved a weary sigh. "I've given serious thought to giving my two part-time workers notice and putting the garage up for sale. It's time for these old bones to retire. Trouble is, who would want to buy this giant maze of brick and crumbling mortar? And I still have a mortgage."

"What about the warehouse and apartment?"

"I'm hoping I can list them separately and a buyer can continue to rent the apartment out. I'm hoping he'd allow Torrie to remain and keep her rent the same."

He picked up a stack of invoices. "I've got to get paperwork together for her to pay bills." He shuffled a bunch of paper into a heap and looked up. "Hey, every Monday night a bunch of us get together for a beer and some nickel and dime poker. Gus, Finn, Lars, Ivan, and Joe usually come. It's at Finn's next week. Why don't you join us? We start at seven p.m. and play for a few hours. You can get caught up on the local news. We'd love to take your money."

Rich laughed. "I bet you would. I'll think about it."

Chapter Eleven

Torrie was not certain her arrival at Rich Redman's house at ten o'clock in the morning with three suitcases was a good idea, but Iris was itching to see Estella and had packed like she was going on a month-long vacation instead of a sleepover. One suitcase alone contained all her stuffed animals, dolls, and toys—as if Estella didn't have enough of her own. The second suitcase was filled with juice boxes and snacks even though the Redman household employed Hickory Valley's best cook, Lucille Smith. And the last contained her clothes—for every occasion imaginable. Sometimes Torrie just felt it was easier to go along and get along than fight with Iris over her packing skills.

Rich, Estella, and Lulu met them at the door. Without any comments or questions or even a raised eyebrow, Lulu hurried them off to the kitchen where she had planned to bake muffins with them, and Rich tossed the luggage at the foot of the stairs. Torrie followed him into the study with a folder and the journal she had perused.

"Did you get Henry's payroll finished?" He gazed at her face, then moved over her body critically. She was glad she had taken the time earlier in the morning to put on a pair of better jeans and a lemon-colored blouse borrowed from Elsa. They stared at each other without speaking.

As usual, he looked like he stepped off a photo shoot for a designer clothing store. His dark jeans, white shirt, and brown canvas vest gave him a totally sexy western look and brought indecent thoughts swirling in Torrie's head.

When he continued to stare, she finally broke the silence and temptation she knew could be perilous to both of them. "What? Do I have dirt on me, again?" she asked.

He shook his head and smiled and walked to the desk, sitting down.

Torrie set her purse on a nearby chair, opened her folder, and got right down to business. They had work to do, and she planned to earn her keep if he was paying her triple her usual hourly rate. She paced in front of the desk as she read from her notes. "I checked all the old newspaper clippings and couldn't find any mention of your great uncle. But I ran into Marlene, and she traced him to Elmira, New York, where he lived before entering a nursing home until his death."

"So it's a dead lead, excuse the pun." Rich frowned and motioned to her to take a seat beside him. Stacked in front of him were piles of Hilda's journals. The papers and books Torrie had moved the other day were still heaped to the side.

"No, not really." Torrie laid her folder on the desk and sat down. "Didn't you say your dad used to travel to upstate New York occasionally?"

Lulu appeared with a tray, a coffee pot and two cups, and what looked like very fattening Danish rolls. She set the tray on the already overcrowded desk. "You are going to need some fortifying food to get through the Hammermill explosion in this room." She peered at

Rich with her wizened elflike gaze. "I'm packing a picnic lunch and taking the girls to the town park to play this morning after we finish baking muffins. If I don't run their little legs off them and tire them out, you'll never get them to sleep tonight. I left sandwiches and a salad on the top shelf in the refrigerator. If Torrie and you want a break, eat in the kitchen, otherwise tote it in here on a tray. There's chocolate cake for dessert."

"Lulu, you are a saint." Rich reached for the coffee pot.

The elderly woman grunted and headed for the door. "And I would imagine saints get extra points, don't you think, Sunshine?"

Rich's laugh bubbled out into the quiet study and followed her down the hall.

"What in the world is she talking about?" Torrie helped herself to a Danish roll. "And why does she call you Sunshine?"

"It's a heck of a lot better than Perry Mason. And it's Lulu's way of telling me she's in charge, especially when I'm in a bad mood. I told her I'd give her special bonus points for any work above and beyond the call of duty or rather above our verbal agreement when she first arrived. They're like frequent flyer miles, only she can turn these in for cash. Now she's started keeping a notebook and writes everything down she believes is not in her job description. Which, by the way, I've yet to see—although she swears she has one." He smirked. "If I have Lulu pegged correctly, I've no doubt she's close to her first thousand points."

Torrie choked on her drink. "I don't believe you're bribing her."

He grinned. "What I'd never tell her is she's the

111

best housekeeper I've ever employed and if she keeps feeding me the way she does, I'll be three hundred lumbering pounds before July rolls around. If I could lure her out of Hickory Valley, I'd take her and her quirky humor back to Texas, but don't you dare tell her. She already has the upper hand and the last word around here." He picked up a pen and tapped it on the desk. "Now what were you saying about this not being a dead lead?"

Rich Redman heading back to Texas was the last thing Torrie wanted to hear, but she pulled herself together and gathered her thoughts. "Your great uncle must have made friends with people in the nursing home before he died. I think someone needs to go up to Willow Tree Assisted Living and poke around and ask questions."

"What are you doing tomorrow?" Rich asked. "We could drive up, make some connections, and be back by suppertime. It's only about two and a half hours away."

"I have to work, Rich. I can't leave Finn in a bind."

"What happens if you get sick?"

"One of Henry's granddaughters usually works for me. Both Danielle and Denise are good at the cash register."

"I'm tripling your wages, Torrie. You can give one of the girls a third of your take, and you're still making double."

"How about you pay Denise's wages and still pay mine?" Her face was stone sober, but her adorable aquamarine gaze twinkled merrily. "If you're serious about wanting me to go," she added.

"Have you been taking lessons from Lulu?"

"No, but now that you mention it, I'd like to try

your point system." She was barely able to keep the laughter from her voice.

He leaned over and pulled her to him. When his lips met hers, he tasted a lingering sweet flavor of cinnamon and sugar. She didn't try to pull away, and he found himself wanting so much more. The kiss lasted way too long before Torrie ended it.

"Well, this alone is certainly worth more than a *few* points." She rose unsteadily to her feet and moved her chair to the other side of the desk, opposite him. "We'd better stick to business."

"Hey, wait a minute." He groaned. "We were just beginning to enhance our working relationship and our interpersonal skills."

"Rich, we're never going to get anything done if you don't concentrate."

"I was concentrating. Weren't you?"

"I mean on these journals of Hilda's. Did you read any of them?"

He looked disappointed. "There wasn't much to read. Hilda seemed to be homesick and kept writing to her cousin to send things from Austria. She mentions doll house furniture she wanted since her husband was making and selling doll houses when he came home at night after constructing the real ones. I don't know if it's important."

"Yes, and she was always requesting teddy bears, designed by Margarite Steiff. Did you know Steiff even designed a Teddy bear named after Theodore Roosevelt? Old German toys before World War I are very pricey and dealers are still interested in them. Some of the bears before 1920 are valued from two to six thousand dollars. Maybe the actual wealth is in your cabinets full of toys, tin cars, and bears dating back to World War I." She rose and walked to the floor-to-ceiling cabinet enclosed in glass where dozens of teddy bears, dressed in all types of clothing, were artfully arranged.

He shrugged. "I doubt it. I think she was homesick for Austria and had an overzealous fascination with toys. Gertie once told me she even made clothes for all the neighborhood children's dolls."

"For the record, just how many people know about these jewels and your father's infidelity?" Torrie sauntered back to the desk and sat down.

"I hope as few as possible. But Marlene Hess knows, and nothing gets past Lucille Smith."

Later, as they sat in the kitchen and ate Lulu's sandwiches and salad, the roar of a motorcycle and rumbling of a pickup interrupted their peaceful meal. Joe Bradley and Gus Larson appeared at the back door, both holding the sides of their heads with their hands as they smashed their noses against the glass and peered in.

"Golly gee," Rich said with a smirk. "Just what I've always longed for—the Sesame Street duo. Bert and Ernie. And on the day we rid ourselves of Lulu and the girls. What luck!" He looked at her with a suggestive glint in his eye. "Do you think if we sit here motionless, they'll think we're wax figures and make like bees and buzz off?"

"For heaven sake, Rich, let them in." Torrie rose, crossed to the French doors, and opened them. "You're just in time for German chocolate cake made by Lucille Smith. It's the prize-winning one she bakes for the church bazaar and county fair." At the mention of chocolate cake, both men wore grins as wide as sock monkeys. Behind her she heard Rich groan out, "Nice work, Torrie. Let's have a party and have all your friends over to eat my food."

Trying hard to hide her amusement, Torrie returned to the kitchen with Joe and Gus trailing behind her like eager taste testers at a holiday bake-off. They scrambled to get a seat at the table and nodded a curt greeting to Rich.

"I thought this would be a good day to check on your ideas for the living room. I just finished up installing a new bathroom sink for Marlene," Joe said. "Lulu's chocolate cake? What an awesome treat. Thank you."

Rich eyed him warily.

"And I'm off from the garage for a few days. Business is tapering off, so I'm ready to tackle any handy work you might need outside. I thought I'd start on the overgrown rhododendron," Gus said. "Man, this is not just a chocolate cake. It's her famous, blue ribbon chocolate cake! What a stroke of luck. Do you have some milk to go with this?"

This time Rich didn't try to hide an outright irritable snort.

Torrie moved to the counter and took out plates. She caught his gaze and laughed, aware of his annoyance. "Hey, Gus," she said as she poured her brother a drink and set the glass and milk carton in front of him, "can you cover for me tomorrow at the landscape center?"

"Yeah, sure, I can help. I was only planning to tune up a few motorcycles."

"I thought you'd start packing for your new job in

North Carolina."

"Not until September, kiddo. I've plenty of time. In fact, I'm a little worried about what I'm going to do with all the motorcycle parts I've stored at Henry's. What's up?" Gus looked at her with a curious expression. "Everything okay?"

"Everything is fine. Rich is headed up to Elmira, and I'd like to ride along. There's some great outlet malls along the way. I figured this would be a good time to get Iris some summer clothes."

His brow furrowed, Joe's face reflected a dubious stare. "I can always take you shopping, Torrie. Wherever you need to go."

"I know, Joe. Thanks." She glanced at Rich and took a deep breath.

He came to her rescue with a smooth convincing voice he often used on his clients. "Actually, I want to interview some people at the nursing home where my late great uncle stayed. I know so little about him. I was hoping Torrie could help me with the female residents."

Joe rose from the table. "Well, we'd better see what you want done with the living room before you leave so I can order materials. I'd like to get right on this. Gus, why don't you help me measure things up before you man those hedge trimmers?"

****

After an hour of conferring with both men about refurbishing and repapering the living room, Rich sent Joe on his way, only to have Lars, Elsa's twin, deliver the new SUV he had purchased. When he finally rejoined Torrie in the study, she was pouring over yet another journal. Outside, the buzz of hedge clippers and the hum of a lawn mower interrupted what he thought would be a peaceful afternoon. He studied her thoughtfully for a moment. Head bent, she was exquisite-looking with her long, blinding white hair flowing over her shoulders in graceful curves and sparkling like tiny strands of lustrous glass.

"You sure have a lot of people safeguarding you from the big, bad male population." He shook his head in frustration. "And we still have one more brother we haven't heard from today. I wonder where he's hiding."

Torrie laughed. "Joe has always been protective, and my brothers are just being…big brothers. We look out for each other."

He picked up her hand and ran his fingers gently up her arm. "I got a great idea. No, I have a *terrific* idea. Let's take a break from this noise and take the new SUV out for a spin. We have a few hours before dinnertime, and if we hurry we can fly the coop before Lulu brings the girls home. It's going to be a long night with Estella and Iris and this girlie sleepover thing."

"You're paying me to ride around with you?"

He shrugged. "Why not? Have you ever pushed aside your worries and the serious side of life and just decided to go with the flow? Taken some time to have fun? Escaped the humdrum and tedium of everyday life?"

She shook her head. "Since Iris was born, my life has been one pothole after another I've had to bump over or around, just to get down the road of life each day."

"Neither have I," he admitted. The last two years since Margaretta's death had been long tedious days and fretful nights. He'd never admit it, but he agonized under the dark shadows of night that he wasn't a good enough parent to Estella, and in the light of the day, he pushed through endless workaholic hours filled with taking care of other people's legal worries. He brightened. "Let's just do something out of character for both of us. Let's waste some time and blow this town."

"What about finding your half-sister and the jewels?"

He waved his hand in the air and circled the study stuffed with books, ledgers, and papers. "No one's found the jewels for over a hundred years. We're never going to examine all this dreadful paperwork in a day. What are a few more hours? Grab a journal if you feel guilty about abandoning work. We'll take it with us."

Minutes later, with the windows down, the moon roof open, and a quilt, a journal, sweatshirts, and a cooler tossed in the back seat, they left Hickory Valley, flying down the road toward Gibson Lake. Torrie had taken off her shoes and propped her feet on the dash. The wind whipped her hair, and she tucked the errant strands behind her ears. The day was sunny and bright and the glorious smell from a hayfield of drying grass wafted around them as fence posts flew by. Rich pulled onto a side road before they reached Gibson Lake and followed an old rutted dirt road ending in a small grassy clearing, protected on all three sides by a stand of hemlocks hugging the lake. He spread the quilt and hauled the cooler from the cargo bed with Torrie following, journal in her hands. When they were seated, he took the journal and tossed it over his shoulder. It landed behind them on the grassy bank.

"Remember, you're paying me for today," she warned him.

"If you don't stop worrying, I swear, Torrie Larson, I'll toss the journal and you in the lake." He stretched out his legs and leaned back, bracing his weight on his forearms as he surveyed the water in front of them. The sun sent slanted rays on the surface and it sparkled like diamonds. Somewhere a duck called and a frog croaked in the reeds.

"How'd you find this spot?" she asked. She lay down on her back, staring at the sky through the branches of the trees. She had propped her head up with a pillow made from one of his sweatshirts.

"My grandfather used to bring me here to fish when I was young. Later, I came out myself when I wanted to get away and have some solitude." He sat up and reached in the cooler for a bottle he had uncorked at the house. He poured two glasses of white wine and handed one to Torrie when she sat up. "To a peaceful few hours and a stress-free night of supervising a sleepover."

She laughed. "To a grand day of finding some clues to your mysterious stash of jewels and discovering new relatives."

Rich watched her take a sip of wine and visibly relax. He wondered how she was able to cope with the sudden death of her fiancé and the frightening realization she'd be the sole parent, responsible for raising an infant. Lulu had told him Elsa and Finn had gone to New York when she was due to have the baby and coached her through the delivery, then packed her up to return to Hickory Valley. He reached out and rubbed a lock of her silky pale hair between his thumb and forefinger. She turned and looked at him and smiled. "Everyone thinks I bleach it until they meet my mom and dad. Then they realize I got a double dose of Scandinavian genes." She took a sip of wine. "I almost forgot. Estella and Iris want to dye their hair pink."

Rich's hand fell from the lock he was caressing. "What?" He set his glass aside, tumbled onto his back, and covered his forehead with the back of his hand. "Holy fright. How do we stop them?"

Torrie laughed. "Take it easy, they just want to put a few streaks of pink in their hair. Most schools don't allow odd colors in their students' hair so all the kids are doing it while school is out for summer. By fall, they would have to have their hair back to its original color."

He peered up at her. "I'm light years behind in this hair coloring thing, and I'm clueless about Estella's clothes. The other day my precious daughter informed me I needed to take a class in fashion—and she said a parenting class wouldn't go amiss either. I feel like a big dope."

Torrie chuckled. "Estella is precious, but she's extremely articulate and way too bright for her age. I can get some washable, colored hair spray, and we can see if they like it first before we make the giant leap to a professional hair dresser." She set her wine glass aside and laid on her back next to him.

"How do you do it?" he asked her, staring at the treetops. "Do you ever feel you're not getting it right? Raising your daughter, I mean?"

"All the time." Eyes closed, she sighed. "Sometimes I feel like I'm not getting my whole life right."

He rolled toward her and brushed a finger across her cheek. She turned her head and looked at him. His gaze was as soft as a caress. He kissed her gently along her neck. "There's some chemistry happening here," he whispered in her ear before his mouth covered hers hungrily.

Chapter Twelve

The kiss was slow and thoughtful, sending spirals of ecstasy through Torrie's body down to her toes. All the memories of her hellish life when she was pregnant, alone, and struggling in New York dissolved beneath his tender mouth and his desire to explore their relationship and perhaps take it to a new level. She would have liked the kiss to go on forever, but she put her hand on his chest and forced herself to pull away. She reminded herself she could not risk her heart. He was not part of her life. He would leave in a few weeks, and she didn't have the strength to fall in love and watch him return to his high-powered lifestyle in Texas. And there was Iris to consider as well.

"This is a bad idea, Rich," she said between a gasp to catch her breath.

"There are a lot of bad ideas in the world, but this isn't one of them." His ash-colored eyes smoldered with fire as he brushed a knuckle over the side of her cheek. "Let's just enjoy the moment." He bent his head and reclaimed her lips, tugging her toward him. Torrie's heart rattled frantically inside her chest and she found herself passionately rising to meet his urgent kisses...until his cellphone rang.

"Noooo," he muttered against her lips. "What fool...what idiot...what insane person...would be calling me now?"

Torrie pulled away and, like a jack in the box, popped up into a seated position and straightened her blouse.

Rich groaned, grappled for the phone in his hip pocket, peered at it, and clicked it on. He drew in a shallow, steady breath to collect himself. "Lulu, this better be an emergency or I'm throwing all those points you're earned into the can and flushing it twice—" He clicked the icon to the speaker and tossed the phone on the quilt between them. "—along with this phone," he muttered under his breath.

Lulu spoke, "Estella fell and is perfectly fine except for a skinned knee, but unless she talks to you, I might as well be in the bathroom with the door closed and earplugs on." He heard the strain in Lulu's voice. "Her persistence would make a diehard spy spill his guts to the enemy. You sure this child came from your loins?"

"What are loins?" a little voice asked in the background.

Rich ran a hand through his hair and heaved an exhausted sigh. "Put her on, Lulu." Beside him, Torrie put a hand over her mouth to muffle her laugh.

He raised an eyebrow and silently mouthed the words, "You think this is funny?"

"Where are you?" Estella whined into the phone. "Iris's Uncle Gus said he saw you and Torrie leaving town in a new car."

"Torrie and you," he corrected her. "We were just taking the new SUV from Iris's Uncle Lars's showroom for a spin to see how it works. How's the knee?"

"Why didn't you take me and Iris?"

"Iris and me," Rich enunciated, then persisted in a

no-nonsense tone. "How is the knee, Estella?"

They could hear Estella take a long, deep breath. "Well, Lulu cleaned it and sprayed it with some first aid spray. I have a Band-Aid on it, but it looks awful."

"The knee or the Band-Aid?" Rich asked.

"The Band-Aid."

"Ah-ha. Then what's the problem?"

"The Band-Aid doesn't match my shorts. They're dark green."

Rich looked heavenward, shook his head to clear it, then glanced at Torrie. He threw his hands skyward in mock defeat.

Grinning, Torrie leaned over the phone. "Hey Estella, your dad and I are on our way home. How about we stop at the pharmacy and pick up some cool Band-Aids? I bet a camouflage one would do the trick. What do you think?"

"Yeah, that would work. Thanks, Torrie. Will you be here *soooon*?" Estella asked. "We have to get the sleepover started."

A sleepover starting at three in the afternoon? Torrie rose and grinned at Rich's sour expression. He looked like he had sucked a tub of lemons. She could tell he was thinking the same thing she was. It was going to be a long night.

"Yes, Estella," Rich said, "*Dentro de poco.* Soon. Tell Lulu to hold down the fort. And do not give her any back talk or grief. Do you hear me?" Before she could respond, he clicked off and rose.

He turned to Torrie. "I'm sorry. I'm really sorry."

"For what?" she asked. "This may have been fate working to save us from a crazy impulsive act. We might have done something we both might have regretted."

"Only one of us may have," he said sourly, adjusting his trousers. "What I was feeling wasn't pangs of regret or guilt."

Amused, Torrie grabbed the sweatshirts and folded the quilt while Rich packed the wine and glasses in the cooler and recovered the journal. They worked silently in tandem and Torrie found herself wondering what it might be like to be married to someone like Rich Redman. Even when Estella pushed him to the limit, he never raised his voice. And his dour-faced expressions of disappointment, disgust, or gloom were sweet and endearing.

****

Rich was not surprised Estella met him at the front door, flying into his legs and wrapping her hands around him as if he'd been on a trek to the North Pole for the last two months. But he was even more surprised when Lulu quipped, "Halleluiah! The reinforcements have arrived."

For her brave conduct under fire, Rich gave her the rest of the day off, while Torrie treated the girls to a girly dress-up party and make-over before they all ventured out to dinner. They now sat in a corner booth of Webster's Burgers and Fries with Estella and Iris opposite them, each wearing streaks of pink in their hair and holding a stuffed giraffe and parrot, respectively. They had even convinced Torrie to color a front lock of her hair a lime green. He was sure he was part of some bizarre psychedelic human circus.

The waitress who had served them at the German restaurant came over to the table with a pad in hand and beamed them a warm welcome. "Hello, Torrie and

Iris," she said. "Wow. Look at you three beauties. You all look chic tonight." She nodded at the little girls. "Nice color of pink, young ladies. What's your friend's name, Iris?"

"Estella," the little girl replied, smiling.

"You know each other?" Rich looked at her, baffled.

The young waitress grinned. She was a lovely girl with hazel eyes. "Yes, I'm Denise. Danielle and I are Henry Jordan's granddaughters. The wait staff at the German restaurant at Gibson Lake is not allowed to make casual conversation with dining guests. We both think it's silly and rather petty, but hey, it's not our restaurant. And it's a job, right?"

"Is Danielle working today?" Torrie asked.

The girl nodded and pointed across the room where a girl with light brown hair stood at the cash register and waved to them. Iris bounced up and down in her seat and frantically waved back. "Look, look! Danielle has purple streaks in her hair."

"Yes, I see. Shhhh." Torrie tried to curb Iris's loud enthusiastic squeals before she brought unwanted attention to them.

"I need a favor, Denise," she said and drummed her fingers on the table. "Gus is going to work for me tomorrow at the landscape center, but I'd like Danielle or you to go in for a few hours and help with the register if you can. He can make a mess of things in short order when the place gets busy, especially around the lunch hour."

"Sure, sure. We're both off tomorrow and Friday. One of us will stop in around noon and work until dinner, or as long as Gus needs help."

When she left with their order, Rich spoke, "So those are Kyle Jordan's twins? Henry's granddaughters? He was so proud of them when I talked with him."

"Yes, though you can't tell it by their looks. Complete opposites. But they are the sweetest gals. Sometimes I get one to babysit for me. Iris is fond of both of them. Keep their numbers on your speed dial. They're always looking for work to make money for college expenses."

The burgers arrived, and they ate quietly. But before they finished, Denise showed up with two very large chocolate fudge sundaes and set them in front of the little girls. "Compliments of Ivan Winters." She pointed toward a booth at the opposite end of the restaurant where Ivan Winters sat with Henry Jordan.

Rich watched a shadow of annoyance cross Torrie's face.

"Please tell Ivan the girls said thank you," Torrie instructed Denise before she left to check on another table of customers.

"I was capable of buying dessert," Rich pointed out, equally annoyed.

He felt her place a hand gently on this thigh. "Easy, Rich. Let's not spoil the sleepover."

"Why? Am I having one, too?" A hopeful expression lit up his face. When she shook her head and laughed, he refocused his attention across the room at Ivan Winters, offering him a brutal unfriendly stare.

Minutes later, just when Rich thought things were as back to normal as they could be for three women with recent makeovers, Ivan sauntered over. He was still dressed in his dark pinstripe banker's suit, dreary gray tie, and shiny black shoes.

"Looks like someone had fun with some hair color." Ivan's eyes circled the girls and came to rest on Torrie's face. For a moment, he just glared at her. "I understand you being lax where Iris is concerned, but aren't you a little old for green hair?" He didn't try to hide the reprimand in his question.

Rich tensed and an overwhelming desire to pop the pompous jerk in the nose rushed over him. He felt Torrie's hand clamp down on his forearm before he could slide out of the booth and do the damage dancing around in his head.

She spoke in a saccharine voice. "Ivan, please don't make me crawl over this messy table and rip your eyeballs out." She smiled at Iris and Estella. "We think we look absolutely fabulous, don't we, girls?" When they nodded their little heads, she forged onward. "You see, we had a make-over this afternoon including a manicure and pedicure. Show him, girls." Twenty little fingers with electric blue nails popped up and wiggled in the air. Torrie jiggled her sea green, sparkly fingers at him and smiled a devilish smile. "And tonight, Iris and I are having a sleepover at Estella's house. With movies and popcorn!"

Ivan's jaw dropped. Too stunned to speak, he stared at her. The message hit home like an arrow hitting the bullseye. Torrie Larson was sleeping over at Rich Redman's house.

And that will teach the dim-witted banker to take a swipe at a mother's child, Rich thought as he fought with every ounce of stamina he had to repress a chuckle bubbling in his chest. But he couldn't halt the satisfied grin spreading over his face.

Flushed, Ivan excused himself and like a crab scuttling across the sand, he made a quick retreat toward the front door.

As the girls waited for the check, Estella sat up straighter, brightened, and looked at her father with an expectant gaze. "So is Torrie staying with us, too?"

Torrie pushed her water glass aside and collected her purse. "Just until after you are all tucked into bed." She nudged Rich on the shoulder to let her out of the booth. "I have things to do back at the apartment to get ready for tomorrow."

Rich slid out and threw a tip on the table. "Dang, I guess it means no dessert for me later tonight," he mumbled under his breath as she stepped close to corral the girls and their stuffed animals.

"Got that right, cowboy." She gave him a sly look to let him know she understood his intent, then hustled the girls toward the door.

****

Hours later, as Rich poured two glasses of wine and waited on the back porch for Torrie to tuck the girls in for the third and what he hoped was the final time, he thought about the day. It had been an enjoyable and fun time with Torrie and Iris. Torrie was a level-headed, down-to-earth woman and mother who only flew into a chilling rage when her child was under attack. He laughed thinking about the look on Ivan Winters's face when he thought Torrie was spending the night at his house.

He looked out over the back lawn and realized he had to make a decision about the rose gardens. All the roses would soon be coming into a full June bloom. Already he could smell the sweet soft scents of the other summer flowers in the air. There was no reason why Torrie couldn't continue with her efforts to propagate the perfect heirloom white rose. In fact, it gave her a reason to come over to the house, and he was looking for every reason he could dream up to have her there.

He had already decided to just repaper the formal living room and refinish the floor, doing as little to disturb its vintage look as possible, but still bringing it up-to-date. He sent the chairs out to be reupholstered and informed the custom furniture shop he would drop in to pick out a sample from the swatches lying on the kitchen table. This way, most of the on-site work would take less than a week. To be honest, Rich didn't care about the stuffy room with its tons of Austrian tchotchkes. And he had no idea what he'd do with a floor-to-ceiling cupboard full of Steiff bears in the study. He just wanted as little disruption in the house as possible so he could work in peace. He and Torrie had used the cozier family room off the kitchen, with its bank of windows facing the backyard and an entrance onto the patio, to entertain the children tonight. The toasted marshmallows made over the brass fire pit outside had been sheer genius on Torrie's part and had kept the girls together in one spot for hours. He could still smell smoke from the burning embers, still see the glowing red coals in the inky darkness.

"A penny for your thoughts," Torrie said, padding out onto the porch in bare feet to stand beside him. In her hand, she held the swatches.

"You're going to need a fistful of coins." He handed her a glass of wine from a small bistro table near the railing.

Torrie took the glass and a sip. "One more burnt marshmallow and I would have exploded."

"Hey," he said, "you were the one who said, 'I'll take it,' when the girls grumbled it was too far gone and charred to a crisp." He chuckled. "What do you think about the swatches?"

"I'd stick with the gold color. I vote for the delicate gold plaid."

He felt a shiver crawl up his back. *I'd stick with the gold color.* The exact words of his grandmother. He peered at her intently.

"What?" she asked. "Don't tell me I have dirt on my face?"

From behind them, the elusive white cat slinked up the porch steps and circled Torrie's legs, purring loudly. "Sheba, where have you been?" She bent to pet her, then stepped away and disappeared inside. She returned with a saucer of milk and placed it by the door. The cat dived into it, greedily lapping it up.

"Torrine Larson. The savior of little children and guardian of stray cats," Rich said.

She moved toward him. "And a coach for men who need to learn the ropes of sleepovers."

"Trust me, I know the ropes of sleepovers." He bent and brushed his lips over hers. She tasted of wine and the faint flavor of marshmallow. "Just not the kind we had tonight. But we could rectify it." He took the glass from her hand and set it on the table and pulled her to him. This time the kiss was more demanding and as his passion grew stronger, he could feel her succumb to the magnetism pulling them together. She curled her hands into the back of his hair and didn't try to disguise her body's reaction. They exchanged kiss for kiss. His hands slipped down her waist and under her shirt and worked their way upward over her smooth soft skin to her breasts. He felt fire spreading over his entire body and he couldn't get enough of her. If they didn't stop soon, he didn't know whether he could stop.

As if reading his mind, she pulled away, panting. "No, not here." She gulped in a breath of air and leaned her head against his chest, breathing hard. "I'm sorry, not here with the girls upstairs. We can't do this."

"You're right. Sorry," he agreed. His breath was as hot and heavy as hers. "But it's inevitable, Torrie. No matter how hard you try to resist."

When she didn't reply, but only looked up at him, he pressed his forehead against the edge of hers, unable to let her go. A huskiness from their interlude still lingered in his tone when he said, "Are you still going with me to Elmira?"

She straightened and lifted up on tiptoe to kiss him gently. "Yes. What time will we be back?"

He encircled her in a hug again, pulling her tight, and spoke into her hair. He knew she could feel his wild beating heart and his arousal. "It might take some time. Do we have to rush back?" There was no mistaking his implied meaning. "Can you pack an overnight bag in case we run late?"

"On purpose?" Blushing, she took a few steps backward toward the door and gave him a knowing look.

"Yeah, maybe. Why not? I've never seen the many waterfalls up there, have you? I'm told they're beautiful." Like you, he wanted to add.

She smiled. "Just a couple. I've been there before, but it was many years ago when I was a teenager. How

132

about I have Denise take over for Lulu after she helps Gus at the landscape center? She's stayed overnight with Iris before and knows the routine.

He nodded, not quite believing his good fortune. He would find every way on God's green earth to drag his feet heading back to Hickory Valley. In fact, he'd book a room in nearby Elmira as soon as possible. Tonight. As soon as Torrie left.

"I have to go." She turned to go inside, but first bent down and petted Sheba sitting beside the milk dish and washing her paws. "Before I forget, your cat is putting on a lot of weight and getting quite chubby."

"What?" He looked at her confused, then laughed. "Are you saying I have a fat cat?"

"Yes, that's one way of describing it." A sly smile crossed her face as she slipped inside the house.

Chapter Thirteen

"My cat is chubby?" Rich wondered aloud as he stood on the back porch after Torrie departed. He scratched his head. "So what?"

"Phfftt. Think about it," piped up a voice from the rocker.

He looked over where the ghost of Grandmother Gertie had taken possession of the rocking chair. "I have. Those darn kids have to stop feeding it so many treats."

Gertie snorted. "Talk to Lulu. You have bigger problems to worry about."

Rich watched for a while as the rocker started slowly, but eventually gained momentum until it was bobbing along in a steady rhythm. "What kind of problems?" he finally asked.

"I'm getting these vibes about a king and queen of hearts, Richard Lee. It must relate to your father and your lost half-sister."

"Dad was never involved with British royalty, was he?" He stared at the empty rocker with a wrinkled forehead. "At least he never mentioned royalty to me."

"No, not that I know of." The rocker stopped suddenly. "You know what you really need to do? You need to see about getting those girls some bicycles to ride. It would give them freedom and something to do in this wonderful summer weather. Remember when you learned to ride in the circular drive out front? I sure miss those days."

"Yeah," Rich smiled. "I remember my poor grandfather running after the bike to keep me upright. I miss those days, too."

Rich leaned against the post at the top of the stairs and shot a penetrating look at the rocker. "Do you think it would help if I called my mother and asked her if she knew anything about a half-sister or the whereabouts of the rubies?" *Now I'm going off my rocker. I'm actually having a conversation with a vacant chair.*

"For earth's sake, no!" Gertie said. "Joyce would be camping out on your doorstep tomorrow, suitcase in hand. She'd be badgering all the townsfolk for information and tearing the house apart looking for the jewels. You know what your mother is like. The woman wrote the definition for the word busybody!"

"Then Torrie is right. We start in New York and see what we can dig up there."

"It's a good start. Torrie's a sharp cookie."

"Yes, she is." Rich sighed and rubbed his face. "I'm done in. Kids are exhausting."

"Tell me about it," Gertie cackled. "Have a safe trip, and don't eat too much ice cream." And with a puff of air, the conversation ended.

With a puzzled look, Rich stared into space. Don't eat too much ice cream? What a strange thing to say.

Chapter Fourteen

It was late when Torrie climbed into the van and headed home from Rich's house with the shower of kisses she and Rich had exchanged still lingering on her lips. She couldn't help thinking how very good looking and virile Rich Redman was and how vulnerable she was to his charms. His energy, power, and sincerity attracted her like a hungry kitten to a pan of milk. She wondered how it was possible for two unlike people to be drawn to each other. He was Mr. Smooth with his sleek, affluent appearance and steady personality. She was practical, predictable, and ordinary—and half the time, she looked like she had rolled in dirt. She didn't know where their relationship was going or where it would end, but she knew she wanted to enjoy the ride for as long as it lasted, even for a scant month. It felt good to be treated like a lady again. To feel someone cared.

Several minutes later, she pulled the van into the driveway beside the warehouse, killed the motor, and grabbed her purse off the front passenger seat along with the spray can of green temporary hair color. Above her, the sky was a canopy of stars with a sliver of a new moon laughing at her. The summer air was still balmy even at such a late hour and smelled lightly of honeysuckle. She barely rounded the corner of the warehouse when she saw Ivan Winter's black sedan parked along the sidewalk below her apartment. He opened his door, and weaving unsteadily on his feet, he circled the front of his car.

"Well, well, so you didn't spend the night with Mr. Rich Guy, huh?" he asked with a slight slur to his speech.

"It's none of your business what I do or don't do, Ivan." She set her chin in a stubborn line.

There was a flush across Ivan's cheeks and forehead. He had been drinking. Torrie thumped down the panic rearing up in her chest. "I'm sorry, Ivan, I'm too tired to quibble with you tonight. Do you need something important? I need to get some sleep. I have an early start at work tomorrow." She heaved an exhausted sigh and turned to leave. She had no desire to tell him she was working for Richard Redman, and they were headed for a nursing home in Elmira, New York.

He grabbed her by her upper arm and spun her around. "Don't you walk away from me!" he growled. "You tried to shame me in the restaurant in front of all those people like I was nothing more than a piece of lint on your jacket. I won't stand for it!"

"Get. Your. Hand. Off me." The words came out in a low, staccato, but ominous tone. Torrie pinned him with a gaze capable of freezing sea water.

"And if I don't, Miss High and Mighty?"

She pointed the can of green hair spray at him. "Remove it now, Ivan, unless you want to look like the Incredible Hulk at work tomorrow." *And you're far from a superhero, you pompous jerk!* Her heart thudded wildly in her chest.

Ivan withdrew his hand, but continued to glare at her. "Listen, Torrie, you're not fooling anyone. I know you're chasing after Redman for his money. But I'm warning you, he's playing you for a fool. He only wants someone to warm his bed for four weeks while he's hanging around Hickory Valley. As soon as he sells the house, he's out of here."

"You don't know anything about Rich Redman or his intentions."

"No, but I do know if you don't take my warning seriously, I can make it so difficult you'll think twice about your intentions."

"Just what do you mean?" Torrie felt fury flare all the way down to her toes, and it took every ounce of stamina to remain calm.

"I'll call in your loan," he said with a slur. He moved so close to her that she could smell the alcohol on his breath and see red rimming his eyes. "And the loan for the landscape center."

"You have no reason to call in any loans." She felt a lump form in the pit of her stomach. "Stop acting like a child, Ivan. We've known each other since grade school. You can't go around bullying people to get what you want." She watched his anger slightly evaporate, and she looked toward the apartment trying to gauge how fast she could maneuver the steps and get away.

"You don't understand, Torrie. I've adored you since grade school. I don't want anyone to cut into my territory until I have time to prove to you we're perfect for each other. You just haven't had time to come to your senses. I'll do whatever it takes to make you realize I'm serious." He glared at her and his voice grew louder and more insistent. Finally he ground out, "I won't take no for an answer!"

A chilly black silence fell between them and Torrie felt increasingly uneasy under his scrutiny. His face was a glowering mask of rage.

"Go home, Ivan, and get some sleep," Torrie said in a calm voice she didn't feel. "You've had too much to drink."

Ivan grabbed for her again, just as the porch light to her apartment came on. He jumped back. "Who's in your apartment?"

"It's probably Finn. He was supposed to look at the ice cube maker on my refrigerator and see if it could be fixed. Good night, Ivan." Heart hammering, Torrie turned away and raced up the steps to her apartment. As she fumbled in her purse for her keys, she glanced back to see Ivan still standing on the walk, annoyance marring his face as he scowled at her.

But it wasn't Finn who opened the door before she could find them. It was Joe. His arm shot out, grabbed her by her upper arm, and unceremoniously dragged her through the doorway into the hallway. He slammed the door and threw the lock shut with a sharp click.

Torrie slumped against the wall and rubbed her bicep. "What is it with you guys and your death grips?"

"Why did you park on the dark side of the building and walk around to the front?" His usual calm voice was curt. His eyes flashed in anger. "You know this isn't the greatest area of town."

He went to the window in the living room overlooking the steps and parted the curtains, peering out. "You should have parked in front. I could've moved the van for you." He came back and looked at her. "Are you all right?"

"Yes. I'm fine."

The motor on Ivan's car started, and she sighed in relief.

She motioned Joe into the kitchen and put a kettle of water on to boil before she allowed her shaking legs to collapse onto a stool by the pass-through counter. Joe went to the cabinet and took out two cups and two tea bags and placed them near the stove. He grunted. "You need to stay away from bozo Ivan. He's bad news. How many times do I have to tell you that?"

Torrie looked at him and wondered if it was a guy thing to warn a female about every person they didn't like. She threw up her hands. "Does it look like I'm trying to be near him? He shows up wherever I go!" She got up, elbowed him aside, and poured hot water over the tea bags in their cups. She opened a cupboard and took out the honey and sugar. The ordinary motions of moving about in her own kitchen calmed her. "What happened to Finn?"

"Your mother needed him for something, so I volunteered. I reset the ice maker and it seems to be working." He took the cup she offered him, crossed to the counter, and set the cup down. Still standing, he paused and cleared his throat. His voice was the old Joe she knew so well. The easy-going, soft-spoken Joe. "Torrie, maybe it's time you settle down. This is no way for you to be living, in this matchbox apartment on the questionable edge of town. Without others around you. Without seeing your daughter half of the time."

She stared at him wordlessly for a minute. Inside her head, a little voice screamed, *Don't say it, Joe Bradley. Please don't say anything to ruin our friendship!*

When she set her cup down beside his, he covered

her hand with his large callused one. He looked at her with clear, gentle eyes. "I have a whole house outside town and lots of rooms to ramble around in and a huge backyard. You know I love Iris like she's my own."

Torrie pulled her hand free. Her eyes were misty when she spoke. "Joe, please. You are my best friend. You were my most devoted ally when I came back to Hickory Valley and had no one to turn to except my family. You *are* family to Iris and me. Please, please, don't ruin what we have between us. Marriage, out of a sense of obligation, would never work for either of us and you know it. I'm flattered you want to protect me. But marriage? Come on. We both know that's not a good idea." They stood, steam rising from their cups between them as they looked at each other in total silence. She thought a shadow of longing—maybe disappointment—crossed his face. Or was it gentle liberation from a chivalrous offer? And an offer both of them would have regretted in the future.

Finally, he cleared his throat and smiled—the old familiar smile she was accustomed to. "Well then, did you ever think about carrying a huge flashlight capable of knocking someone to his knees?" he asked. "Or maybe a Taser or some pepper spray?" He gestured to the spray can on the counter. "I don't think green hair spray will stop an attacker, maybe only make it a little easier for the police to apprehend him."

A small bubble of laughter started in her chest and rose upward until she laughed outright.

When he joined in, she gave him a rib-shattering hug. It was a huge sense of relief, knowing they were on safe, even ground again.

****

It was early morning when Rich tiptoed downstairs with an overnight bag. He went straight to the kitchen where Lulu had coffee already made. She was dressed in bright orange with yellow stripes, and she was filling a picnic basket with a thermos of coffee and some breakfast foods. "You said you wanted to get an early start. I thought you might want to stop along the road a few hours into your trip and have something light to eat. How did you make out with the girls and the sleepover?"

Squinting at her, Rich poured a cup of coffee at the counter and added a splash of milk. He blew out a breath of air. "Why is it called a sleepover? Those kids didn't sleep. They were giggling like hyenas all night. Torrie and I put them to bed three times. I finally gave up when my brain and body begged for sleep so badly, I couldn't see straight. I'm betting they won't be up before noon." He shook his head in exasperation. "Where do females get enough fuel to keep a conversation going for an entire night?"

"You're a big shot lawyer, and you're asking me?"

He sauntered over to the table and slumped down. "I guess I should warn you, they have pink hair and blue nails." He took a sip of coffee, fell silent, and peered at her, wondering why he was warning someone about pink hair and blue nails when she was decked out in colors that could blind an average person wearing sunglasses.

"What's eating at you now?" Lulu asked. She came over and sat down across from him, her bony fingers interlinked while she waited for him to speak.

"Do you think a person can have a second chance at love?" he finally asked.

"Ahhh," she replied. "This sounds like some deep soul-searching question needing the perspective of a clinical psychologist to come up with the correct answer." She pursed her lips. "From my experience, the answer is plain and simple. Yes." She rose and went to the bread drawer and took out a lemon muffin and set it in front of him. "Eat! You have a long drive to Elmira."

"That's it? Yes? A simple y*es*?" He looked at her in disbelief and started to unwrap the paper from the muffin.

Lulu shrugged. "Let's do this backward, Sunshine. Do you honestly believe—in this whole universe of over 7.2 billion people—there is only one perfect person for each of us to love and marry?"

"Well, when you put it so simply, it certainly increases my chances," he agreed and took a big bite of the muffin.

Lulu shook her head in exasperation and went to the window.

"One more thing. I think the girls are feeding the cat too much food." He mumbled his words through a mouthful of muffin. "She's getting fat. Even Torrie thinks so." He paused, chewing. "Fat. Just like I'm getting after eating all this mouthwatering food you make."

Lulu snorted. "You big dope. Sheba is going to have a litter. Of course she's getting chubby."

Rich choked on the last bite sliding down his throat. "Say what? Kittens? How'd that happen?"

"Goodness gracious, you don't want me to answer such a ridiculous question, do you?" Lulu bent closer to the window overlooking the backyard and squinted. "Richard Lee Junior, there's something odd-looking about one of the flowerbeds in the backyard. Maybe more than one. It looks like someone has been cutting Torrie's roses with a shovel."

His chair scraped the floor as he rose, and together they both headed for the back door at the same time.

Minutes later, with a look of sadness and disgust, he was dialing the police and Torrie Larson.

****

Frowning, Torrie surveyed the damage. She squatted before a row of roses chopped off near the base. The stems and flower buds were tossed about and stomped on. Her heart sank. An entire bed of grafted bushes was lost. She would be lucky if the root bases were hardy enough to regenerate this summer for grafting next year. She thought about the long hours she had spent taking cuttings from the Austrian plants and splicing the bud eyes onto the understock. Then came the long two and a half years of babying the plants, fertilizing, and winterizing them from the northern cold. Two and half years wasted on this bed alone. She looked forlornly at the scattered parts of the bushes. She had been hoping to pot and offer them for sale. She had planned to take cuttings from the others to add to the root roses she was growing in the greenhouse at the landscape center.

Beside her, Rich and the town police officer searched the ground nearby looking for any evidence or footprints. "I would suspect it was kids starting their summer rebel rousing," Officer Powers said, flipping the top down on a small notepad where he had jotted down contact information. "I don't think we'll find anything to give us a hint of who did this. I'll try to have a patrol car make a few passes by your house late

144

at night and keep an eye out." He turned to leave and glanced at both of them. "Maybe you should spend a few minutes searching your memories to determine whether there's someone who might have issues with either of you?"

Speechless, Torrie stared at him. Enemies? If last night was any indication of having enemies, Ivan Winters was the first person on her list. But somehow she didn't think Ivan would stoop so low or even take the time to actually sneak into someone's backyard and destroy a bed of plants. He would never get his lily white banker's hands dirty. And someone knew what they were doing, judging from the plants scattered everywhere. They had chosen the roses, and they would have had to wear leather gloves or they were walking around Hickory Valley with a million scratches on their hands and forearms.

When they were alone again, Torrie put on a brave face. "Well, there's not much we can do here. Let's get started for Elmira. We're already late. I'll phone Finn, and he'll have someone come over and clean up this mess. Joe or he will be able to determine whether there's any salvageable stock for re-grafting or rooting, and they'll take the cuttings back to the nursery to preserve them."

Rich pulled her toward him and squeezed her shoulders. "I'm so sorry, Torrie. I know how much these gardens mean to you, but especially the roses. Are you sure you still want to go to New York?"

She nodded. She had been banking on selling some of the Austrian roses to help with her expenses. There was no way now she was not going to Elmira and triple her pay.

Chapter Fifteen

Willow Tree Assisted Living, just outside Elmira, was an upper crust, one-hundred-and-fifty-acre nursing home shaded by giant elms and crisscrossed with a maze of connecting walkways. Torrie and Rich wound their way between picturesque cottages and a showy condo complex for self-sufficient residents, complete with patios and two pools. The assisted living building they arrived at contained not only single person rooms, but also a multitude of facilities, including a library, common gathering room, exercise and craft rooms, and a reading salon.

Rich was prepared to jump through hoops to find out information about his grandfather's brother, Walt Redman, but was surprised when the manager at Willow Tree not only offered his condolences about his great uncle's passing, but also pointed out Walt's favorite companion, Mrs. Winifred Fox, who was at the moment in the reading salon beside the library.

A stately-looking woman with long, well-manicured fingernails, Winifred had short, snow white hair clinging to her head like a helmet. Rich approached cautiously and politely introduced Torrie and himself. With the grace of the cultured, Winifred regally closed her book, careful to place the bottom edge of the book mark exactly on the paragraph she had finished reading. She placed the book on a stack and straightened them so all the corners were squared and orderly before she motioned with a bejeweled hand for them to take a seat.

"We're so pleased to be able to meet you. We were hoping you could tell us a little about my Great Uncle Walter," Rich said, cautioning himself to tread lightly, not knowing what type of impression his uncle might have made. For all he knew, his great uncle could have been a sly scoundrel or the world's most renowned womanizer.

"Are you researching your family's history?"

"Yes, you could say that," he admitted.

"Well, Walter Redman was a charming man." She had a clear, genteel voice that spoke of wealth and privilege. "He loved to laugh and tell jokes. He was a voracious reader, and he enjoyed following politics, never missing the nightly news and Sunday review of the Washington D.C. scene. And my, oh my, he could dance." She looked around the room and motioned to a tiny woman with a sharp little nose sitting a few feet away, reading the *Elmira Star Gazette*. A rosewood cane was propped beside her chair. "Couldn't he, Ethel?"

"Who?" Ethel lowered the newspaper and stretched out her thin birdlike face, squinting over the reading glasses perched on her nose.

"Walter. Walter Redman." Winifred thumped her hand on the arm rest, disgruntled to have to repeat the question. "Couldn't Walter dance? Why, he had every lady in here wanting to be his partner."

Ethel nodded in agreement, then tilted her paper to cover her face and resume her reading, but not before Rich caught her rolling her eyes toward the ceiling.

"Well, it seems I learned something new about my

great uncle. Does the king and queen of hearts mean anything to you?" Rich offered her a tentative smile.

"Yes. Yes, it does." Winifred's face lit up like a Happy Lamp. "Walter and I were selected King and Queen of our facility's Valentine's Day celebration two years in a row. We were like Fred Astaire and Ginger Rogers. Everybody said so. Didn't they, Ethel?"

Ethel lowered her paper. "What did you say, Winny?"

"I *said,* everyone thought Walter and I danced like Fred Astaire and Ginger Rogers. Didn't they?"

"If you say so." Ethel raised her paper to continue reading.

"Why, you old fool, of course they did!" Winifred grew agitated.

"I'm sure they did." Rich tried to soothe her.

"We could fox trot better than any couple in the entire Willow Tree community."

"I have no doubt," Torrie interjected lightly. "You have the lovely, lithe figure of a dancer."

"I'll have you know I took ballet when I was a young girl."

"And I bet you were one spectacular ballerina." Rich waited a moment, hoping for her anger to diminish and serenity to prevail. He slumped back in his seat in a relaxed positon so as not to seem impatient.

Finally, he asked, "Did my father, Richard Redman, ever visit Walter?"

Winifred looked at him, her face changing from irritation to suspicious caution. "Yes, why do you ask?"

'I was wondering if he was ever accompanied by a lady friend."

"If you mean my niece. Why, yes. They visited us

together on many occasions. I can't say I held your father in high esteem." She stiffened. "It's not like he didn't treat Walter with total respect. There were just other factors involved. Why, the Redman fellow was fifteen years older than Anne and was not divorced when they first came to visit, mind you. How tasteless, don't you agree?"

Rich glanced at Torrie. She flinched and gave him a cautious look. If there was more information to garner, he had the feeling it would not be forthcoming from Winifred Fox. Together, they watched Ethel rise, tuck her folded newspaper under her arm, and shuffle from the room. Her rubber-bottomed cane squeaked as she made her way across the tiled floor.

Torrie spoke up in a soothing tone. "What was your niece's last name, Mrs. Fox?"

"Why do you want to know?" She stared at them with a grim look. Her voice grew distant, cold, and sharp. "I think it's best if you leave. I see no reason to start digging through dirty laundry."

"No, no, please." Torrie said. "We're just trying to locate a family relation."

"Well, if it involves Anne, I've nothing more to say." She opened her book and bent her head, dismissing them.

****

Rich rose and took Torrie by the arm and escorted her to the door of the salon. "Well, that certainly went well," he whispered, leaning close.

"It's my fault, I shouldn't have pushed her for a name." Torrie frowned. "I guess I stirred the pot a little too quickly."

"Nah, getting information from the old gal was as

much fun as hugging a rabid porcupine. She was a real pain in the—"

"Rich!"

He scrubbed his face with his hands and cranked his head to look back at Winifred. "Well, the old gal wasn't about to give up anything worthwhile we could use."

"True, but now we know where your dance genes came from. Great Uncle Walter." Torrie giggled.

He looked at her, eyebrow raised. "That's all you gleaned from the entire conversation?" He shook his head. "I'm heading back to locate the manager and see if he can supply us with any more information or leads."

Torrie nodded. "Why don't I just poke around here and see if I can shake down some of these old folks in the sitting room?"

They parted, Rich heading for the manager's office.

For a minute, Torrie lingered at the doorway and scanned the main gathering room. She turned back to see Winifred pretending to read, but surreptitiously glance up at the salon door where she stood. Every fiber in her body told her the wily old woman had played them for fools. Irritated, she stomped back to where Winifred sat, head still bent over her book. She would have made a pitiful actress and Torrie had doubts about her dancing skills as well.

"You know," Torrie said in a low voice, "kind acts put off until tomorrow may become only bitter regrets." When Winifred refused to look at her, she persisted, "The man you just refused to help is an only child looking for his half-sister. He's one of the kindest and most honest and giving persons I've ever come to know. There's a trust set up for her, and he could easily have disregarded the request of his dead grandmother, let time play itself out, and take her share, which will be due him in a year. But he chose to honor his grandmother's wishes."

She turned to go, then whirled back, her voice rising in volume. She didn't care if the whole reading salon heard. "And my mother always used to say the best sleeping pill in the world is to lay down each night with a clear conscience. So sweet dreams, Winifred Fox!"

Back stiff, she walked into the main gathering area where people were watching large flat screen televisions in three corners of the huge room. On one screen, a game show host interviewed a contestant, and from another corner, a station blared out the weather report. Near a glass exit door, Ethel frantically flapped her hand to motion her over.

"You'll never squeeze an ounce of information from sour-faced Winny," Ethel declared in a low chiding tone. "I never knew what Walt saw in her. What a shrew."

"Maybe her ability to dance?" Torrie leaned down closer to the little woman. "Is there anything you might be able to tell me?"

"No, no, no," Ethel crowed. "It's not that easy, my dear. Information will cost you."

Torrie straightened. Were all these old women at Willow Tree as crazy as bats? Her arms flew up, palms smacking the air in front of her. "I'm not a rich woman, Ethel. I've come here because I'm helping Richard Redman while he's in Hickory Valley. He desperately wants to find his half-sister."

"No, my dear, not money. You misunderstand me. I want to go to the ice cream shop down the road."

"What?" Torrie's eyes widened in surprise. "Ice cream shop? Why?"

"For some soft ice cream. Why else?"

"Are you allowed?" Torrie could envision the headline now: rich Dallas attorney and poor landscape owner arrested for kidnapping elderly woman from an Elmira eldercare facility. "Aren't there some rules for residents leaving the property with strangers? You don't even know me."

Ethel patted her on her upper arm. "No, no, my dear, there are only restrictions for those with directives issued by a doctor or their family. I assure you, I don't have mental incapacities or any health restrictions. My mind is sound. And you, my dear, look pretty harmless. All you have to do is cosign with me at the desk. You state the location where we're going, time, and sign your name. Then I sign beside your signature to indicate I'm in agreement." She looked at Torrie like she was missing half a brain. "This isn't a maximum security prison, my dear. It's a respectable retirement community."

Rich approached them, frowning. "Any progress?"

Torrie blew out a breath of air and tugged him off to the side. This was truly going to sound like she had half a brain. She pulled him farther into a corner until she was certain they were out of earshot of the other residents. "Yes, we're taking Ethel for ice cream at the local ice cream shop."

"We're what?" He stared at her, speechless. "Why?"

"Come on, Rich. It's just down the road a bit." Torrie shot him a hopeless look.

"Why don't you just shoot me? We're going for *ice cream*? I can't believe you're letting these little old ladies bamboozle you!"

"Shhhh. Let's not announce it to the world," Ethel scolded, startling him as she hobbled over to stand beside them. She squinted at him with shriveled little blue eyes. "You want half this room to pile into your car? What's the problem? Don't you like ice cream, Dreamboat?"

"Yes, of course. And my name is *Rich*." He shot Torrie an agonizing look which translated to: Tell me what I did to deserve this?

Ethel poked him on his chest with a scrawny finger. "Well, since Torrie and I need to talk, I suggested we go out for ice cream, and she agreed." She turned to Torrie. "Didn't you, my dear?"

Torrie sighed, but some sixth sense nagged at her, telling her this would not be as hopeless as she earlier thought. "Yes, I did." She glanced at Rich who now looked somewhat dazed; but like the gentleman he was, he propelled the little woman with her cane toward the front desk.

Humming a soft polka tune, Ethel scribbled her name beside Torrie's, then turned and spun her cane like it was a baton. "I used to be a dancer, too, when I was younger, you know. What's your favorite flavor of ice cream, Dreamboat?"

"I guess vanilla," he admitted. "The name's Rich."

"Then let's get a move on. At my age, even minutes are precious." Taking his arm as if he was her knight in shining armor, she limped gleefully toward the exit.

Minutes later, flying down the road to the local ice cream shop with an old romantic tune from the fifties blaring from the car's speakers, Rich shot Torrie a withered glance. "Tell me again, why are we going to the ice cream shop and, more specifically, why are we listening to this crap on the radio?"

Torrie sat up straighter. "Shhh. Ethel likes the oldies and wanted Tom Jones but this is all I could find when I searched the stations." Torrie patted him reassuringly on his upper arm. "Be nice, Rich. Let's make this a fun time for her. Maybe she'll tell us something we didn't know about Walt."

Rich stole a peek in his rear view mirror and watched Ethel, in the backseat, humming and swaying along to a song with a male singer begging someone—perhaps a former lover—to release him and let him go. Boy, was he saying a mouthful, he thought. He turned to Torrie. "You know," he said, "one of us in this car is close to going off the deep end."

Torrie snickered. "For heaven's sake, you're just sore because you didn't get enough sleep last night."

"Which brings me to another point," he grumbled. "When explaining the finer details of a sleepover, you neglected to tell me the participants don't sleep."

Torrie couldn't help but smile. "If I had told you all the particulars, you might had chickened out, *Dreamboat*."

Minutes later, with a huge banana split with extra whipped cream sitting in front of Ethel, Torrie leaned forward and addressed the little woman like they were co-conspirators. "Okay, girlfriend, we made a deal. Spill the beans. Tell me what you know about Richard

Redman and Winifred Fox's niece, Anne."

"Her name was Anne Alexander." Ethel dove into the ice cream with gusto. "She often came with Richard when he visited Walter Redman. She was a beautiful, sweet girl, at least fifteen years younger than him. Now all this happened a good seventeen years ago or more, so my memory is not as good as it used to be."

"I understand. Tell us what you know," Rich coaxed.

"Well, rumor has it Anne got pregnant, and Richard, your father, was responsible. Ten months later, she shows up alone to see Winifred. Again, rumor has it, she gave the child up for adoption." Ethel stopped eating, wiped a ring of whipped cream from her upper lip, and looked at them with a serious expression on her face. "It was a good thing, too, because a few years later, Anne was involved in a winter automobile accident up by the Finger Lakes and died."

Rich remembered that just before his first year of college, the fighting between his parents escalated. He would bet money his mother suspected his father was seeing Anne when he came to Hickory Valley.

"Do you have any idea what happened to the child?" Torrie shoved the dish of chocolate ice cream she was eating aside.

"A local doctor by the name of Winters in Hickory Valley supposedly handled the adoption, which I understand was kept private. The child was placed out of state, much to the disappointment of Winifred."

"Do you recall what the child was named?" Torrie asked.

Ethel shook her head. "No, I don't. But I knew as soon as I heard the name Redman, you were probably looking for your half-sister." She reached out and touched his hand. "Don't be disappointed in Winifred. She may have hated your father, but Anne never revealed any details about the adoption, and Winifred would have liked to have known her grandniece since she never had any children. She lost her only sister, Anne's mother, to cancer before all this happened, so she's quite alone."

"Could you give us an approximate date when Anne returned without the child," Torrie asked. "It might give us an idea about the time of the child's birth."

"She had the child on May 12th."

"How can you be so certain?" Rich asked.

Ethel looked at him with a grim look. "When Anne waltzed in to visit Winifred later in the summer, I overheard her tell Winifred the child was born on Mother's Day. Her exact words were, 'Don't you think it's some kind of strange karma, Aunt Winny?'"

Rich rose. "You have been very helpful, Ethel." He handed her his card. "If you ever need anything, anything at all, feel free to give me a call."

"I wish you luck." Ethel reached for her cane propped against the table. "It's difficult to be alone. It's tough to know you have family out there you can't locate."

He nodded and gave the old woman a warm hug before depositing her back at Willow Tree Assisted Living with two quarts of soft ice cream to share with her friends.

****

"So what do you think?" Rich turned his coffee cup around and around in his hands. They were sitting in a nearby diner having coffee.

Torrie drew her lips in thoughtfully. "I think our next step is going to be a challenge. We need to talk to Ivan's father. I'm hoping Dr. Winters won't stonewall us and his records haven't been destroyed. Nathan Winters has been retired quite a while now. He's getting up there in years. He may not even remember the specific adoption."

Nodding, Rich looked out the window where a slight breeze caused the flowers in the urn outside the diner to bounce and bow their heads as if they too knew the troubles ahead. If the adoption of the child was a private one, not only would Dr. Winters be involved, but also a lawyer. In private adoptions, paperwork was often difficult to track down and even more difficult to obtain. Many times, it was easily and conveniently misplaced upon the request of those involved. It could include certain agreements about when a child might have access to his records—upon request of the birth mother or the adoptive mother. There were a multitude of legal scenarios he didn't want to think about.

"There is something interesting I did find out after glancing through the ledgers last night. I skimmed the last five before your dad's death and one afterward." Torrie's voice shook him out of his reverie.

His lips thinned in exasperation. "Burning the candle on both ends? You're not supposed to be working after hours, Torrie. Make sure you keep track of the time so I can pay you."

She waved him away and bent closer. "Don't worry about it. What I did find out was every month, before your dad died, various monthly sums of money were paid to Henry Jordan at Henry's Garage."

"How much?"

"Anywhere from one thousand to three thousand dollars, and usually in even amounts."

"I'll bet he was making payments on a car for my grandmother. Perhaps paying for repairs. Or maybe Dad bought a vintage car from Henry. Henry was always getting good deals on used vehicles from the local dealers. And Dad was a car fanatic."

Torrie raised her eyebrows. "Don't you think it's a lot of payments for a car? And I've never heard of monthly repairs to the tune of thousands over years and years. The payments stopped after his death."

"Hmmmm, interesting." Rich leaned back. "I guess you and I will be poring over ledgers when we get back to Hickory Valley." He studied her thoughtfully for a moment. "Let's not talk about work. We're here to enjoy the rest of the afternoon."

"Okay." Torrie gave him a small endearing smile. "Do you know we're in Mark Twain Country? The Clemenses spent their summers here, just outside Elmira at Quarry Farm where the sister of Twain's wife lived. Her name was Olivia."

"And he wrote here?" Rich looked at her animated face. She was so beautiful when she talked about the arts. Her eyes held a glint of wonder and passion.

"Yes, this is where he wrote portions of some of his most acclaimed works like *The Adventures of Tom Sawyer*. He's buried here in Woodlawn Cemetery in Elmira." Torrie paused to catch her breath.

"Do you want to explore the town?" he asked. "Today's supposed to be our day together. No kids. I'll do whatever you'd like." He rubbed his thumb gently over the top of her right hand and the delicate ring she wore. "Tell me, Torrie. Do you miss designing jewelry?"

She shook her head. "There was a time when I thought I did. But once Finn and I decided to open the landscape center, it drifted farther and farther from my mind. I found I missed the outdoors and feeling of the sun and wind on my face. Then, when I started floral arranging, I realized I had a real talent for working with flowers, shapes, and colors. You can apply the same design techniques in most art forms, but my creations are special because they're not cardboard copies of stock arrangements—they're all original bouquets and arrangements, although some people do request the same composition once they've seen one of mine at a friend's house. I keep pictures of all my designs in a scrapbook to be safe."

They left the restaurant together, strolling up the street. "Do you like Hickory Valley?" she asked.

Rich pulled her close, his arm around her waist. He was amazed how comfortable they were in each other's company. "Yes, and I envy you because Iris can be brought up in a small town surrounded by a large loving family." He pulled her closer and kissed her gently beside her ear.

"Would you consider relocating from Texas?"

"It would be difficult. I own a firm with two partners and eight other practicing lawyers back in Dallas." *But most of the time, Redman, you are on the road and work with a computer. It could be possible,* a little voice in his head whispered.

They stopped near where the car was parked across from a small floral shop. Torrie went to the display window and looked at the bouquets and arrangements.

159

"We can go in and look around," Rich suggested. "We only have to be at Seventh Heaven Bed and Breakfast at Montour Falls by dinnertime. It's about a half hour drive. I have a bottle of wine on ice waiting for us." Torrie saw the reflection of his smile in the glass.

"Seventh Heaven?" she squealed and turned to face him. "Overlooking Shequaga Falls?" Eyes shining, she grasped his hand and yanked him toward the car. "Let's go. I haven't been there since I was a teenager."

Chapter Sixteen

Torrie couldn't believe her good fortune. Upon their arrival at the bed and breakfast, they had hurriedly stashed their luggage to take advantage of the warm afternoon to see three of the many falls in the surrounding area. Torrie felt like a princess with Rich squiring her from one beautiful place to another, and he had been attentive, caring, and kind. Not only did he reserve a tranquil, spacious room at the elegant bed and breakfast, but he had also requested dinner and wine be served on their private screened terrace overlooking the lush gardens, sparkling fish pond, and pergola. Never once had he brought up the problems of the destroyed flowerbeds or his problems with the jewels and his lost half-sister. He had promised her the entire afternoon and evening would be set aside for their enjoyment, and he had meant it.

Now, as they sat on the patio outside their room in peaceful silence with empty wine glasses and only the occasional songbirds to interrupt the calmness of the descending evening, Torrie could feel the sexual magnetism hang in the air between them. She wondered what it would be like to always have someone so self-assured to stand by her side when life got tough. It would be comforting to have someone she could lean on and who could reassure her when problems arose. Someone who would wrap his arms around her and make her feel protected and safe.

"What are you thinking?" A tiny smile curved the corner of his mouth.

"Wouldn't it be awesome to have this perfect Norman Rockwell world go on forever and ever?" She sighed and leaned back in her seat.

He reached over and took her hand, squeezing it gently and sending delicious shivers up her arm. He bent near her and placed a kiss on her cheek. "Then let's not destroy the perfect moment." His gray eyes brimmed with tenderness and passion.

Torrie met his gaze. Her heart hammered in her chest. She was not a fickle female who didn't know when a man's eyes were full of desire. All of a sudden a shadow of alarm washed over her as her snug safe world tilted on its axis. What had she gotten herself into? What was she thinking when she agreed to accompany him and stay overnight? She wasn't a woman who did one-night stands. She was Torrie Larson. Responsible, steadfast, and predictable. The girl who never colored outside the lines all her life. Single mom. Mother of a young daughter who led an uneventful, innocent life for the last six years. Even though she was attracted to Rich Redman, she still couldn't bring herself to believe a relationship between them had a chance. They were so totally different and from different backgrounds. He was rich and she was poor. He was mature, worldly, polished, and sure of himself. She was a jumbled mess of insecurities and broken dreams. So what was she doing here?

"What's the matter, Torrie?" he asked softly.

She swallowed hard, trying to manage a feeble answer that was honest, but not insulting. "I guess I can't decide whether I've made a good decision." She bit her lower lip. "I've never done this before."

He smiled at her with his utterly stunning lips. "And do you think what we're doing here is wrong?"

She shrugged, afraid to look him in the eye. She stared at the stone patio instead. Panic like she never felt before rose up. "I…I think…I think we need to call our girls," she stammered.

"Torrie, look at me," he said. When she met his gaze, he spoke with a voice filled with a knowing and gentle calmness as if he could read her mind. "Torrie, this night is for you to enjoy. Trust me, you needn't feel frightened or pressured to do anything you don't want to do. Yes, we need to call the girls." He rose and offered her his hand, helping her up. "I have to make a few calls myself. Why don't you use the shower and afterward, I'll take one."

He pulled her into his arms. His comforting embrace felt so right. She leaned into him, feeling his warmth through his shirt. She could hear the soft beating of his heart. When she pulled away, he kissed her lightly on the lips and looked into her eyes. "I want you to shower, and put on those sexy stilettos and the hot electric blue dress I saw in the garment bag." When her eyes widened, he laughed and said in a low, husky voice. "It's not what you're thinking. We're going out on the town…dancing, my dear."

An hour later, after a short taxi ride to the Still Waters Lounge, Torrie and Rich were seated at a table in a private corner of the room, away from the noise of the bar and the possibility of loud music from the band. A bottle of champagne was waiting for them when they arrived.

"Rich, this is fabulous. It's like a fairytale." Torrie swept her hands in the air and looked around at the lavish room trimmed in polished brass, dark walnut paneling, and lush red carpeting. The dance floor at the front was lit with overhead spotlights of blue, aqua, and pink. Behind it, a slightly raised stage held a multi-piece band, complete with violins and brass, already playing a soft waltz.

A waiter appeared, opened the champagne, and poured two flutes. Rich raised his glass to Torrie's. His shark gray suit emphasized his gray eyes and turned them from smoke to charcoal in the dim light. "You look stunning tonight, Torrie." He winked. "A toast to us for health and happiness, and some excellent music and romantic dancing."

"And sleuthing," she added, beaming.

Moments later, she was swept up in his arms on the dance floor where he held her close and smoothly twirled her in a soft waltz across the room. Within minutes, it was obvious others on the dance floor were watching them. Oblivious to everyone and the spectacle they were making, Rich kept his gaze pinned on her face alone. He was so incredibly handsome and charming, she let herself go, melting into his arms, enjoying the music, the beat, and powerful attraction between them.

"How did you learn to dance so well?" she asked. "And don't tell me it was natural talent inherited from Great Uncle Walter."

He grinned and spun her toward an isolated area on the dance floor free of other dancers. "It was my grandmother's idea. When I was in junior high, the local YMCA of Hickory Valley was giving summer dance lessons. My grandmother knew I wasn't comfortable around women…well, girls back then. She told me if I learned to dance, every female would look at me in a different light since all women love to dance." He offered her an arresting smile. "Of course, she hinted a new baseball bat and mitt might be forthcoming if I managed to suffer through all the lessons. What she didn't tell me was she wanted to expose me to the YMCA and to more people my age who later became my friends when I transferred for my last two years of high school. She did the same with sports in school and our church group. Because I was an only child, I think she always worried I wouldn't fit in. I wouldn't have friends."

A lull fell and Torrie snuggled closer, feeling blissfully happy and alive. She kept in perfect step with him as if they were made to be partners. She remembered Elsa telling her Rich could be so unbelievingly charming when he wanted to be and depending upon how much mischief he was planning for later. "So tell me, did the females look at you in a different light?" she asked.

He chuckled, expertly twirling her around in the opposite direction. "If they did, I didn't notice. But I met your sister and her twin brother there. Elsa was often my dance partner. She refused to dance with Lars."

"Ah, ha. So that's how she knows so much about you."

"Hmmm, I guess."

"Lars still has two left feet." Torrie smiled.

"True, but he's one of the funniest guys I've ever known. We became close that summer, and have been best friends ever since."

"He's a car salesman, for goodness sake. He'll sell you the wheels off your own vehicle and joke about it."

"Well, I know a Texan who'll do that."

Torrie's laughter was warm and carefree.

"I also met Ivan Winters there."

This time she stiffened and faltered, but recovered her step. Her smile faded. "On that cheerful note, let's take a break," she suggested.

Back at their table, Rich pulled out her chair and casually slid his hand across the back of her bare shoulders, caressing her before sliding into his seat. "Is everything okay?"

Torrie nodded, afraid to speak. Afraid she would blurt out secrets even her family didn't know about.

****

Rich felt Torrie's change in mood the minute he mentioned Ivan Winters. He wondered what caused the shift, but he knew how secretive Torrie was with her personal life, so he dismissed her sudden reaction and focused on putting her at ease. This was a night to romance Torrie Larson.

A waiter arrived at their table with a tiered plate arranged with a rich assortment of elaborate hors d'oeuvres, fruit, and small sugared treats. Rich leaned back in his chair and chose a chocolate-dipped strawberry from the tray. "So tell me what it was like to live with three big brothers." In truth, he often wondered what living in a large family was like. The many times he visited at the Larson household, it was a beehive of activity with Regina, Torrie's mom, organizing the family of children with quiet but unwavering authority.

He remembered she had a house rule. No one was allowed to leave the house until his chores were finished. Often Rich spent time in their backyard helping Lars so they could get out on a Saturday night in record time. He remembered mowing the lawn, washing the family's van and pickup, and chopping and stacking wood for the woodstove in the downstairs family room. Most households had only one axe or one shovel, but with four males in the household, the Larson family had multiples of everything, including two lawn mowers and snow blowers. Most of all, Rich envied the camaraderie only a large family experienced. There was always laughter and ribbing and quibbling, and sometimes downright fighting. When he went home to his grandmother's house, it sometimes seemed empty, silent, and lonely.

"The noise. There were days when I hated the noise," Torrie confessed. "Being the youngest, I thought everyone lived in a home with continual racket and commotion." She sipped on her champagne and chose a piece of chocolate. "When my mom finally realized I needed quiet time for myself to sketch or read, she had Dad convert a space under a dormer window up in the attic into a small room with an overhead light and a desk so I could create in peace. Dad even put a lock on the door to keep my brothers at bay. When I wasn't in my treehouse, I was up in the attic."

"But you played sports and played them very proficiently. Soccer, volleyball, basketball," Rich pointed out. "So all your free time wasn't set aside for only art projects."

Torrie took a small bite from the chocolate square.

"When my brothers didn't have enough people to fill out a team or needed a spare player, they always came looking for me." She shook her head. "No, I'm not being honest. Those knuckleheads pounded on my attic door until I gave in. Then they humored their little sister until their game was over. Otherwise, they ignored or teased me." Her aquamarine eyes pierced the distance between them. "I played sports because my parents believed exercise was good for your health. I was often enlisted by high school coaches who needed to fill out their teams. When you play with rough and tumble older brothers, coaches figure out quickly you can handle the game better than a beginner because you've survived your holy terror siblings. They think you're fearless."

"But the Larson boys looked out for you. And they still make it a point to check up on you."

"Yeah, well, it wasn't a big plus when you're trying to date in high school." She frowned. "Every guy who didn't make muster by big brothers' standards didn't even get to wink at me."

"Your mother was a saint. I never heard her raise her voice."

"No, she never raised her voice or her hand. She gave you her cold Scandinavian stare. She believed in far greater punishments. She heaped additional chores on us if we stepped out of line."

A flash of humor crossed Rich's face. "Tell me about it. I'll never forget the time we had to wash all the outside windows before we could go down to the local hangout because Finn and Lars hid a video game from Gus."

"Mom always liked you. She thought you were

well-mannered. I know she'd love to see you." Torrie inclined her head. "I'll try to find a time when I know the others are busy and out of our hair, and we'll go over with the girls for dinner." She yawned and glanced at her watch.

"It is getting late and you're getting tired," Rich said, signaling for the waiter. He asked for the check and gave instructions to call a cab. While they were waiting, the band began its second set with a soft romantic Spanish waltz.

He stood, holding out his hand. "Come, let's dance," he coaxed. "This is a favorite of mine by Eros Ramazzotti. The lyrics have been translated into Italian and Spanish."

He led her to the dance floor and pulled her into his arms, his fingers aching to touch her all over. Her nearness was intoxicating. They fell into the rhythm of the song like they had been dancing together for years instead of hours. With Torrie Larson pressed close to him, Rich felt like a prince. Like the lyrics of the song, he felt like she belonged to him and him alone.

Chapter Seventeen

On the cab ride back to the B&B, Torrie snuggled close to Rich and laid her head on his chest, inhaling his spicy aftershave. A million thoughts swirled through her head, each colliding with the other:

He's out of your league and he'll be gone before summer even ends, a little voice in her head warned her.

But why couldn't she have a short fling, no strings attached? she countered. Nobody was going to get hurt when it was over. They were adults, just two people, enjoying each other's company for a few weeks. And enjoying each other's bodies.

But can you handle it? the contrary first voice asked.

Minutes later, as they climbed the steps to their room, Torrie thought the fairy tale evening had ended, but she was even more astounded when they entered their bedroom. The lights had been turned off and a dozen candles in crystal globes shed shimmering light around the room, bouncing off the walls and mirrors. Two dozen white roses in two crystal vases gave off a sweet intoxicating smell she had come to recognize and love.

"What on earth, Richard Lee Redman, have you done?" She turned to face him and felt the familiar sizzle jump between them. Before she could decide the many reasons why this was all wrong, she threw caution to the wind, cupped his face in her hands, pulled it to hers, and kissed him. His mouth responded hungrily and shivers of desire spiraled through her. His arms looped around her waist and he drew her up off her feet while they kissed and kissed. Finally, he set her down and pulled away ever so lightly, then yanked her close so she could feel his arousal.

"Yes or no, Torrie," he groaned against her lips in a tortuous tone. "You're killing me here. Is it a warm bed or a cold shower for me tonight?"

She knew she surprised him when she stepped back and laughed a buoyant, provocative laugh, toeing off her high heels and sending them sailing across the room. She let her eyes say it all. "What are you waiting for?" she whispered and crooked a finger at him.

Breathing heavy, his eyes widened.

"First one naked calls the shots and chooses who gets top or bottom," she said with a devilish grin.

"You're on. And I'll go easy on you," he sputtered. "Jewelry doesn't count."

Her heart fluttering wildly in her chest, Torrie yanked at her dress, pulling it over her head. "You're toast, cowboy," she muttered through the fabric. "Try to remember who had more experience in sports and could beat the pants off any competitor."

"Really? Bring it on, sweetheart." His low ripple of laughter filled the room. His tie, shoes, and belt hit the floor together. He had always been skilled at multi-tasking.

****

The morning arrived too soon for Torrie as she awakened, her head lying on Rich's chest. The sun was already sending a slanting golden band through the end of the curtain to fall across the foot of their bed. They had made love several times through the night until they both had fallen asleep in each other's arms. Quietly, Torrie slipped out of bed and into her robe and rounded the bed, just as she heard him say softly, "Sneaking out on me?"

"We have to get started for home," she whispered coming to stand beside him. A hand snaked out and grabbed her, pulling her on top of him and rolling her onto his side, pinning her in place. "Why are we whispering?"

Laughing, she stammered, "Rich, stop it. We have to get dressed." She raised herself on an elbow and asked, "So? How are we going to handle this?"

"This? I think we're handling *this* really well at the moment. Don't you think so?" If he heard nervousness in her voice, he chose to ignore it. Instead, he pulled her gently back down, kissing her forehead at her hairline. He ran his other hand over her hair and down the side of her shoulder.

She nudged him in the ribs. "You know what I mean. When we get back to Hickory Valley."

"Your hair is beautiful," he said, his hand toying with a strand. "Silky and soft. Like satin. Flaxen-colored satin."

"Flaxen?" She snorted. "Who taught you the color chart?" She tapped him on the chest. "Concentrate, Richard Lee Junior. We were talking about what happens when we go back to Hickory Valley." She rolled on her stomach and looked him in the eyes.

"If you think this is just a fling or one impulsive day of sexual dallying, Torrie Jane Larson, you're wrong. You're sorely mistaken." His eyes flashed.

Realizing he was on the verge of becoming angry, she reined herself in. "I just would like to keep our little tryst out of the town's gossip pipeline. Understand?"

"Little tryst? Is that what you want to call this?"

Torrie squeezed her eyes shut. Oh, brother. This was not going as she had expected. She tried a different, straight forward approach instead. "Okay, I don't want the kids, my parents or brothers and sister to know. Not yet."

"Elsa already suspects there's more than camaraderie," he pointed out.

"Rich, we need to figure out where we're going with our relationship without everyone jumping in to give advice."

"Fine," he conceded. "But I'm not going to walk on eggshells or avoid you like you've got the mother of all diseases." He rolled on top of her and kissed her—and his phone started ringing.

****

This time Rich was really aggravated. Why couldn't he catch a lousy break? What was with the darn phone interrupting at the most inopportune times?

Cursing, he rolled over, sat up, snatched the phone from the nightstand, and checked the number. He swiped the answer screen. "This better be important, Marlene." He frowned, watching Torrie slip off the bed and tiptoe into the bathroom. So much for his quick morning romp before a long drive back.

He had called Marlene last night before they left for the Still Waters Lounge to see if she could find someone who had the inside track with Dr. Winters.

"What are you doing working so early in the morning?" he asked.

"I could ask you what you're still doing in Elmira," she shot back with an amused tone to her voice. "Car break down again?"

"Hah, I'm in Montour Falls."

"Hah to you, I'm not at the office."

"If we're going to waste each other's time with 'who's on first,' I'd rather you give me the information you've found out and hang up."

"So I *did* interrupt something."

"Spit it out, Marlene!"

"Well, Joe says—"

"Whoa, are you at Joe Bradley's house? At six in the morning?"

His eyes grew large in lust and awe when Torrie pranced out of the bathroom in a sexy black bra and panties. Hers widened as well when she figured out the drift of their conversation and she realized Marlene's early morning whereabouts. She gave a two-thumbs-up gesture, then she bent and started picking up loose clothing from the floor, tossing his on a nearby chair, and throwing him a pair of silk boxer shorts. He caught them one-handed and frowned at her, obviously disappointed by the turn of morning events. She grinned impishly at him, collected a pair of jeans and shirt from her suitcase, and sashayed back to the bathroom.

"It's is none of your business, Rich Redman," Marlene's clipped voice was cool and disapproving.

"Touché," he replied.

Silence descended, and Rich knew she was regrouping her thoughts.

Finally she spoke. "Okay. Truce. Here's the scoop. The two people who were close to Ivan's mom and dad were Joe Bradley's father and Lucille Smith's late husband. Joe told me they once collectively owned a hunting cabin up in New York by the Finger Lakes. Here are my thoughts. You approach Dr. Winters with one of the women, either Joe's mom or Lucille Smith, and you might have a better chance of shaking him down for information."

"You're a gem, Marlene." Rich bent and picked his belt off the floor. "Tell Joe I said hello."

"Tell Torrie I said hey, too."

"I will when I see her later this morning for breakfast."

"The hole you're digging is getting deeper by the minute," Marlene warned. "Have a safe trip back to Hickory Valley."

Chapter Eighteen

Rich drove along U.S. 15 south toward Hickory Valley with Torrie sitting quietly beside him, hardly making a sound. He wondered whether she was thinking about the information involving Dr. Winters and his half-sister's adoption, or whether she was mulling over the night they spent together. She had been insistent they take both vases of white roses. Perched in a box on the back seat, the roses permeated the inside of the car with a sweet intoxicating smell. Torrie had also insisted they skip breakfast and stop only for a quick, fast-food hamburger since the trip would take over three hours.

"Why the silence?" he asked. "Come on, Torrie, tell me what's bothering you."

"The girls." She frowned. "Surely they will be asking why we didn't drive home last night."

"That's it?"

"Well, it might be awkward to lie and tell them we were too tired to drive back."

Rich threw her a quick glance. Was she was feeling guilty? Having second thoughts about their relationship? Or was she truly concerned about the girls and how to explain a night away from them?

"We'll tell them the truth, Torrie. We wanted to have some time alone. We went to see the falls. We had a nice dinner. I was exhausted, especially after the sleepover." He stopped, then added, "Anyway, Estella is used to me being away."

"But Iris is not. At least, not in another state where I can't reach her."

He sighed. A twinge of annoyance crept into his buoyant demeanor. "Okay, what do you want to tell them?"

"I don't know. I know I don't want to fight. I don't want us to make commitments we can't keep. We've spent one night together. Maybe we were just caught up in the moment. Maybe this was a rash decision."

"Rash decision? Where do you come up with all these disastrous thoughts? Last time it was fate working to save us from a crazy impulsive act. I don't know about you, but last night was no rash decision. I was caught up in the moment, and I want to be caught up in a lot more of them, sweetheart." He picked up his phone from the console pocket beside him and handed it to her. "Here, look up the name of the bicycle shop I saw in Mansfield on the way up. Get me an address."

"Whatever for?" She punched at the keyboard. "And you better not call me sweetheart in front of the girls."

"Insurance, babe. The kind you like."

"Can you be more specific?" She looked at him with a puzzled expression. "Maybe *babe* isn't such a good idea either."

He drew in a long breath. The woman had the ability to be exasperating without much effort. "Insurance so our time away will never cross their devious little minds. The girls need something else to do at the house besides pestering the poor cat and asking Lulu enough questions to fill a half-hour game show. So I thought we'd pick up bicycles for them in Mansfield."

He recalled his conversation with Gertie's ghost on the porch. He wasn't about to tell Torrie that his grandmother had made the suggestion. He had noticed the bicycle shop on the way up.

"I loved to ride my bike at Gertie's," he admitted aloud. "I'd start at the back of the house where the lawn sloped downward. If you could get a fast start, you could come down into the circular drive and around the house to end up almost where you started. And barely pedaling! I wore a path around the place."

Torrie slapped a hand on her knee. "I can't let you buy Iris a bike, and I can't afford to get her one yet."

"Will you stop?" he begged. "Please stop with your tedious desire to be so independent. Why can't the girls have fun together? If it will help to end your unrelenting guilt trip, I'll tell them the bikes must stay at the house." His black mood shifting like the wind, he offered her a conspiratorial wink. "And that only means Iris will be bugging you like a gnat on a hot summer day to spend more time with Estella, and you'll be forced to spend more time with me."

Torrie stared at him. "Does anyone ever win against you?"

Yes, he wanted to say. *You did. You stole my heart, messed with my head, and made me the most confused, love-struck creature in the state. You belong to me, Torrie Larson. Now all I need to do is convince you.*

"Not usually," he admitted instead and reached over and ran his hand tenderly over the top of hers. "Torrie, I don't want to bicker."

"Well, we'll have to get two bikes exactly the same

and exactly the same color," she said, conceding. "You better hope it's possible. Otherwise, you're going to see two little girls quibbling, instead of sailing around the house in mind-numbing circles."

"Are you serious? You think they care what color they are?"

Torrie laughed. "Ah, Rich, you have a lot to learn about kids in groups of more than one, especially girls. Mom used to say raising kids is like working with one hand tied behind your back. Even my brothers would argue over new baseballs, bats, kick balls, soccer balls—even the color of their T-shirts. When she could, especially with sports equipment, Mom used to buy everything exactly the same, right down to the same manufacturer, then write their names on everything with a permanent marker so there'd be no mistaking who owned what. When someone's baseball turned up missing, you'd find her checking everyone's baseballs to make sure there was no pilfering taking place among her sons."

Hours later, when they pulled into the driveway and unloaded their luggage, it was only Lulu who joyously greeted them at the door. "Welcome home, Richard Lee," she quipped as he piled the luggage inside the entranceway. "Good trip?"

When he nodded, she waved at the family room in the back of the house. "Iris is resting on the couch with a book, and Estella is upstairs with Denise who's doing an elaborate series of braids in her hair. The girls were up most of the night according to Denise, and it was really another wide-awake, rambunctious pajama party. Danielle came over to help and join in the merriment, but Denise should get a gold star. She deserves a few bonus Redman points. She worked like a mother hen to keep them in tow. And trust me, they were a sugar-induced handful when I left."

"Noted," Rich said. "Anything else?"

"Well, I think Sheba's approaching her due date."

He frowned.

Lulu grinned. "Estella asked again how we were going to locate the father when the blessed event occurs. She seems to think he'd want to know."

"And what did you say?"

Lulu headed for the kitchen. "I told her to ask you."

Rich groaned. "What am I missing here? You're from a farm. Who better to explain the birds and the bees?"

"Me?" Lulu snorted. "Explaining the propagation of felines was never mentioned as part of my job description, so I'd better not lose one stinking point." She marched down the hallway and disappeared into the kitchen.

"I never got a copy of that job description!" Rich yelled after her.

"Lunch will be on the table soon. Gather the troops," she shouted in reply.

"Well played, Rich." Torri's laughter billowed out as she headed for the family room. "Can't wait to see how you handle cat reproduction."

Frowning and disgruntled, Rich climbed the staircase, halting at the top to listen to Denise and Estella chatting like magpies inside the front bedroom. From his vantage point, he could see Estella sitting on a chair, her small hands clasped demurely in her lap as she looked out her dormered window. Behind her,

Denise stood, pins in her mouth, her hands deftly parting Estella's hair, braiding, and coiling the braids into a fancy creation exactly like she was wearing. Not wanting to disturb their antics, he decided to silently stand and eavesdrop instead.

"Denise, do you ever feel different?" he heard Estella ask. She held her little head ramrod straight as Denise wound another braid into a fancy knot by her ear.

"Like how?" Denise asked, mumbling around the pins in her mouth.

"Well, since Mommy went to heaven, sometimes I feel all alone—like I don't always belong because I don't have a mother like all the other girls. And I don't have any sisters or brothers. Sometimes I feel like I don't fit in."

Denise nodded. "Hmmm. Yes, sometimes, I do. Even with my sister, I sometimes have a feeling like *I don't belong*. I think everyone does. Danielle and I've discussed it and she agrees everyone gets those thoughts. I guess it's quite natural—to sometimes feel all alone, I mean." She chuckled. "But then, I know my mother and dad love me, and you know your dad loves you, too. That's what important, Estella. Someday, you'll get a new mommy and she will love you very, very much."

"But how can you be sure?" Estella asked. "What if she hates me?"

"No, Estella. No, no. Your dad would never marry anyone who didn't love you as much as he does. He's a wonderful father. You must trust him."

"All right," Estella said in a resigned tone. "I guess you're right." She brightened. "Wouldn't it be wonderful if my dad married Torrie? Then Iris could be my sister and I wouldn't be an only child anymore!" She squirmed excitedly in the seat. "Then they could have a baby and I could have two sisters. I'd make a good big sister. I try to take care of Iris sometimes."

"Hmmm," Denise said, removing more pins still in her mouth. "Maybe you ought to take this subject up with your dad. Hold still, I'm almost finished."

With a heavy heart, Rich looked at the two and sighed, turning to sneak back down the steps. He had no idea Estella worried about not belonging. About being alone. About not having siblings. He knew those feelings himself when he was growing up.

He swiveled slightly to take one last look at Denise Jordan who was winding the last braid onto Estella's hair-do. She was getting a huge bonus for babysitting today. She was a peach, like Lulu indicated.

****

While they ate a quick lunch together of toasted cheese sandwiches and tomato soup with walnut brownies straight out of the oven, the girls chattered gaily, taking turns telling Rich and Torrie about their sleepover, the Parcheesi board game they had discovered in the trunk of toys, and how Denise had taught them the rules so they could play. Estella then promptly instructed everyone about the royal game of India and how it was once played on large outdoor boards using colorfully clothed servants of the royalty household as game pieces. She had looked it up on the Internet, and she wondered whether it was possible to make a board game with chalk on the circular drive out front and enlist everyone in the neighborhood to be human players.

But it was Iris, as Torrie earlier suggested, who whined, "Why did you have to spend the night in New York, Mommy? What were you doing there? I missed you." She punched out her lower lip, ready to mope.

Rich and Torrie's gaze met for a suspended moment, and Torrie felt a sinking feeling right down to her toes. She could never lie, but at the moment, even a plausible excuse eluded her.

Rich pushed himself from the table. "Well, we were getting important business taken care of, but we did manage to find time to buy you both a surprise." He offered them an endearing smile.

And in a flash, the tide of events changed as both little girls threw off their glum expressions and jumped up, following Rich and Torrie out to the SUV in the circular drive. They squealed as he withdrew two new shiny pink bikes with white fenders and sparkling handlebar streamers.

"For the two most beautiful princesses in Hickory Valley." Rich pushed the bikes to an open section of the driveway away from the car and shrubs.

Estella clapped her hands and looked in awe at the bikes. "Yippee! It's just what I wanted. I've missed my bike so much since we've been here."

"For me?" Iris asked, taken off-guard by the generosity of the gift. "Is it really, Mommy?" She ran and wound her arms around her mother's legs and hugged her.

Torrie nodded. "But there are restrictions," she said firmly, pushing the girl's pale bangs from her forehead. "You must keep the bike here at Estella's house and they must be ridden in the back of the house, here on the front circular drive, on the front sidewalk, or on the driveway leading to the garage. Under no circumstances are you girls to leave the property with them. You cannot ride them downtown. Do you understand?"

"But how will we tell them apart?" Estella asked.

Rich withdrew two decals of sparkling silver and pink, one with the initial "I" and the other with the initial "E" on it and waved them in the air. "These go on the back fender."

"Can we try them out? Now?" Iris asked, jumping up and down.

"Yes, but let's be careful," Rich cautioned.

After he and Torrie separated each girl at an even greater distance, they held the bikes upright while the girls got their bearings. It was Iris who sailed away first, grinning, pedaling the bike with relative ease down the drive, adeptly turning and racing back, her hair flying out behind her. "This is so much better than the bikes at Aunt Elsa's," she yelled, referring to the bikes of her male cousins. She glided to a smooth stop and hopped down, giggling, before setting off again.

"They're having a blast," Torrie said and looked over at Rich standing with hands in his back pockets. "You're a very generous man, Rich." *And a very handsome, but devious one.* "They've completely forgotten we were away for a night."

"Uh-huh." He came to stand beside her and looped an arm over her shoulder, rubbing the side of her cheek with his thumb. The single act of disguised affection turned her heart over. She gazed up at him and wanted so much to stand on tiptoe and kiss him. She wanted so much to stand there all day in the sunlight beside him. To be happy like this forever. But she refrained from making any romantic gesture, content to just watch the girls and listen to their innocent riotous giggles fill the summer air around them before she headed off to the potting shed in the backyard to see what could be saved of her precious rose cuttings.

****

Later in afternoon, after lengthy telephone conversations about business, Rich wandered onto the porch and took in a breath of clear, clean summer air. Somewhere far off and to the north of where he stood, someone had mown a field of hay. After all these years, he was surprised he still could recognize the smell of freshly cut alfalfa and clover, a smell so sweet and so unique to rural living. Beside him, a chickadee chattered and two swallowtail butterflies flitted on a bush. He gazed toward the potting shed where Torrie had been laboring for the last few hours.

He ducked back inside, poured two glasses of Lulu's homemade lemonade, and carried them across the yard. He found Torrie sitting on a stool before a bank of south windows. Head bent, deep in concentration, she was carefully examining and sorting the pieces of broken rose clippings Joe or Finn had salvaged and tucked into squat buckets of water to keep them fresh for grafting or rooting.

He set a glass beside her. "Is there anything I can do to help?" A multitude of flats holding four-inch pots filled with dirt lined the farthest end of the long counter.

Torrie looked up surprised. "You want to help?"

Rich watched her gaze travel from his scuffed cowboy boots to his faded Levis and on up to his plaid shirt before they rested on his face. He had purposely dug through his closet and donned the oldest clothes he could find in hopes of convincing her.

"This is a dirty job, Rich."

He shrugged. "So is a lawyer's job at times. Only a different kind of dirty." He swept his hands over the counter and the buckets of rose clippings. "This whole mess is probably my fault, Torrie. Someone wants me to sell the house and hightail it out of Hickory Valley." He went over to a far bucket and fingered a shiny leaf on a rose stem. "And anyway, babe, I just finished up a heap of legal business by computer and phone, so I'm your landscape slave until dinner time. Tell me what to do and how it's done."

Torrie shook her head, trying to look annoyed by his interruption, but finally slapped a pair of soft leather gloves against his chest. "First, we don't want any thorns to harm those soft velvet hands, counselor. Some people knock the thorns off when they're handling cuttings, but I prefer not to wound the plant any more than necessary."

He nodded, slipped on the gloves, and grinned. "Yes, these velvet hands can work magic, don't you agree?"

"Rich." The tone was reprimanding.

"Okay, okay." He chortled. "No wait. Just one more, *please,* Torrie. This one is good, I promise." He held up his gloved hands and wiggled his fingers at her. "So now for the first time in my life, I can safely say I'll be literally handling things here with kid gloves."

This time, she gave him a doleful shake of her head. "I give up. You do know where Estella gets her clever but never-ending ability to annoy people, don't you? Are you here to hinder or help?"

"Sorry." He tried to look repentant, but couldn't

186

quite wipe the grin off his face.

She motioned him closer. "Since I don't want you to play with knives and this one is very sharp"—she waved it in the air while he feigned being frightened and took a step backward—"I'm going to give you a six-inch stalk which is cut on a diagonal at the bottom and which has two sets of leaves attached. I will wound the rose stem at the bottom along the stalk as well."

"Wound? Sounds like you have to be a little spiteful to do this. You sure you're up to it?"

She raised an eyebrow. "Luckily for you, I've become adept at ignoring your snarky comments."

"As are the girls, Lulu Smith, and even the darn cat."

She shook her head again and persevered. "Now, try to focus. You'll take each cutting, dip the bottom and the wound in this rooting hormone, and plant one in each corner of a pot farther up the counter, being careful to push them only half way into the soil." She grabbed him by his shirt on his upper arm and pulled him along as she planted the first cutting. "See? It's simple."

He squinted at the pots of soil. "What's the shiny stuff?"

"Perlite. The soil in the pot is half soil and half perlite. The high water content of volcanic glass lends itself perfectly for rooting plants."

They worked for the next hour with Torrie explaining to him the difference between bud and cutting propagation methods and other landscape techniques and problems. He could tell by her animated gestures and the excitement in her voice how much she loved her work, enjoyed the outdoors, and liked watching things grow—but at the end of the day, she really loved the roses and flowers above all.

"You never grow tired of this?" he asked when they were finishing up.

"There are some things you never grow tired of," she admitted.

"Or people."

He fixed his gaze on her. She didn't try to look away, but her cheeks burned from pink to red. He realized he could watch her for the rest of his life. He loved the way she moved so efficiently and athletically, almost gliding around the potting shed. Her fingers were delicate but agile when she worked on the rose stems. Despite the lack of jewelry, except the ring she designed and some small hoop earrings, she possessed a raw beauty mixed with natural earthy qualities.

When at last they were done, and two pairs of leather gloves lay side by side on the wooden counter, he pulled her to him and kissed her gently, lovingly on the lips. She didn't resist, but snuggled in against his chest. Around them, the scent of roses and earth filled the shed.

"Torrie," he said in a tortured voice, laying his cheek along the side of her hair, "would you ever consider marriage someday? I need you so much in my life."

She pulled away slightly and searched his face. "How on earth would it ever work?"

He sighed, but still held her by both arms. "I've been on the phone for the last few days with the other attorneys in my office. What if I told you I'd consider staying in Hickory Valley, but just travel to Texas when needed? I'd put someone in charge of the Dallas office."

"But what about Estella?"

"Estella? Estella is in love with this town, this place, the outdoors. She adores Iris and that flea-bitten, pain-in-the-backside cat. And she is thriving here more than when she was in Texas. Lulu is like a grandmother to her. Who knows, maybe my half-sister is living somewhere nearby. I still have to find her."

"Oh, Rich, I don't know what to say. Can you give me some time to think about all this? Some time to think things through? There's so much that needs to be sorted out and discussed, so many questions to be answered. I have to consider Iris and what's best for her. This is more complicated than you can imagine."

He kissed her mouth, tenderly at first, then more insistently with growing ardor. He pulled away. "Then I take it your answer is not a *no*?" He kissed her again. "How about we just get engaged and see where it takes us?'

"Rich, you're pushing," she whispered against his lips.

"If I keep pushing, will you cave?" he asked softly. He ran his index fingers over her lower lip. "Let me put a ring on your hand. Say yes. You're driving me wild."

Standing on tiptoe, she brushed her lips over his again. "I'll give it serious thought. How about you give me two weeks?"

"You aren't making it easy for me, you stubborn sexy minx."

From somewhere behind them, Estella asked, "What's a *sexy mink*? And are you two kissing each other?"

Rich jerked upright, groaned, and felt Torrie stiffly

pull away. Semi-shocked, they found both girls standing in the doorway of the shed.

"Oh, brother," Torrie muttered under her breath. "See what I mean about complicated?"

Chapter Nineteen

The next morning rolled in dismal and wet. Leaving Torrie to watch the girls at her house, Lulu and Rich set out to talk to Dr. Winters at an appointed time Lulu had somehow magically secured. The red brick mansion of Dr. Winters sat back from the road on a side street of Hickory Valley with an imposing chimney on each end and a black wrought iron fence protecting a large, well-manicured property of leafy maples, oaks, and gigantic elms. Old rhododendron reaching to the sky and knee-high ferns added to its stately charm and distinction. Colorful gold, bright yellow, and orange marigolds sprinkled beside the long walkway led guests to a gigantic porch and a large white front door with leaded glass sidelights.

A curtain of gray rain pounded down around them as Rich escorted Lulu from the car and up the walk. Wearing a bright pink raincoat, the little woman grumbled as she trudged along under an umbrella Rich held over their heads. Earlier, she had told him to keep the blasted thing away from her. She didn't melt in the rain, and when he laughed and admitted he often wondered about it, she sent him a scorching look and warned he'd never get another bite of her blue ribbon chocolate chip cookies—the ones he always begged her to bake as soon as the cookie jar was empty—if he didn't behave.

They stopped in front of the door and Lulu peered up at him. "Okay, big shot attorney, how do you want this to go down?"

For a bare second, she caught him off-guard.

"Lulu, this isn't a sting operation," he said. And if it were, he thought, her gaudy pink raincoat with her lime green handbag would have blown their cover before he turned off the car. "I just need to get the dear doctor to allow me to see the adoption papers of Anne Alexander and my father." He pushed the doorbell and muttered, "And let's hope Ivan isn't around to throw a few wrenches in the old man's gears."

A tall, slender woman with steel gray hair answered the doorbell on the first ring and smiled widely when she saw Lulu. "Why, hello, Lucille. Come in. Come in! I haven't seen you in a while. We missed you at cards the last couple of times. I heard you were working at the Redman house." She gestured to a corner of the entranceway where an ornate brass coat tree stood ready to handle their soggy coats and umbrella. "Dr. Winters is most anxious to see you. He's been fretting about refreshments and your arrival for over an hour. And you must be Rich Redman. All grown up, I see!"

Lulu spoke. "Do you remember Nancy Decker?"

"Ah, yes." Rich smiled. "Your son, Paul, played quarterback for our high school, I believe. How is he?"

"Fine. Fine." Nancy nodded. "He coaches football at Ohio State now. Paul's married with three children." She waved them toward the hallway. "Come. This way. Dr. Winters is in the sunroom at the back of the house."

As soon as they entered the three-sided, glassed-in sunroom overlooking a well-kept vegetable garden and lawn, Nathan Winters rose and made his way across the gray slate floor to sweep Lulu into a polite hug. "Lucille, so nice to see you. It's been a long time. Too long. How have you been?" He held her at arm's length and continued, "I know your husband's death must have been as troubling to you as my wife's was to me. It's hard to lose a spouse."

Lulu nodded in agreement and untangled herself from the doctor's embrace. "Yes, it is. But I'm fine, Nathan. Just fine. I'd like you meet Rich Redman. You remember his grandparents, Gertie and Matthew Redman, don't you?"

"But of course, of course. Please sit. I'll have Nancy bring some coffee and some sweets." He took a seat in a wicker chair and gestured for them to take a seat on a matching wicker couch across from him. Beside him on the floor was a banker's box of what looked like medical files.

"I must admit, I wasn't totally surprised to hear Rich wanted to talk to me. But I was truly delighted to hear Lucille's voice on the phone the other day." He smiled and tapped his fingers lightly on the arm of his chair.

"Then you must know I'm searching for my half-sister." Rich decided to get straight to the point. "I know Dad had a child with Anne Alexander, and the child would be just over eighteen years old now. I have money in a trust Grandmother Gertie left and which justifiably belongs to her. But if she's not found in the next year, then it reverts to me."

Dr. Winters frowned. "And you think I was involved?"

"I know you were involved with the adoption,

yes."

"And how can you be so sure?" Dr. Winters's voice took on a cautious tone.

"I spoke with her aunt, Winifred Fox…and some residents of Willow Tree Assisted Living."

Dr. Winters paused, pondering his next sentence. 'Wouldn't it be in your best interest if the money was just returned to the trust?"

"I have a letter from my grandmother which she wrote just before she died." He withdrew it from his jacket. "It was her wish my half-sister and I meet." He held it out.

Waving it away, Dr. Winters spoke. "I believe you. That would be just like Gertie Redman. She was a righteous and honest woman. To be fair, though, I'd need to reread the adoption records and see what specific instructions were included before I divulge any information. Sometimes things are better left alone, Rich."

Rich forced his lips to part in a stiff smile. "Maybe so. But there's a sizable trust due the young lady, and quite frankly, I want to meet and know my half-sister. I was raised as an only child. For me, money from the trust is secondary to finding a blood relative."

Commotion from the front room brought everyone to attention. Nancy rushed into the room without the coffee and refreshments. She halted, wringing her hands. "Ivan's here. I told him you were having a meeting, Dr. Winters, but he insisted he needed to see you immediately."

"It's okay, Nancy." Nathan Winters rose and went to the doorway. "Send him back here."

Beside Rich, Lulu groaned and elbowed him in the

ribs. "For pity's sake. Just what we didn't need—Ivan the idiot to muck up the works."

Ivan appeared in the doorway, dusting water droplets off the shoulder of his impeccable navy blue suit. "Well, well, what have we here? A meeting? Don't tell me I'm interrupting something?"

"Lucille Smith and Richard Lee Junior asked for an appointment to discuss some business," replied Dr. Winters. He gestured down the hall toward the kitchen. "Why don't you grab something to eat? I won't be long."

Ivan sauntered farther into the room. "This meeting is basically over anyhow, Father. I know exactly what Rich Redman wants." He sneered, showing sharp thin teeth. "I don't think we need to turn over rocks, open old wounds, and go searching for long lost relatives. He's only in Hickory Valley to stir the pot."

"I don't think it's any of your business." Rich stood and used every ounce of restraint to maintain an outward calm demeanor. His phone vibrated in his pocket, and he removed it, glancing at the text message.

"I think some civility might be in order here, Ivan," Dr. Winters urged, offering Ivan a somber gaze.

Ivan brushed aside his father's remark. "Could I have a private word with you, Redman? It'll only take a few minutes. I think we share something in common we need to discuss."

"Now?" There was nothing Rich wanted more at the moment than to pop the meddling banker squarely in his pompous nose. He was sorry Torrie never let him have the pleasure at Webster's Burgers and Fries the other day. How dare the jackass interfere again? But years of training and dealing with disgruntled people had taught him to shy away from creating a scene even when it was warranted. Upsetting Dr. Winters would not get him the information he wanted.

"We'll use the study," Ivan said, sneering. "This will only take a minute."

Rich handed Lulu his phone, bent down, and whispered, "Please call Torrie and see what she needs. She just texted me she can't find Estella's bathing suit at the house and wants to take the girls to the community pool as soon as the rain stops." He looked up. "I apologize, Dr. Winters, for all these interruptions."

Dr. Winters waved away the apology. "This just gives Lucille and me more time to get reacquainted."

Bewildered by the turn of events, Lulu nodded and took the offered cellphone.

The second Rich stepped inside the study and closed the door, his voice changed to a cold, steely tone. "Just what do you mean by interrupting an appointment we had with your father? An appointment, I might add, which is of no concern to you, Ivan."

Ivan whirled on him. "Everything in this town concerns me. Everything everyone does concerns me! And what concerns me the most is *you*. Isn't it about time you finish playing around with your grandmother's house, sell the damn thing, and go back to Texas where you belong?" Ivan stomped to the window. Red-faced, he barely could keep his temper in check. He looked out. "And I should warn you. You need to leave Torrie Larson alone, too," he muttered under his breath and whirled to face him.

"What did you say?" Rich shot him a feral glare.

"I said to leave Torrie Larson alone."

"And why should I?"

"She doesn't need someone waltzing into Hickory Valley and giving her false hope or stirring up senseless dreams that only serve to hurt her once you head back to Texas. Leave the poor woman alone!"

"Listen, Winters," Rich ground the words out through teeth clamped so tight they hurt, "I don't need anyone telling me what I can and cannot do. My relationship with Torrie Larson is none of your business."

Ivan's nostrils flared with fury. "Torrie and I grew up together. I want you to back off, Richard Lee. I'm warning you. I could make your life and Torrie's miserable if I choose to."

"Are you threatening me?" The cords along Rich's neck stood at attention. "I don't know *how* you think you can threaten me." He scoffed, his voice low and dangerous. "I don't scare easily, Ivan. You're certainly irritating, but you're about as terrifying as a sack of garbage." He turned and stalked out the door, slamming it as he stormed down the hall.

"Garbage? Are you calling me garbage?" Ivan rushed after Rich, snorting like an angry bull. "How dare you?"

He entered the sunroom on Rich's heels. "I hope you're not going to divulge any information without speaking with a legal firm, Dad," he sputtered. "You may find yourself in a lawsuit if you don't handle this correctly. It's time these people leave."

Dr. Winters looked curiously at Ivan. "As I've already told Lucille, I'll get back to Rich after I locate and study the papers and have them reviewed by legal counsel. Settle down. These people are my guests.

There's no need to be alarmed, Ivan."

Lulu jumped up like she had springs on her feet. "Richard Lee, I think it's best if we leave." She turned to Dr. Winters. "It was nice seeing you again, Nathan."

"Oh, no. Stay, Lucille. Please stay for some coffee and refreshments. Nancy has made a delicious lemon cake. We're all adults here. And you and I have so much to catch up on." He looked at her with obvious disappointment.

"Yes, why not stay, Lulu?" Rich urged. "I can pick you up later."

"I can drop Lucille off as well," Dr. Winters offered.

Lulu shook her head vehemently. "No, thank you. I think it's best if I leave now. I have an idea, Nathan. Why don't you stop by Gertie's house some morning and have one of my fresh baked muffins and some coffee? I'll give you a call, and we'll pick a convenient day."

"Sounds good," Dr. Winters acquiesced in a disheartened tone. He escorted them to the door.

The sun was out, drying the wet lawns and streets and sending out a muggy pallor over the land as steam rose up. With their raincoats over their arms, Rich had a hard time keeping up with Lulu who was racing down the long walkway to their car like she was being chased by a pack of Rottweilers. They stopped by the passenger side of the SUV.

"What's gotten into you?" Rich glared at her. "You should have stayed. Maybe you could have shaken down the good doctor for some information."

"With you and Ivan looking like you wanted to start a donnybrook?"

"You know I can't tolerate the pompous jerk. He told me to stay away from Torrie." Rich ran his hand though his hair. "So what's our next move, Watson? Because Sherlock here is plumb out of ideas."

Lulu handed him the phone. "We go home and look at the pictures I took of the documents in Anne Alexander's folder."

"We what?"

Lulu shrugged. "Well, while you were tangling with the village idiot, Dr. Winters went to help Nancy get the refreshments ready, so I figured a quick peek in the good doctor's banker box couldn't hurt our cause."

"You know how to use the camera on my cell phone?"

"Land sakes, Richard Lee Junior, the girls are using Torrie's phone constantly when she's around and they're taking those face pictures together. You know. The ones where they smash their heads together and make ridiculous funny faces and gestures at the camera. What are they called?"

"Selfies?"

"That's it!"

Lulu's final words barely spilled out when Rich scooped up the little woman like a sack of feed and twirled her around. "You are really something, Lucille Smith. Never let anyone tell you differently!" He peered up at her, her toes still off the ground.

"Listen up, you overgrown brat, if you don't put me down this minute, I'm going to wallop you alongside your head with my purse."

Laughing, Rich set her down gently and hugged her. "Lulu, you have just been awarded a wheelbarrow full of Redman points." He opened the car door for her and she slipped into the passenger's seat, folding the pink raincoat and placing it on her lap.

"Let's not get too carried away," she mumbled, glancing at him as he slid behind the wheel and shoved a key in the ignition. "We don't know what's in those photos on your phone."

He handed the phone back to her. "Put it in your purse. I have the feeling it's safer with you than with me. Everyone heard me tell you to use my phone and call Torrie."

Lulu nodded and slipped the phone into her lime-colored handbag. "Wait a second. Why do I have to keep the evidence? I did all the work. What if there were cameras in the house?"

"Ah, Lulu, I highly doubt there would be surveillance cameras in the sunroom. And no one would ever expect you to be devious. However, in celebration of your stellar sleuthing performance, I'm buying you lunch and then we're going to the jewelry store."

"Jewelry store?" She looked at him confused. "Are you crazy?"

"I'm working on it. I need a woman's opinion." He drove away merrily belting out the off-key words to the famous country and western song with the same name as Lucille Smith.

From the passenger seat, Lulu curiously eyeballed him. "Are you certain, Richard Lee Junior, you were only drinking orange juice this morning?"

****

The first thing Rich noticed when he returned to Gertie's house was the tomblike silence pervading every corner of every room when the girls weren't there. There was no scampering of little feet overhead or up and down the halls. No shoes pounding on the wooden stairs. No shouting and no giggling. No stuffed animals abandoned in every nook and cranny. Even the coloring and reading books were not littering the counters or kitchen table.

He felt a queer stab of loss. It was the same dreaded feeling he hated when he was an only child growing up—emptiness and silence.

He looked around at the floor. Not even a single squeaky toy of Sheba's was lying around to step on by mistake. He even missed the wretched cat.

"I'll put on a pot of coffee," Lulu offered, hanging her raincoat in the hall closet and scurrying back to the kitchen. "Torrie and the girls must have headed to the pool. When they get back, those little girls will be hungry."

Rich dropped the umbrella in the stand by the door. "Did Torrie say how long they'd be gone?" He followed her down the hall when the house phone on the kitchen counter startled him with its sharp ring. It was Torrie's number, and he picked it up as the roar of truck engines and sirens wailed in his ears. The frantic shouts of people drowned out what he thought was Torrie's voice. Finally, she screamed above the commotion, "Rich, can you hear me? Are the girls at the house?"

"Barely," he said. "I thought the girls were with you at the pool."

He could scarcely understand her through her frustrated sobs, but seconds later, she was shouting again to be heard. "No, a fire started in the warehouse below my apartment. Everything is ruined. I smelled it shortly after we came back from the pool to change into street clothes and collect the girls' belongings before heading to your house. I sent the girls outside to the front yard and dialed 911 for the fire company. Then I went down the back stairs to try to find the source. When I finally made it to the front yard, the girls were gone. Rich, I can't find them. Help me find them. Please!"

"Stay there," he yelled back into the phone. "Stay calm. I'll check to see if their bikes are here, then start down through town. Take it easy, Torrie. They couldn't have gone far. And they know enough to stick together. Estella is street smart from living in the city. She'll go to a place where it's safe." He could feel his heart pounding in his chest even though he forced himself to remain calm and reasonable.

"Okay," she said coughing. "I have to move. The smoke is blowing in my face. I'm going to get Finn and Gus to start scouring the area." She clicked off.

Relating the dilemma to Lulu, Rich dashed out the door, keys in hand, and searched the front lawn before he rounded the house to find the girls' pink bikes neatly parked side by side on the back walk. He raced back to the front, jumped into his vehicle, and followed the route to Torrie's place, scanning the streets for Estella and Iris as he went. When he pulled up near the apartment, amid a crowd of milling people, three fire trucks, and two police cars with lights on, Torrie rushed over to him. "Rich, I can't find them!" She flew into his arms. "Where can they be?"

He slumped against the side of the car with her in his arms as the fire fighters extinguished the last of the flames. Torrie's apartment was charred black, and water gushed from the roof, spilling down the sides to puddle in the street. Around them a gray haze filled the air. If Rich were a betting man, he'd guess most of her belongings were smoke- or water- damaged or destroyed along with the apartment and warehouse. Luckily, the morning rain had helped to keep the building from burning to the ground.

But what he noticed as well was the huge number of town folk who had turned out—Henry Jordon and his son, Kyle, and his granddaughters Denise and Danielle were there. Ivan Winters stood off to one side and Torrie's siblings, Finn, Elsa, and Lars, were opposite him watching the spectacle beside the fire fighters who had extinguished the flames. On one of the fire trucks, Joe Bradley was working the controls for the ladder while another crew member aimed his hose to wet down the building beside it. Amid the commotion, Torrie's phone vibrated and without looking to see the caller, she held it to her ear. "Hello," she shouted above the din.

She shook her head and handed it to him. "I can't hear a thing. I think it's Marlene."

Rich took her phone and spoke, "Hello?"

"Rich, this is Marlene. I was waiting for a call from Torrie and when I didn't get one, I decided to call. I heard about the fire."

"We can't find the girls, Marlene. We're about to organize a search party."

"No, don't bother. They're with me. Didn't Joe tell you?" Marlene's voice was laced with disbelief. "They were smart enough to notice I had a 'Safe Home' sign in my front window when they walked past so they stopped and asked for help when they couldn't locate

Iris's mom. They were worried she may have been hurt. They said they tried to call out to her above the sound of the sirens, but the smoke billowed out into their faces and eyes. The noise, police sirens, and sounds from the fire engines frightened them. When they didn't get a response after trying to shout above the din, Estella headed to town with a hysterical Iris to try to find help and someone to calm the child down."

Marlene took a breath. "Joe immediately went to help fight the fire. I told him to tell Torrie or you that I had the girls with me. Do you want me to keep them or bring them down to you? I'm assuming you're at the scene of the fire."

"Wonderful news, Marlene. How can I ever thank you?" Rich breathed a huge sigh of relief. "Yes, we're at the fire. Tell the girls that Torrie is safe. And please keep them until she or I can pick them up. We need to talk to the fire chief as soon as he's available."

"You got it, Richard Lee."

As soon as Rich clicked off, he relayed the information to Torrie. "I don't know why Joe didn't tell you about the girls' whereabouts," he said in a disgruntled tone.

With a sigh of relief, Torrie slumped farther against Rich and started to cry into his shoulder. "Thank heavens. At least we know they're safe," she blubbered through her sobs.

"Hey, hey," he said, murmuring near her ear. "We found them. Think about what's important. Some of your belongings are probably ruined, but some might only need to be cleaned. There's nothing we can't replace. It'll be all right, Torrie. You'll see." He rubbed her gently on her back. From across the lot he saw Ivan turn and look at them, an angry sneer on his face.

"I was so scared," she cried. "I was afraid someone took them. Why? Why didn't Joe *tell me*? I was here the whole time. It's not like him to be so careless."

"He probably was waylaid running the equipment when he first arrived." He hugged her and tried to make light of the situation. "Torrie, darling, don't think about it. They're safe. And face it, anyone who'd take Estella would bring her back within a half hour, after she pounded and hounded the poor soul with a dozen questions."

Soon it was over. Fire fighters hustled to pack up the equipment and repack the hoses. Town folk slowly drifted away. Joe Bradley came over and removed his helmet and gloves, wiping a sooty hand on his forehead. "The chief seemed to think the fire was set," he said and shook his head ruefully. "I think most of the contents of your apartment may be ruined, Torrie."

"As long as everyone is safe." Torrie peered up at Joe, "Why didn't you tell me that Marlene had the kids?"

"Didn't Ivan tell you?" He looked at her with wrinkled brows. "When I arrived on scene, I immediately began setting up the ladder in case it was needed for rescue, so I told Ivan to make sure you knew the girls were at Marlene's house and were safe." He swore a string of expletives. "I'm sorry, Torrie. I didn't know."

They all turned to look for Ivan who had slipped away, stalking to his vehicle up the street.

Joe and Rich both took off at a run to catch him. Rich reached him first, grabbing him by the arm and spinning him around. "Hey, jackass," he ground out, "you were supposed to tell Torrie the girls were safe at Marlene's."

"Yeah, I guess I forgot," Ivan said, shoving Rich away. "So what's the big deal, fellas?"

"What's the big deal? Here's what the big deal is. Two little girls were scared and needed their parents," Joe spit out. "How could you be so cruel? So thoughtless, Ivan?"

Torrie had come up beside the men. "Yes, Ivan, I'd like to hear your excuse. You had to know I'd be frantic with worry."

Ivan shifted his gaze to the door handle of his car. "Sorry, Torrie. I didn't mean to alarm you."

"Well, you did!"

Ivan opened his car door. "If you need a temporary place to stay, give me a call. I can help. And I need to talk to you. It's important." He slipped into the driver's seat and started the engine. His passenger window was down and he glared at Rich. "I'm not finished with you, Redman. You need to know when to high-tail it out of town and leave our women alone."

He hit the button on his window, gunned the engine, and tore down the street.

Chapter Twenty

A somber group circled around the kitchen table at the Redman house after the fire. Despite Lulu's best efforts to mother the weary group and ply them with coffee and tea, sandwiches, and chicken noodle soup, no one was in the mood to eat. Even Estella and Iris sat picking morosely at their food.

"Why would someone set a fire?" Estella asked as she played with some fruit salad, pushing a piece of pineapple around the plate and making swirls with her fork.

"I don't know," Rich admitted and saw the cautious look on Torrie's face. He glanced at Iris. Without warning, the tears began to slide down the child's face. She broke into muffled sobs. With the back of her hands, she tried to wipe the tears away with brusque angry motions. She burst out through sniffles, "All my clothes and toys are ruined! All my stuffed animals are…gone. Everything we have is burned or wet or smelly." She hiccupped through the last sob. "Mommy, what are we going to do?"

Before Torrie could rise to comfort Iris, Estella popped up and draped an arm around the little girl. "Don't cry, Iris," she said, patting her on the back. "I'll give you some of my toys, and I have loads and loads of stuffed animals—a whole garbage bagful. You can even have some of my clothes." She looked up at her father. "You can fix this, can't you, Daddy?"

He heaved a sigh. "Not everything, but yes, we can fix some of it, Estella." He reached and ruffled Iris on the top of her head. "Hey. Not all your clothes are ruined, honey. We just need time to get them cleaned."

Lulu interrupted, "Maybe it would be best if I take these girls upstairs and give them a bath. They smell like smoke. We'll find some clothes for Iris to wear until we can take her shopping." She clapped her hands softly. "Come. Let's go, my little ladies. Time to raid Estella's closet and play dress up."

Estella jumped on the idea like a dog on a bone. "Yes, Iris, let's go. You can pick out whatever you want to wear from my things. And tomorrow we can go *shopping*!" She grabbed the little girl by the hand and yanked her from her seat. "This will be soooo much fun. We can pretend we're sisters. And guess what? Another sleepover!"

Rich gave Lulu a grateful look as she followed the gleeful girls into the hallway and up the stairs. Then he heaved another weary sigh and leaned back, staring at an equally exhausted Torrie. He wondered how all the disastrous events had come about. He was not surprised to hear the fire was deliberately set. Someone was either angry at Torrie, or someone was irate with him and trying to get to him through her. Or someone had a vendetta against Henry Jordan who owned the building. He recalled the conversation with Ivan. Surely he wasn't crazy enough to resort to destroying Torrie's property, just to break up a relationship she might be having. Traumatic mishaps had the ability to bring people together, not push them apart.

Elsa arrived later, just long enough to drop off

Torrie's suitcase from her trip to Elmira and a change of clothes Torrie routinely kept stashed at the landscape center for when accidents happened or she was caught in the rain. Luckily, although Torrie had taken the suitcase from Rich's SUV and transferred it to her van, she had never taken it inside her apartment. Hugging Torrie, Elsa warned her not to fret. She had planned a family meeting and would rally all the brothers and Lars's wife to help gather the necessities she'd need to start over. She also told her she'd round up more clothes from her closet and drop them off in the morning. Rich was thankful she had discouraged their parents and brothers from coming to try to commiserate with Torrie. He knew Elsa realized the event was traumatic enough, and Torrie needed time for emotional recovery and later, some sleep. There would be plenty of time to worry about fire reports, insurance claims, and help with clean-up.

Once the girls had left, Rich sat up straighter in his seat. "Torrie, we need to talk."

"I need a place to stay."

"You're not going anywhere. You're staying right here. Lulu has cleaned my grandmother's downstairs bedroom, and she's made up the bed. There's a small private bath there as well. She'll help you with anything you need once the girls are bathed. It's a perfect set-up until we figure out what we're going to do. Estella is thrilled to have Iris stay with her."

"People will talk, Rich."

"People are already talking about us. Who cares?"

"I do! They're talking about *me*!" She pounded her chest with a fist. "Now they'll start referring to me as a loose single parent."

"What do you care what anyone in this town thinks or says? It's small town gossip. People are thoughtless, cruel, and clueless. They know your family and what good people they are, and yet they gossip. Hell, Torrie, they gossip about me. Admit it. They do, don't they?"

"Yes, because they're jealous," she shot back, "not because they think you're single and promiscuous."

He ran a hand through his already rumpled hair, resisting the urge to pull it out. "I can't win with you!" He rose and paced to the open French door and looked out at the backyard where a cardinal started to scold from a far pine tree. A wind had kicked up and sent the sweet smell of flowers filtering in through the screen. His voice dropped in volume. "Torrie, I need to know what's going on with you and Ivan Winters."

She rose and went to the coffeemaker and poured herself another cup, leaning against the counter. "It's a long story, but to make it short, I owe him a little less than ten thousand dollars." When Rich stared at her, failing to react, she continued, "It was to pay off a personal debt I owed for expenses and land I needed to quickly sell in New York when Daniel died so I could move home. Now he holds it over my head, and I wait every day for the dreaded moment when he calls it in…or asks for some favor I can't grant."

"So it's a simple fix. We pay it off."

"I can't take your money."

"No way! You're not going to start with that, are you?" His gray eyes were stony with anger. "So you'd rather be indebted to Ivan Winters than take the money I'm offering? Are you in love with the damned monkey on your back?"

"No." She took her coffee back to the table and

slumped down. "You don't understand. It won't be easy, even if I agreed to take your money and pay him off." She fiddled with the cup's handle. "Ivan Winters controls this town," she explained, "and he doesn't let anyone forget it. If I pay off the loan and anger him, he'll call in our mortgage for the landscape center. Or he'll refuse loans to folks who want to buy cars at Lars' dealership. Marlene crossed him once and now she sends everyone who buys homes or real estate over to Center City to get a mortgage. Lucky for her, her father was already set up with one of the lending institutions over there. She has no use for Ivan Winters."

She covered her face with her hands and shook her head, her long hair flying around her head like a curtain. "Dear God, I don't know what to do. Everything's a mess!"

He moved to her and sat down beside her. His warm palm caressed her back. He wanted to tell her everything would be all right. He wanted to tell her the truth...he was in love with her. But this was not the right time. "We'll work it all out," he said instead. "First thing, we pay off the loan."

"But...I have no money."

"No buts, Torrie. I have the money. Please just let me handle this. For God's sake, just for once let me take care of this. I'm tired of this town and a dictator who thinks he has the right to rule every person once they've signed on the dotted line."

A sob escaped her throat and she flung herself into his arms. She started weeping, her voice muffled against his shirt. "Rich, I have nothing. Iris is right. Everything I have is ruined."

"Ah, Torrie, no," he whispered in her hair. "You

have me, babe."

"Rich, I'm so mixed up. You've been more kind to me than anyone in this town. You don't deserve all the trouble I'm handing you…and I don't deserve you.'"

He chuckled against her hair. "Well, to be honest, I like a little trouble every so often to keep me on my toes."

The minutes slipped by as he cradled her in his arms and stroked her hair. Peace settled around them like a warm winter coat. "You know," he murmured, "we could tidy up this whole mess without a lot of frustration. You could marry me. I'm not falling in love with you, Torrine Jane Larson. I *am* in love with you. And I know it's not what you want to hear right now."

"Whoa, Rich." She looked up at him and touched his face lovingly. "How would it ever work?"

He dipped his head and found her lips. They tasted sweet and a little smoky from the fire. He pulled away and looked at her. "We'll figure it out. Trust me, we'll—"

Just then the thundering of sneakered feet on the stairs brought them to reality.

"I know where Sheba is!" Estella screamed and streaked past Rich and Torrie with Iris hot on her heels wearing a too-large, blue summer outfit with the shorts hanging down below her knees. "She's in the carriage house. I just saw her go around the back of it from your upstairs bedroom window when I went to show Iris your cowboy hat. I'll bet she gets in through the hole in the broken window. I'll bet she had her kittens." She tugged at the sliding glass doors.

Rich stood and moved toward the door. "Wait. Just wait a moment." He turned to Torrie. "Holy moly, just what we need. A horde of kittens. I wonder how many a cat can have?"

"I've heard they can have as many as ten," Torrie said.

"Ten?" he bellowed. He looked around wildly and shouted into the air at the front of the house, "Lulu! Where are you? We're going to need some animal husbandry advice in the carriage house."

Lulu emerged from the hallway with an old fashioned key in her hands. "Stop shouting, you goofball. You're going to need more than just me if Sheba has a large litter. You're going to need kitten food, feeding bowls, clean bedding, litter boxes, and some very loyal friends." She hurried out the back sliding door calling after the girls, "Wait. Let me go first. Let's see if the cat's up in the top level of the carriage house like I suspect. I have the key to the door."

"Loyal friends?" Rich's eyebrows rose as he gazed at Torrie.

"To take the kittens off your hands."

Minutes later, the group huddled in the far corner of the carriage house watching Sheba, nestled in a pile of old rags, feeding six newborn kittens.

Iris and Estella squatted several feet away, enraptured by the sight of the tiny babies. Two of them were snow white, one was black, and the remaining ones were black and white. They squirmed around like one massive ball rooting for a place to suckle.

"Look, Daddy, there's one for each of us." Estella exclaimed in a jubilant whisper and clasped her hands together. "I wonder who the father is?"

"I'll bet his name is Tom," Rich muttered under his

breath and felt Torrie's sharp elbow connect with his side. "What? I'm taking a wild guess here. And I'm also guessing he has black fur." The elbow nailed him again.

"Can we touch them?" Estella asked, peering up at the grown-ups behind her.

Lulu shook her head. "No, sorry, honey. Not today. They're newborns and their eyes haven't opened yet."

"How long before they can see?" Iris asked and moved to stand beside Lulu. "Does it hurt them not being able to see?"

"About two weeks." Lulu put an arm around Iris's thin shoulder. "And no, it doesn't hurt them. It's nature's way to give their delicate eyes time to grow and be healthy. We should leave them alone for about four weeks before we touch them. If we don't, we could put a human scent on them and confuse the mother. And if you girls come up here bothering Sheba all the time, she'll hide them. We have to make her comfortable so that doesn't happen."

Lulu turned to Rich and Torrie. "We need to get a big box with some towels and holes in it and put it close by. Sheba will want to move them into a safe place. She knows she has to keep them away from sunlight so it won't bother their eyes once they start to open."

Estella popped up from the floor. "Goody! Goody! I'm so happy. Now we don't have to go home for another month." She placed her hands on her hips and stared at her father. "We're staying right here in Hickory Valley until I can play with them, aren't we, Daddy?"

"Good grief." Rich looked at the cats with a wilted gaze.

But Estella was far too excited to wait for an answer. "How can we tell if the kitten is a girl or boy?" she asked.

Only Estella, Rich thought, with her thirst for details, would ask such an awkward question. He felt like sinking into the floor. Beside him, Torrie snorted out a soft laugh.

"Lulu, a little help here," Rich drawled and pointed to the squirming balls of fur.

Lulu patted Estella on the back. "We have to be patient. It can take over a month before we can really figure it out. Their bodies need to grow, too."

"Then we really have to stay." Estella turned to Iris and grabbed her shoulders, jumping up and down and grinning. "Did you hear what Lulu said? We can be make-believe sisters for a looong time."

Rich snuck a peek at Torrie, who gave him a corner-of-the-eye glance. This time it was she who muttered, "It's going to be long month, isn't it?"

The evening shadows were dense and gray by the time Torrie and Rich and the girls carried old towels, a box, and food out to Sheba. It was even later when Estella and Iris were calmed down enough to finally eat. Lulu had gone home and Torrie was cleaning the kitchen when Rich took the girls into his study and unlocked the floor-to-ceiling cabinet holding the collection of teddy bears.

"It's a special night, girls," he announced and motioned to the cabinet shelves where all the Steiff bears of Great Grandmother Hilda Redman stared back at them. "Pick a teddy bear you want to take with you to bed tonight."

Iris's eyes were huge and round. "You mean I can

choose any of these?" She brushed her hand along the lower shelves. Rich nodded. "Even those on the top shelf. I'll get it down for you. You need to go to sleep with a smile and a cuddly bear to keep you company."

After several minutes of serious deliberation, Iris chose a honey-colored bear with a brightly colored plaid bow around his neck, and Estella chose a light taupe one with an orange scarf.

From her place at the kitchen sink, Torrie spoke up. "Are you crazy, Rich? Many of those bears are worth hundreds of dollars."

"And they're all sitting in a case gawking at me while I work," he yelled back through the doorway. He had plans to have Lulu take a picture of each of them and box them up. He needs extra shelves for work. "Anyway, this is a special occasion. Iris needs a stuffed animal of her own."

Torrie came into the study, wiping her wet hands on a dish towel. "You're an old softie." Without warning, he reached out and pulled her close to him. He kissed her lightly on the lips. "Why don't you go take a shower and get ready for bed? I'll take the girls upstairs, read them a book, take a quick shower myself, and come back down. We'll have a glass of wine on the back porch."

"I'm sorry, Rich," she said, leaning her head against his shoulder, "the shower sounds wonderful, but I'm emotionally beat from the fire and Sheba's kittens. I just want to get cleaned up and go to sleep. It's been an exhausting day."

"Understandable." He dredged up a faint smile as disappointment fell over him like a dark shadow, blocking out the anticipated joy of being with her—and the anticipated joy of giving her the diamond ring burning a hole in his pocket.

Chapter Twenty-One

Fresh from the shower, Rich wandered past Torrie's closed bedroom door and out into the kitchen. If he was disappointed she didn't want to spend a few minutes alone with him, he also understood how traumatic, chaotic, and tiring the day had been. He was mentally and physically exhausted himself. He poured himself a glass of red wine and carried it out to the porch, where he took a seat in the rocker. His mind flashed back to the encounter he had with Ivan Winters, and then it dawned on him his phone was still inside Lulu's handbag and on its way to her farm outside town. He groaned into the shadowy night. How could he have been so stupid to forget about it?

"Fine pickle you have yourself in now, Richard Lee Junior," a voice said from beside him.

"Dammit!" Rich jerked in his seat, splashing wine down the front of his T-shirt and onto the porch floor. Heart banging like a drum inside his chest, he zeroed in on the rocker beside him which set itself in motion. "You have to stop popping up without warning, Grandmother Gertie! You just wiped five years off my life. And look at the mess I've made!"

He stepped over the puddle of wine, swiping at his shirt, as he skidded away to the top of the steps.

"Don't swear, Richard Lee Junior. It's not refined. It's not polite, especially in front of your elders. Think about this. How would you like your whole earthly life to be finished, like mine?" she groused. "You think it's sheer joy to keep popping up on this silly rocker?"

"There must be a good reason why you've decided to harass me after a day like today." Rich took a sip of wine, thinking he should have grabbed the entire bottle and maybe, just maybe, the rocking-chair apparition of his grandmother might be more tolerable.

"You need to clean up the mess with Ivan Winters," she scolded. "He's going to hell, you know, unless he gets off his keister and walks the straight and narrow."

"I plan to deal with him in the morning when I send the girls out shopping. I have Marlene on it. We have a plan—loose as it may be. And there is no doubt he's going to hell, no matter what I do."

The rocking chair moved and creaked for several seconds as if Ghost Gertie was in deep thought. Finally she spoke, "You love Torrie, don't you?"

"Yes, of course."

"Then why can't you figure out how it's supposed to work for both of you, and put a ring on her finger?"

"Ah, how sweet. Now you're a relationship therapist, too? I did ask her, and she's stonewalling." He shot the rocker a withering glance.

"I figure there are two little girls who need a good home and there's a wonderful woman who could be your better half."

"Whoa, Grandmother. *Better* half? What about me?"

"As always, Richard Lee, it's not your humility that gets you in trouble."

"Okay, I agree, but it's an occupational thing. It

only happens occasionally. Tell me, what will get you off my back so you'll disappear?" Frowning, he leaned against the post connected to the porch rail.

"Occasionally?" The rocker moved more spritely this time. "Find the jewels, find your half-sister, and find real love. *Real* love, Richard Lee."

The rocker stopped. A breeze kicked up and the world around him fell silent again.

Chapter Twenty-Two

Rich lay beneath the covers, arm bent beneath his head, as he pondered what his grandmother had said. No matter how hard he tried, he couldn't divert his thoughts about Torrie from running through his head. He loved her. And he didn't need the ghost of his grandmother to tell him. He also loved Iris as much as he loved his own daughter. He tried to imagine what life would be like as the girls grew into teenagers and young adults. Electrifying and mystifying. Tumultuous, even strenuous. Everything he had come to love over the past few weeks.

The bedside clock said 2:38 a.m. when he finally convinced himself he had to get sleep or he'd be useless in the morning. Drifting off, he almost missed the light rapping on his door. It sounded again, then the door creaked open and a head peeked around the edge. "Rich," Torrie whispered, "are you awake?"

"I am now," he said and resisted a chuckle.

She tiptoed in, then eased the door closed behind her. "I can't sleep." She stood in the moonlight glowing through the window. Her hair cascaded down over her shoulders and the milky white color made her appear angelic. She was dressed in the same sexy black lingerie she had taken to New York. It highlighted every perfect curve on her delightful body.

He threw back a corner of the covers. "Come

here," he said softly. She slipped in alongside him and he drew her close, her head resting comfortably on his shoulder.

"It's so quiet down there," she said, "and I don't want to be alone tonight." She laid a hand on his chest. "I just want to be held and have someone tell me everything will be all right."

"Of course, it will." He kissed her on the corner of her forehead.

"I never asked what you learned from your visit with Dr. Winters?"

"Ivan tried to disrupt the entire meeting, but Lulu foiled his plans and got some pictures of the files. We'll find out tomorrow. She took my phone home with her." He stroked her arm lying on his chest. "I want you, Lulu, and the girls to go shopping for clothes tomorrow."

"But…but…I have no money and—"

"Shhh," he whispered. "I don't want to hear it. You're taking a fistful of cash and getting some clothes until we can figure out what can and cannot be saved in your apartment. There'll be no discussion about this."

Torrie snuggled closer, yawning, and mumbled. "You know, Richard Lee Junior, I think I'm falling in love with the belligerent side of you." She looked up at him in the dark and she found his lips, kissing him. It was gentle at first, but then became more insistent and he gave himself up to her seductive powers. Her hand slid to his waist and then downward, stroking his abdomen and silk shorts, then slid lower.

He captured her hand with his and said, "Torrie, we both desperately need sleep. We'll be worthless walking zombies tomorrow."

"Not if we hurry," she whispered and stretched up for another kiss while her hand proceeded downward to caress the exact spot she had been looking for before the interruption.

"Heck," he said and pulled her on top of him, sliding his hands down her back. "Sleep is overrated anyway."

****

Lemon yellow sunlight forced its way through the bedroom blinds and fell in a slotted pattern across the foot of the bed where Rich and Torrie were sleeping. Through a stupor of partial wakefulness, Rich heard what sounded like giggles floating out on the air…maybe somewhere nearby, maybe filtering under the bedroom door. His eyes popped open when his brain registered the noise came from across the hall and the girls were wide awake. He looked over at Torrie lying beside him. She slept deeply, soundlessly, and as motionless as a rock. Face down, her luscious hair fanned out on the pillow beside him. He rose up on his elbow and caressed the tresses, so soft they felt like silk. As much as he hated to arouse her, he leaned down and whispered, "Hey, babe, I think we have to get up and get moving."

One eyelid opened and an aquamarine eye peered at him through her blonde curtain of hair. "Why?" came the voice in an exhausted timbre.

"'Cause our girls are awake."

Her instant response caught him by surprise. "Oh. Oh! Ooooh nooo!" She gasped and rolled her naked body expertly over the top of him like a frightened gymnast and landed on her feet in front of his night stand, righting herself. "Rich, I need clothes!" She pushed back her hair flying around her head in a tousled disarray. Frantically, she searched the bedroom and probably would have wrapped herself in the nearby drapes if he hadn't gestured to the chest of drawers in the corner.

"There are clean T-shirts and a pair of sweat shorts in the top drawer," he said through a yawn.

She jerked on the dresser knobs and pulled out a pair of gray running shorts with a drawstring waist. She danced a little jig as she hurriedly jammed her feet into the pant legs. Still topless, she drew the cords until they bunched at her waist and knotted the ties, her hands shaking.

A series of footsteps in the hall jerked their heads upright. They heard Estella's clear voice tell Iris they should check with Rich before they headed down to breakfast to see what time they needed to be ready for the shopping excursion.

"They're going to be here any minute." Torrie waved a frenzied hand at him. "Stop them," she whispered with a hysterical hiss. She stepped closer to the bed and shook her finger at his nose. "And get out of that bed, Rich. Now!"

"Women," he mumbled and rose, searching the room for a pair of jeans.

Still in a state of panic, Torrie dived back into the drawer and yanked out a charcoal T-shirt. She dragged it on over her head and squinted at herself in the dresser mirror, grimacing. "Do I look pathetic or just homeless?" Her anxious eyes found his calm ones in the mirror as she finger-combed her wild hair.

"You look gorgeous," he whispered and tugged on his jeans, snapping the waist before he crossed the room and put his hand against the door to prevent it from opening. Footsteps sounded outside, drawing near, and the doorknob turned.

"Daddy, the door is stuck," Estella shouted. She pounded on the door.

Torrie shot across the room.

"Daddy, let me in!" Estella screeched.

When Rich swung the door open, pajama-clad Estella with a bear in her hand stumbled in, and he caught her, setting her upright.

"There's something wrong with the door," she whined.

"Why are you yelling?" He spoke in a calm but firm voice.

Behind Estella, Iris peeked into the room, with her teddy bear in tow, but also with a doll exactly like the one left in Estella's room when she arrived. This one had blonde hair like Iris and aqua-colored eyes.

"Look what I found this morning," Iris exclaimed with a dazzling smile. "Thank you. Thank you!'

A shiver went up Rich's back as he eyed the doll. Gertie was at it again. "You're welcome, sweetie," he said.

Estella peered around him, her gaze circling the room. She zeroed in on Torrie, who was now standing in his walk-in closet. The wire hangers squealed on the rod as Torrie pushed them aside.

"What's Torrie doing in here?" Estella asked. She stared at her father with little round suspicious eyes.

"She's…ah…she's looking for some clothes to wear."

"I thought we were taking Iris and Torrie shopping today," Estella pointed out. "Lulu, too."

225

"You are," he agreed. "But Torrie was wondering whether I might have a few everyday clothes she could borrow when she went to the gym or wanted to work in the rose beds."

Estella gave him a disbelieving look and shook her head, sending her mop of dark hair flying. She reached for Iris's hand and pulled the younger girl to the doorway. "Come on, let's go see if Lulu is here. Maybe we can get her to make some blueberry waffles and hot chocolate."

"Great idea," Rich said. "Tell her to put the coffee on. We'll be down in a minute."

Seconds later, the clomping of little feet resonated on the stairs.

From where they stood in the bedroom, Rich and Torrie sighed in relief, but not before they heard Estella say in a low conspiratorial voice, "I sure hope your mom doesn't wear that horrible outfit of Daddy's in public. She looks like my Barbie doll in fat lady's clothes."

"No," Iris replied in a serious whisper. "I think she was just trying them on to see if they would fit. Anyway, Mommy doesn't like gray. She said it makes her look washed out. What does that mean?"

"I'm not sure. Like maybe she just came out of the shower?"

****

Rich waited until Lulu, Torrie, and the girls were on their way to the local department store, before he scanned his phone Lulu had returned to him. Puzzled, he looked at the paperwork she had taken pictures of before calling the Jordan house. Laura Jordan, Kyle's wife, answered the phone.

"I was wondering how long it would take before I got this call," she said. "I told Kyle you would eventually figure it out once you realized I was Dr. Winters's nurse before we moved to Michigan."

"I don't think I have it figured out completely. Can you meet me somewhere and talk?" he asked.

"How about Webster's Burgers and Fries for dinner," she said, "and I'll explain everything then."

Minutes later, Rich telephoned Marlene and after a lengthy discussion asked her to meet him at the First National Bank. Sorting through the suits in his closet, he finally chose a crisp white shirt and brown lightweight suit to match his favorite Justin dress boots. If you were going to do banking, you had to look your best, he decided. And if you're going to get down to some real serious business dealings, you need to look like a serious-minded businessman—or lawyer, he amended his thought. Smiling, he snatched up a shoe brush and shined his boots until every inch of leather sparkled from the lizard skin toes to the hand-tooled leather shafts.

The drive down to the First National Bank took only minutes.

Marlene was waiting outside the bank when he parked the SUV across the street and strode over. She wore a stunning suit of kelly green along with white and silver four-inch heels. They flashed in the sunlight like mirrors.

"I don't know why you need me, Richard Lee," she said and threw the strap from her handbag onto her shoulder. "But I have the feeling you may need a witness." She straightened her suit jacket and looked down at his feet. "And since you're wearing those audacious-looking boots, I imagine you're not trying to hide your Texas ego either. I'm surprised you didn't wear your big white Stetson."

"Mine is a *tan* Stetson with a pinch front crease," he replied with a sour expression. "I don't know anyone who wears a white hat, unless he's impersonating the Lone Ranger or he's an unscrupulous car salesman."

"Well, excuse me." Marlene rolled her eyes. "Joe warned me to stay out of trouble if I was in cahoots with you."

"Cahoots?" Rich's forehead wrinkled. "I don't know if we even use that word any more in Texas. I'd prefer collaboration."

This time she laughed outright. "Ah, this is going to be fun. You have the temperament of a rattlesnake this morning."

"You don't have to get involved if you don't want to."

"You know I couldn't resist. You know how much I adore this two-bit bank and its good-for-nothing president. Where's Torrie, partner?"

"I sent Lulu, the girls, and her out shopping for new clothes." Rich patted his chest where his check book was tucked into an inside breast pocket. "I don't want her involved with any of this. She's afraid of Ivan Winters, and there's no point in putting her through any more trauma than she's had to experience with her roses and the fire."

"Do you think Ivan had anything to do with them?" Marlene asked.

"Well, we'll find out when we go in, won't we?"

"He'll never admit it."

Rich only raised an eyebrow and offered her a

slight smile of defiance.

"I don't like the look on your face." Marlene shook her head. "By the way, I called the police department and fire department, and as we speak, they are accompanying the restoration company to get most of Torrie's belongings sorted, removed, and cleaned. They gave me an update and said most of the clothes in dressers could be easily dry cleaned or washed without any smoky residue. The fire inspector is certain the fire started in the basement of the building in a pile of old rags soaked with gasoline."

"Thanks, Marlene. You're a saint. I hope Joe knows he's got a good woman." He winked at her.

"I hope so, too," she said. "I also rented a storage unit. Once everything is cleaned, it can be properly stored. Unfortunately, a lot of Iris's stuffed animals are ruined as well as the couch, pillows, and anything with padding or stuffing in it."

"Not a problem." He figured Estella had enough of those fuzzy things to hold hands and encircle the earth.

Rich looked at his Rolex. "Well, it's nine o'clock sharp. Banking hours have begun. Let's go pay a visit to Ivan Winters and pay a loan."

Like a true gentleman, he took her gently by the elbow and ushered her through the double glass doors, bypassing the tellers at the front and proceeding down the hallway to the offices in the back. They stopped at a receptionist's desk positioned before Ivan Winters's office. Engraved letters on a brass placard attached to a solid oak door behind the receptionist announced his position as president of the bank. Two large, plate-glass windows flanked the door, blinds drawn shut.

"We came to see Mr. Winters," Rich said to the

receptionist.

A petite young woman in a smart black business suit with matching black glasses perched on her nose looked up. "Do you have an appointment?"

"Just tell him Richard Lee Redman is here to see him."

The receptionist rose, knocked softly on the door and returned, minutes later. "I'm sorry, but he's busy. You'll have to make an appointment."

Rich leaned down next to Marlene's ear and whispered. "This is the part where the fun begins." Aloud, he spoke respectfully to the receptionist, "I don't think so, ma'am. I have important business to discuss." He strode past her desk to Ivan's office door with Marlene behind him as the receptionist leaped from her chair and scolded, "Wait! You can't go in there without his approval!"

The door swung open.

Ivan's feet barely made it off the polished cherry desktop where they had been resting. "What's the meaning of this?" he sputtered. He reshuffled his feet on the floor and inched his body upright in his chair. His face glowed red. "I told my secretary I'm not taking any appointments."

"Ivan, Ivan. Working hard again, I see." Rich grunted out a derisive chuckle. His gaze circled the room from the posh leather couch by the wall to the ornate framed pictures of what looked like Paris, France, on the far wall. He spied a round glass trophy on the corner of Ivan's desk, given to First National Bank for its donation to the local Sportsmen's Club.

Finally, his gaze settled on Ivan again. "Nice office. Do you give tours?"

"I would suggest you make an appointment," Ivan said in an icy tone. "We give tours on Fridays."

"I guess I'll pass." Richard removed the checkbook from his coat pocket, ripped off the top check, and dropped it on the desk in front of Ivan. Behind him, he heard a click as Marlene locked the door. "I came to give you a check for the remainder of what Torrie Larson owes you."

"What Torrie Larson owes me is none of your business." Ivan stood up and rounded the desk, heading for the door.

Rich yanked him by the back of his suit jacket as he passed, spun him around, and pushed him up against the front edge of his desk. "Let's get something straight, Winters," he ground out. "You're finished terrorizing this town and all the people in it—Torrie Larson included."

"Let me go." Winters unsuccessfully struggled to push him away. "I own this town," he choked out as he wiggled from Rich's grasp and tried to slip past him.

Rich spun him around again, yanking his arm behind his back and pinning it. "Now, let's chat, Ivan," he said in a dangerous low voice. "Who tore up Torrie's rose beds at my house?"

"I don't know," Ivan hissed.

"Don't make me hurt you, Ivan," Rich muttered and tightened Ivan's arm at his back.

"All right. All right. It was me," he confessed through a groan. "I hired a high school kid to do it. I figured if Torrie realized the beds were in jeopardy, she'd stop hanging around Gertie's house. But I didn't start any fires."

Rich released him, pushing him away.

Ivan stumbled, caught his balance, and staggered up. "I'm going to call the police and have you arrested," he hissed through clenched teeth. He brushed himself off and pulled his suit coat sleeves over his shirt cuffs. His expression was callous and defiant as he glared at him.

"For what?" Marlene asked. "For asking a question? For paying off a loan?" She hooted out a long musical laugh. "Good one, Ivan."

"So you're in on it, too? You were always a troublemaker, Marlene. I'll see you both never do business in this town again."

His haughty attitude only infuriated Rich more. "Quite the contrary, Winters. You're washed up around here. I've spoken with the First Federal Bank in Center City, and their board agreed to refinance any loans people have at your bank at a lower rate with better terms. Marlene has contacted all her fellow realtors who have, in turn, contacted customers having past and recent real estate transactions to tell them the good news. Letters went out yesterday announcing the spectacular refinance rates."

Rich smiled. "I also called your board members to let them know as long as you're president, I'll take all my money and my grandmother's money out of town, and I'll ask every businessman I personally know to remove every penny from this bank."

That was when Ivan grabbed the glass paper weight and charged at him, hand raised to strike. "Why you good for-nothing piece of sh—"

Rich ducked and sidestepped as Ivan rushed him, pushing a chair directly into his path. Ivan tumbled over the chair and nosedived onto the floor with the glass paper weight slamming into his jaw as he landed. Not a splinter of glass fell off the paperweight as it rabbit-hopped across the floor and landed with a thud against the wall.

"Ouch," Marlene uttered.

"Whew, that's some paperweight," Rich drawled. "Remind me to high-five a local sportsman next time I see one."

He looked at Marlene, shook his head, and grinned.

"Brought down by his own award." Marlene stifled a chuckle and opened the office door where a startled group of people had gathered and silently gaped at them as they walked out. From somewhere among the crowd, a person started clapping, and then everyone burst into an earth-shattering applause.

"How do they know?" Rich glanced at Marlene with a confused look.

"Speaker phone," she said, smiling. "I clicked it on when you were getting cozy with Ivan. I figured a few more witnesses couldn't hurt."

Chapter Twenty-Three

Rich never heard anything as pleasant as the giggles and laughter of all the women in his life barreling through the front door. Plastic bags rustled and everyone talked over each other as they dropped their precious cargo in the entranceway and headed into the kitchen where he was scarfing down one of Lulu's cinnamon muffins to tide him over until dinner. He stood at the kitchen sink with a glass of cranberry juice.

Torrie rushed up to Rich and put her arms around his waist. "We had a splendid time with your money."

He swallowed his last bit of muffin. He snuggled her closer and felt an unexpected comforting warmth surge through him. He was surprised at how much he missed her when she wasn't nearby. The scent of lemon and flowers filled the air to torture him and he whispered, "I hope you bought something like the slinky black thing you wore for three minutes the other night."

Torrie laughed.

"Guess what? We bought Iris some more stuffed animals," Estella piped up. She and Iris were each holding the bears Rich had given them and which had accompanied them on the shopping trip. "Go find the bag with the hippopotamus, Iris, and show it to my daddy."

The little girl dropped her bear on the chair beside

her and darted down the hallway. Returning, she dragged a large shopping bag behind her. When she reached the kitchen, she stopped and pulled out a chunky gray hippo with round, doleful brown eyes and a pink bow around its neck. She handed it to a smiling Rich.

"See?"

He squatted down before her. "This is a very handsome little dude, don't you think?"

"It's not a dude," Iris corrected him, giggling. She pointed to the pink bow.

"Okay, my mistake. A dude-ette? Is there such a word? So what are you going to name this little lady?" He grinned at her.

Iris giggled again and took back the hippo he offered her. "Heidi. But she's a hippopotamus so she's big."

Rich ruffled her silky head. "Good choice. Heidi the hippo. Good name."

He straightened and looked at Torrie and the two little girls. They were all becoming family to him. Iris and Estella were good for each other. They were playmates and friends…and maybe in the future they could be sisters. As an only child, he had no one to share his secrets with, no one he could share his feelings of sadness or joy. He couldn't believe how much he loved both the little girls.

"Iris, Oscar's bow is untied," Estella pointed out in a disgruntled tone.

"Oscar?" Rich asked.

"Yes, we named the bears. Mine is Olivia since she's a girl, and Iris's boy bear is Oscar." Estella reached for the bear on the chair the same time Iris's hand lunged for it. Iris held tight to its front paw.

"I'm just going to retie the bow for you," Estella said, tugging on the bear head. "I just want to help."

"No, it's my bear and I'll do it," Iris insisted, refusing to let go. She yanked harder. "I can do it. I know how. I'm not a baby!"

"But I can tie it better," Estella pointed out.

"Girls," Rich warned in a firm voice, wondering if this was the first of what might be many disputes between the two. But neither girl heard him, so caught up in a tug-of-war with the poor bear.

It ended abruptly—with Iris holding onto a front leg and Estella hanging onto the remainder of the bear.

"Girls, girls! Now look what you've done." Torrie sprang forward. "This is a genuine vintage collector's bear—"

She never had the chance to finish. Three red rubies flew out of the bear and tumbled onto the floor near Estella's feet.

Awestruck, five people stepped back and fell silent, staring at the red jewels twinkling in the sunlight.

"Well, kids," Lulu said, finding her voice while the group stared mutely at the jewels, "this could be a totally new twist to *The Three Little Bears'* fairytale." She squatted and retrieved the rubies off the floor while Rich took the bear from Estella, and shook it.

Another two jewels fell out, and the girls scrambled to pick them up.

"What are these?" Estella asked.

"Rubies. Very expensive jewels," Rich explained, and held out his hand.

"What about my bear?" Iris looked at her mother with a gloomy scowl.

Torrie stooped and hugged Iris. "Honey, Oscar can be stitched back together and he'll be just like new."

Later, when girls ran off to play, the grown-ups sat around the table drinking coffee, each deep in his own thoughts. Finally Rich spoke, "I never once thought about the shelves of bears. I thought they were a nuisance." He looked over at Lulu and Torrie. "Do either of you know anyone in town who would be willing to X-ray a horde of bears?"

"We could go out to the airport and walk a few bagsful through the TSA scanners," Torrie suggested and laughed. "No, seriously, there is no way I'm letting you rip any more of those bears apart. They're collectable antiques and much too precious."

Lulu exhaled a long sigh. "I never thought when I came here to work my life would be like a twenty-four hour soap opera. Who would have thought those bears held jewels after all these years?"

"For nearly a hundred years," Torrie said. "Do you think Gertie knew?"

"About the tale?" Rich shook his head. "Of course she did. The whole family did. When my parents were still married, I remember my mother repeating the story of the Redman rubies. I just passed it off as a colorful family legend."

"I have a friend who might help you." Lulu peered up at Rich.

"Why am I not surprised?" He had learned from his short stay in Hickory Valley that Lulu Smith knew over half the people in the town.

"He's a veterinarian and has an X-ray machine in his office. How about I give him a call and set up some type of appointment to scan them?"

Nodding, Rich said, "Set up the appointment. What's it going to cost me?"

"The vet will probably do it for a generous donation to the animal shelter." The little woman grinned. "But my involvement will be up for negotiation."

A groan slipped from his lips. "Again, why am I not surprised?"

****

Webster's Burgers and Fries was doing a brisk business when Rich arrived for dinner accompanied by Torrie. They found Laura Jordan and Denise and Danielle sitting at a round table in the far back of the room away from the noise and commotion of the rowdy crowds out front.

"I asked the girls to reserve us a quiet spot to talk," Laura said as Torrie and Rich slid into seats opposite them. She glanced at the girls with the look only a devoted, loving mother would give to her daughters. "The girls know this story. They're only here to help bolster me while I try to relate it to you."

"Well, it's always a pleasure to have these young ladies around." Rich nodded, urging her to begin.

Laura swallowed and found her voice. "I was working for Dr. Winters as his nurse when Anne Alexander realized she was pregnant by your father, Richard Redman Senior. Together, your father and she made an appointment for her to be checked. They turned to Dr. Winters here in town, inquiring about what their options might be. He told them he would support them in any decisions they made—whether Anne chose to raise the child as a single parent or give it up for adoption. Your father was trying to get a divorce from Joyce, your mother, but a lot of red tape and lawyers were holding up the final decree. Anne decided she wanted to give the child up for adoption."

"So that's how you figured into the picture?" Rich asked.

"No, not exactly." Laura paused. "I had married Kyle a year before and was also pregnant when I found out we were moving to Michigan where he'd taken a new job with a prominent car manufacturer. Ironically, I was carrying twins, but even more ironically, both Anne and I gave birth within a day of each other. She was in Hickory Valley's community hospital and I was in a hospital outside Detroit. Anne's heartache was she was giving the child up for adoption. My heartache was one of my twins, we later named Dana, only lived a few hours out of the womb. Just long enough for me to hold her."

"I'm so sorry," Rich said quietly.

With watery eyes, Laura nodded, cleared her throat, and continued. "The delivery was complicated and as a result, I was told I could never have any more children. Dr. Winters learned of the death of Dana, and was going to place Anne's baby in a foster home here in Hickory Valley until he could find suitable parents. He contacted Kyle to see how I was doing." She looked up at Rich. "Kyle refused to come today. He said he can't stand going over this one more time. Both girls are his daughters, and he has nothing more to say."

Rich nodded. "I understand completely. It must have been difficult for him as well."

Laura continued. "So the long and short of it is, Kyle and I decided we'd adopt Anne's baby." She turned to Denise and patted her hand. "We named her

Denise and raised her with Danielle as twins. No one in our small development outside Detroit ever questioned anything. I brought two babies home, just as planned. Dr. Winters and a nurse personally drove Anne's infant to me while I was still in the hospital and arranged for Denise to be taken home with Danielle."

Rich stared at Denise. She sat looking back at him with serene, calm eyes. He didn't know why he didn't see it a long time ago. She resembled his father with her straight nose and hazel eyes. And it certainly explained why his father sent a check to Henry's garage each month while he was alive. He'd bet the money was forwarded to Laura to help with costs for adopting and rearing Denise. "I see this it isn't a surprise to Denise. When did you tell her?" he asked.

Denise spoke up. "I didn't know you were my half-brother until yesterday when Mom told me. But she told me I was adopted when I was twelve. I had an appendicitis attack, and she was afraid I'd look at my charts in the hospital, as curious as I am about medical procedures." She paused and looked at her mother. "She was certain I'd eventually figure it out since I'm an AB blood type and my sister, dad, and she are A positive."

"AB, huh? Like my father and me," Rich said. "So I understand you want to be a nurse?"

Denise nodded. "Yes, I've always wanted to be a nurse, just like Mom."

"Well, there won't be any trouble with tuition costs for either of you girls. You'll inherit more than enough to give you and Danielle a superb education. I'll have to speak with both your parents, and we'll decide how you might best access your inheritance." He shook his head woefully. "I don't know why I didn't see it."

"How could you, Rich?" Torrie asked. "We all assumed they were Laura's twins."

Denise rose, wringing her hands. She asked, shyly, "Can I hug you?" A tear slipped down her cheek. "I don't know what to say to an older brother I didn't know I had. And there are so many questions I have to ask about my biological father."

Rich rose and rounded the table, meeting her half-way. He scooped her up in his arms. "You can hug me all you want, Denise. It's a terrific feeling to find out I have a sister, but it's even more heartwarming now that I've found you. And of course, you realize, you're an aunt now. Estella may drive you absolutely crazy once she finds out."

Denise laughed. "You mean all the things she's done so far don't count?"

****

Later, after Torrie, Danielle, and Laura left to give Rich and Denise some much needed time to themselves, Denise nervously folded and refolded her paper napkin until she had a tiny square. Then she unfolded it and started again.

Rich looked at her curiously. "What's the matter?"

"I need to ask a favor. And it's a big one."

"Looks like this is going to be the evening for surprises. Tell me."

"I think my Grandpa Henry set the fire below Torrie's apartment."

Rich's body stiffened, and he glanced at her in disbelief. "Henry? Why would he set a fire in his own building? And what makes you think he did?"

Denise sighed and closed her eyes for a second.

241

"Because I was at the garage the morning before the fire started."

"Go on," he urged.

She frowned, her face bleak and sorrowful. "I stopped into Grandpa's office to pick up a stack of invoices Torrie wanted me to deliver to her at the landscape center. She planned to look them over in her down time before she went to the office to process the billing online. While I was collecting them, I noticed a can of gasoline and a pile of old rags behind a stack of boxes in the office. The gasoline can must have been recently refilled because the odor was strong—like maybe it was splashed onto the outside of the can. Otherwise, I wouldn't have noticed it. I didn't think anything about the can or rags until my dad said the fire chief believed it was the cause of the fire." She fell silent a moment and looked down at her hands.

Rich blew out a long breath of air.

Denise plunged onward. "I overheard my dad telling my mom that Grandpa was worried about the mortgage he had taken out on his house to cover the last addition to the garage. Business was declining, and when he went to see Ivan Winters at the bank, he came back very upset. I knew he was disappointed he couldn't help Danielle and me with tuition and costs at the local college."

"So you think he burned the building to get insurance money?"

Denise shrugged. Her eyes were troubled. Her voice was pleading when she spoke. "Please don't tell anyone I told you this. I know he never meant to hurt Torrie or Iris. I don't think he knew they were inside the apartment. I think Grandpa was desperate. Out of sorts. Is there something you can do to help?"

Rich pondered the question for a moment, then nodded. How could he deny his just-found sister her first request? "I'll see what I can do, okay?"

Denise smiled shyly. "Okay, big brother."

Those last two words were two of the best ones he'd heard in a long time.

Chapter Twenty-Four

Rich paced, circling the confines of his study like a lion trapped in too small of a cage. In the week since he learned Denise was his half-sister, he threw himself into the work piling up from his Dallas office. He tried desperately to push Torrie and her inability to make a commitment out of his thoughts as he also struggled to play the white knight of Hickory Valley. He had to discover a way to help Henry Jordan recover from financial ruin while still keeping the old man's secret from becoming part of the public pipeline and ruining his reputation. But the women in Rich's life had other plans.

On Monday morning, Iris tiptoed into the study to interrupt his work with her adorable shy smile and her burning question: Did he ever consider becoming her daddy? And when?

On Tuesday, Lulu interrupted him to ask what he planned to do with all of Sheba's kittens—and when was he going to seal the deal and give Torrie the huge allotrope of carbon she helped him to select? He found himself looking up the word allotrope and discovering carbon had many of them besides diamonds, including graphite and coal.

On Wednesday, Elsa popped in to tell him Estella had approached her to ask if Rich and Torrie were planning to make her and Iris sisters. It was, as far as

Rich was concerned, a very legitimate question, although he was loath to mention it was Torrie who was dragging her feet. He had promised he would give her the time and space she had requested. They had made plans to go out to dinner on Sunday night, and he was hoping her answer was forthcoming.

By the time Thursday rolled around and both Denise and Marlene stopped by to ask him if the rumor was true about Torrie and him being an item, and also whether he had devised a plan to deal with Henry Jordan and the fire at Torrie's apartment, Rich was certain he was in need of some serious mental rejuvenation. If there was a modern day, female-inspired Inquisition, he had no doubt he had been the target and, like the whirligig outside, he found his brain churning as fast as it could, but going nowhere and coming up empty.

It was late afternoon, later that day, when he called an urgent meeting of the Larson brothers. A man could only suffer so much without some male empathy over a good beer. The Crazy Lady Bar was doing a vigorous business when he parked three blocks away and walked into the dimly lit interior, pushing his way past the regulars crowding around the sleek black granite bar. He found all three brothers sitting in a spacious booth in the back of the narrow dining area and nursing their first drink. They looked up with quizzical gazes as he slipped in beside Lars with a manila envelope in his hands. Across from him, Finn and Gus nodded a sober welcome.

A tall stick-like waitress with frizzy gray hair tied into a messy bun on the top of her head made a beeline for the group. She slipped a stack of menus onto the table, asking, "What'll you have to drink, honey? I see the Larson comedy team has started without you."

Honey? Rich smiled. It was the first sweet word he'd heard all week.

"A medium amber, please." He offered her a faint smile and turned his attention to the men. "I appreciate everyone coming. There are a few things I need help with."

"If it's with my sister, I'm clueless, pal." Lars took a sip of his beer, squinting at him over the frosted mug with still-sober eyes. "Trust me."

"Ditto here," Finn chimed in as a rousing cheer erupted at the bar and was followed by the birthday song crooned loudly and off-key by some very spirited regulars. "Torrie's a complete enigma and I don't want to tick her off. You know I have to work with her, right?"

The waitress interrupted their discussion with a frosted mug of beer, and he nodded his thanks.

Gus gave him a sideways glance of utter dread. "Hey, don't look at me." His tone was solemn but held a hint of alarm. "News flash. Torrie has never…ever…taken any kind of advice from me."

"Well, why am I not surprised?" Rich grinned at the youngest Larson brother, who was always the brunt of his older brothers' playful jesting. "You've never had any worthwhile advice to give." He clicked glasses with Lars while sharing a conspiratorial wink.

"Knock it off, will you?" Gus frowned and shook his head. "I have absolutely no idea why you lamented the fact you were an only child when we were growing up." He tipped his mug of beer toward his two older brothers, who were grinning. "I ask you, who needs this kind of abuse?"

"If it's any consolation," Rich admitted, "your sister's not listening to me either." The ring was still burning a hole in his pocket as proof. Besides needing more time to think about their relationship, she was also carrying around a lot of old baggage and wading through a lot of issues. The fire did little to help the situation.

"She'll come around." Lars thumped him on the back. "Torrie has been a little gun-shy with men since she's had Iris. You two are perfect for each other. You've always been her hero even when we were in high school."

"Yeah, true." Gus admitted. "To be honest, I haven't seen her this happy in a long while. I don't know how you got Ivan Winters to fall onto his own glass paperweight, but word has it he was last seen leaving town with a bruised jaw."

"Your final hurdle is the Forresters," Lars said. "Their denial of Iris as their grandchild has eaten at Torrie for six years now."

Finn spun his mug around and around slowly in his hands and shook his head sorrowfully. "Talk about a couple of dimwits. Who wouldn't want to know their only grandchild?" He squinted up at the men.

Rich straightened in his seat. "Well, on such a jovial tone, I guess I'll tell you why I'm here. I need one of you to hand deliver a package of material to them at their residence in New York and help me with my final hurdle." He shoved the manila envelope into the center of the table. "Inside are duplicate DNA samples of their son, Daniel, that I was able to get through a bit of legal manipulating, and DNA samples of Iris, as well as a series of recent pictures of her. I think it would be more effective if an uncle made the contact instead of a lawyer with a vested interest in Torrie as his future wife. I want to make one last attempt before I give up and convince Torrie to write them off and let go."

"I'll go," Lars volunteered. "Finn needs to run the landscape center. It's his busy time of the year."

"And I need Gus's help this weekend," Rich said. "Why not take Elsa with you?"

"I thought Torrie was planning to take Iris and Estella to stay with her for the three days when you're away in Dallas," Lars said.

Rich smiled. "Yes, but with Elsa helping you in New York, she can ask Torrie to babysit her boys along with our girls. It'll be the perfect opportunity to keep her away from my house in town. I want to set up a surprise for her when I come back on Sunday."

"Well, babysitting those four rascals should keep her occupied." Lars grinned.

"And if anyone can be persuasive with the Forresters, it's your sister," Rich pointed out. He remembered all the chores she used to hoodwink her brothers into doing for her when they were growing up.

"But it's not the only reason I'm here." Rich felt a sick empty feeling in the pit of his stomach and forced himself to continue. "I think I know who started the fire in the warehouse below Torrie's apartment."

Silence filled the booth and somber faces stared intently at him while he related Denise's suspicions about Henry Jordan as a likely suspect. When he finished, he was met by eerie silence. Three pairs of cautious eyes stared at him.

"Come on, guys," he broke the stillness. His gaze circled the table. "I need some help here."

Finn blew out a long breath and sat up straighter in his seat. "So Henry did it for the insurance money? Whew, I need another beer."

"Me, too," Lars agreed. He shook his head sorrowfully. "*What* was he thinking?"

"Order a shot with mine." Gus groaned. "I knew he was struggling with cash flow, but I never thought he'd be desperate enough to go to extremes."

Silence enveloped them again like a wet blanket thrown over roaring hot flames.

Finally, Gus spoke. "Well, I don't want to see Henry Jordon accused of arson. If Henry had a lapse of judgment, it was probably the result of the steep mortgage and pressure from Ivan Winters. I don't want to see the old man in trouble. He's been helping folks all over town when they were down on their luck since he started that dang garage. I can't tell you how many people had their vehicles repaired on credit or who couldn't pay and were given a special Henry Jordan discount. There were others he wrote off, knowing they'd never be able to pay."

"I'm certain Torrie doesn't want Henry to be reported to the police and come to any harm," Finn admitted. "She's been responsible for his bookkeeping for quite a few years now. And she says no matter how tight the budget was, Henry was always a man of integrity, making certain all the employees were paid even before he was."

All three brothers' heads bobbed in agreement.

"Well, considering he's my sister's grandfather, I'm not one for stirring up any dust either," Rich admitted. He remembered Torrie telling him Henry had let her slide on her rent a month or two when she was short of cash. With a hopeful gaze, he regarded the three men who were like brothers to him. An idea had been simmering in his head all week. "Do any of you know what the warehouse site is zoned?"

"I believe it's commercial and a portion was grandfathered in as residential," Lars admitted. "That's why the apartment is still there."

"What does the town need if the building was razed? Maybe we could join forces, buy the warehouse, raze it, and build a business complex which we could collectively share and profit from."

Gus's face came alive. "Hmmm. Not a bad idea. Once demolished, we could build a car wash on one end, and on the other, I'd rent space for a motorcycle repair shop. Or we could set up space for storage rentals. The town is in desperate need of those. I'm guessing everyone here is agreeable to throwing in some cash for this?"

Around the table, everyone nodded.

Rich picked up the stack of menus and distributed one to each brother. "But I thought you wanted to go to North Carolina and work on race cars, Gus."

"My first love has always been motorcycles." Gus took a sip of beer. "If I had the choice of staying here or moving away, I'd choose Hickory Valley and you clowns, hands down."

"Then it's settled." Rich smacked his hand on the table and signaled for the waitress. "Gus and I will present our plan to Henry before I fly out to Dallas late tonight. I'm in for my share of costs for whatever it takes to buy the building, demolish it, and establish a legitimate business you fellas come up with. Let's order and brainstorm while we eat. I'll be back on Sunday. Watch out for my girls, will you? Torrie said something about an amusement park with Elsa's boys, and she was going to enlist your help on Saturday."

A series of groans and snickers spewed out from Gus and Finn's mouths.

"And one more favor."

"Sure, man." Gus gave him an evil look. "What can be worse than spending an afternoon on thrill rides at an amusement park with four squealing, sticky-fingered kids?"

With a smug grin, Rich's gaze flashed around the table. "I need you to find homes for six kittens before your precious niece and my darling daughter get permanently attached to the little fur balls."

"You are really pushing your luck, man," Gus said.

****

Torrie sat at Elsa's kitchen table with her hands propped under her chin and an unfinished slice of cinnamon toast beside her. Outside, a pale, uncertain Saturday sun struggled to heave itself over the horizon to greet the day. Faint rays peeked from behind low early morning clouds to shine weakly on the damp summer lawn. Soon its rays would light up the kitchen windowsill and the array of herbs Elsa cultivated in colorful pots.

On the table, a vintage white rose, one of the first of the season, stood in a cut-glass bud vase. From the backside of the house, Torrie could hear the whispers and giggles of Elsa's boys and those of Estella and Iris as they roused themselves awake. There was excitement in the air ever since she had told them, when she arrived with the girls yesterday, she was taking all of them to an amusement park. By late morning, it would be a glorious day for enjoying rides, French fries, ice cream, and lots of giggles at Thrills and Spills Wonderland. She only hoped she and Gus could keep everyone happy, and she could devise a plausible excuse to escape riding any of the four roller coasters at the park. She hated heights and open cars on rails traveling at breakneck speeds.

But it wasn't amusement rides troubling Torrie the most. All week she pondered her dilemma with Rich Redman. He had flown out on Friday evening to Texas to finish some business. He was planning to take her to dinner on Sunday night when he returned. She suspected he would choose the German restaurant beside Gibson Lake where they had first dined.

Torrie knew it was time to make a decision about their relationship and his offer of marriage. She was being unfair to him. If the truth were told, she was in love with him and his precocious little daughter. Even though they had only been together again for four weeks, the pull between them was indisputable. She had to admit she had harbored a secret crush on him since she was eleven years old and hung like an idiot upside down on her monkey bars, daring him to best her. He was one of the most generous men she'd ever met. Thanks to him, she no longer had to worry about Ivan Winters and her loan. Rich unselfishly offered security, continuity, and stability. And not only for her, but for Iris as well. It was wonderful to be around someone who found the details of your average, everyday life fascinating, or could sit around a table of females with cardboard crowns on their pink highlighted hair and stuffed animals under their arms and be completely relaxed and comfortable. And his crooked, sexy grin would melt any woman's insides. So why was it so hard to take the plunge? Maybe because for the second time in her life, she just might be in love. And it was absolutely terrifying.

"Have you brooded long enough?" Elsa asked, stirring Torrie from her thoughts as she came into the kitchen, slipping on a pair of silver hoop earrings to accent her tailored blue suit. "You're on breakfast detail. I promised Lars I'd meet him in a half hour at the dealership to help with some business he has in upstate New York."

"Gee whiz, Elsa, I don't know what to do." Torrie sighed.

"With the roses? With your life? Or with Rich Redman? I need a little direction here before I offer some unsolicited advice." Elsa smiled, slipped the carafe from the coffeemaker, and poured them both a cup. She sat across from Torrie and shoved the cream and sugar toward her. "You know, worry is like being stuck in deep mud. The wheels keep turning, but nothing happens."

"But did you ever worry about giving up your freedom? Your independence?" Torrie asked.

"Well, there were no bells clanging in my head as a reassuring sign Neil and I were meant for each other." Elsa gave a half laugh. "And I never thought about giving up any freedom, but rather how terrific it would be to have someone who cared for me—to have someone to share my accomplishments with and someone to bolster me in my failures. Neil gives me a sense of belonging. He's not a person who would

253

demand my undivided attention and devotion only to him. And Rich Redman is the last person who'd ever steal your freedom from you. I have the feeling he likes strong independent women. And he's a romantic at heart. He'll love and treasure you to the ends of the earth." Elsa took a sip of coffee. "Maybe it's time you moved on with your life."

"I know." Staring into the coffee cup like it was a crystal ball, Torrie took another teaspoon of sugar and stirred it into the brown liquid.

"Marriage is not a fifty-fifty union," Elsa said. "It's one-hundred percent merging with another hundred percent to make two-hundred percent. And it has to have flexibility because sometimes, as a wife, you'll have to carry more than a hundred percent of the workload, and other times those numbers drastically flip-flop. It's give and take, Torrie. The question you have to ask yourself is: Do you love him?"

Elsa rose, went to the window and looked out, then turned and smiled. "So if you're going out to dinner again on Sunday night, how about you rummage through my closet while I'm gone and pull out my aquamarine dress to wear? And shoes. Wait until you see what I bought. A pair of silver sandals with four-inch heels. Together, they'll make Rich Redman think he's the luckiest man alive when you two reconnect tomorrow! So lucky that hunky Rich will rue the thought of taking you to dinner and wasting time eating in a restaurant."

"Gee whiz, Elsa, you have to stop playing up the sex angle."

Elsa laughed. "I'm a married women with two kids. Please let me have my fantasies."

Chapter Twenty-Five

Rich Redman paced the kitchen from the French doors back to the sink and over to the oven and back again where Lulu was finishing up washing some pots and pans. On each pass, he stopped long enough at the sink to jingle the change in his pocket before setting off again.

Lulu's sudsy hands flew out of the sink, sending bubbles into the air. "Would you stop the infernal pacing!" she scolded. "For criminy sakes, you're making *me* nervous. Everything is ready. The dinner will be perfect." She wiped her hands on a kitchen towel and tore her yellow apron off from around her slight frame. "All the food is warming nicely in the oven. Just keep the foil covers on until the last minute when you serve the food onto the plates."

She glanced over at Rich, who was back at the stove, peering into the oven with the inside light on. "What do you hope to see in there? Oven imps? Trust me, Richard Lee, you can't mess this dinner up. A child could serve roast beef and vegetables."

"Lulu, have you ever seen me cooking anything?" Rich slumped against the counter and crossed his arms, watching her put away the last of the bowls and pots she had used.

"No, come to think of it, I don't believe I have."

"Case closed. I could mess this up without any

effort."

"You're telling me that you've never cooked *anything*?"

"Do Ramen noodles count?" Rich pinched the bridge of his nose and looked down at the little woman.

"Oh, boy." She looked at him like he had grown two heads, but she recovered quickly.

"And I want this to be perfect."

"It will be perfect." Lulu grabbed her purse from the counter and went to him, patting him on the arm. "You'll be fine. Once she sees that gigantic diamond, she won't even be hungry. At least not for dinner."

"Lulu!"

"For pity's sake, Richard Lee Junior, get yourself a stiff drink to calm your jittery nerves. Use some of that expensive whiskey hidden in the study and go outside and cool off. Try counting the number of twinkle lights you had Gus string all over the back porch to look like Disney World. Meditate or star gaze. But please settle down. I'll see you tomorrow."

"Thank you, Lulu." He wrapped an arm around her thin shoulders. "You're the best. I owe you!"

"You *finally* got that right, knucklehead." She winked and headed for the door.

Minutes later, Rich went out to the decorated porch with a glass of whiskey on the rocks. It was a perfect night for a romantic outdoor dinner. The air was balmy and overhead stars, bright as the twinkle lights on the porch, were scattered across an inky sky.

"Lovely night, Richard Lee," a voice said from the side of the porch.

Caught off guard, Rich jumped and choked on a mouthful of his drink. He swallowed so suddenly the whiskey burned a trail clear down to his toes. He coughed, his eyes watering, and fished out an ice cube, popping it in his mouth to soothe his throat. "For the love of Pete, you have to stop popping up like this, Grandmother Gertie. You have to go to the next dimension or I'm going to go crazy. What don't you understand about heaven and hell?"

He drew in a huge breath. "I finished everything you requested in the letter. I found the jewels and I located my half-sister. We have the vintage roses robustly growing from both grafting and cuttings. What more do you want? See all those stars up there?" He waved his hand frantically at the sky. "Go find them. Go find cloud nine. Please go to the Light. Cut me a break and pleeeeese go to the Light or tell me what I need to do to get you out of my hair forever."

"Get a grip, Richard Lee," Gertie scolded.

"No, I'm serious. Dead serious. No pun intended. Must I smudge every room in this old house with sage? Call a priest to sprinkle holy water? Get a shaman with divination skills?"

Gertie snorted. "Like a little sage is going to scare me! Have you ever heard of the phrase 'it's like heaven on earth'? That's what I've had while I've watched you find your way back to Hickory Valley."

Rich leaned against the post and stared at the rocking chair which was slowly and methodically moving on the tranquil, windless night. One niggling question still bothered him, erratically surfacing from his thoughts. "Tell me, did you put those dolls in Estella's room?"

Gertie's chuckle was light and lilting. "I thought the girls would like them. I thought it would make them feel a little more at home. They were from your Great Grandmother Hilda's collection in the attic."

"Ah, ha. I see." Rich rubbed his chin. "So tell me. What more do you want from me?"

"Nothing more, Richard Lee. Just stopped by to offer some parting words of wisdom to you."

"I can't wait."

"Remember the heart often sees what the eyes cannot."

"Both my heart and my eyes want Torrie Larson for my wife," Rich admitted. "They have from the moment I saw her in those oversized coveralls with blue nail polish on her fingernails."

"Then ask her. Convince her. '*Keep love in your heart. A life without it is like a sunless garden when the flowers are dead.*'"

"Oscar Wilde, your favorite writer." Rich leveled his gaze toward the flower gardens out on the lawn, visible through the dim light shining from the gazebo. The roses were starting to bloom and their white buds shone as if someone blew luminous bubbles through the air and they drifted downward, floating just above the ground. They were exquisite. The smell was intoxicating.

But when he turned back to the rocking chair to mention it, the rocker stood unmoving.

Silence surrounded him.

"Gertie?" he asked.

Chapter Twenty-Six

Late Sunday afternoon in Elsa's bedroom, Torrie ran a hand over her aquamarine dress and looked in the mirror, straightening a loose strand escaping from the fancy clip she had used secure her hair on the top of her head. Purse in hand, she headed out to the kitchen and passed the family room where both Gus and Neil were now sitting on the floor among a half dozen plastic boxes of Legos and four rambunctious children. Elsa had called to say she and Lars were running late from their business trip to upstate New York, but Gus had gladly stepped up to help Neil babysit until Elsa and Lars returned.

Rich Redman had called her and the girls every day he was away. If the truth be told, Torrie missed him more than she cared to admit, and she was looking forward to seeing him. Estella was staying one more night with Iris at Elsa's house. Gus had rented an old *Star Wars* film and popcorn was on the list of many things for movie night with the children. Torrie stopped and peered in, watching them noisily playing and showing off their elaborate creations to each other.

Gus glanced up from his Lego design of what looked like a misfit starship and caught her gaze. "Wow, you look spectacular, Sis. Like a princess. You're gonna make every guy at the restaurant jealous of Rich Redman."

Torrie smiled and stepped into the room. "You guys have this movie night under control, right?" She stooped to kiss Iris and Estella on the top of their heads.

Neil looked up and whistled under his breath. "Whew, Gus is not kidding. Looking good, Torrie. And yes, this isn't my first rodeo babysitting a bunch of kids on a sugar surge." He smiled. "Go, go. Have a good time. Tell Rich we said hey. We'll be sure to get the girls back to the house on Monday morning."

On the drive to meet Rich, Torrie pondered her life over the last few months. In just four short weeks, Rich Redman had turned it upside down and filled a void she thought would never be filled. It was nice to feel safe and protected. Nice to trust someone. Torrie felt like a dozen butterflies were fluttering around in her stomach. She had to come to a decision about their future relationship. To be fair, she had to do it tonight.

****

Rich Redman waited at the front of the house, apprehensively pacing the front drive like a man about to scratch off a lottery ticket in hopes it was a winner. For the last three days, all he could think about was Torrie Larson. He had deep feelings for her, even though he wasn't sure how or when they started. Maybe it was a collective realization that crept up on him. She was a beautiful woman who had courage, strength, tenacity…and yet a sweetness and warmth about her. And tonight, he was not going to let her stall or throw up barriers to justify why they couldn't be together forever. "*'Keep love in your heart. A life without it is like a sunless garden when the flowers are dead,*'" he repeated under his breath.

Minutes later, when Torrie pulled her vehicle up to

the house, he went to the door and helped her out. His heart skipped a beat just touching her. She was luscious and sexy and her four-inch heels accented legs men would die for. The aquamarine dress she had chosen, the same color as her eyes, wrapped her up into one stunning package. He kissed her lightly but possessively on her lips. "I've missed you," he admitted. "A lot."

"I missed you, too," she said and stepped backward, "and I have exciting news. The roses are starting to bloom!"

"I know, I saw them when I arrived home." The word home reverberated in his head like a beating drum. Home. Home. Home. He had really started to think of Hickory Valley as home.

"Isn't it wonderful?" She laughed, then dangled the car keys in front of his face. "Do you want to drive? We really need to celebrate. Where are we going?"

"Nowhere." He took the keys, pulled her abruptly against his body, and soundly kissed her again, this time more possessively. He was surprised when she returned the kiss just as passionately. "We're dining in tonight. Just us," he whispered against her lips.

He led her up the front walk and through the house to the kitchen, redolent with the warm spicy smell of food, until they reached the back porch which had been elaborately festooned with tiny white lights hanging from the railing and twined around the posts. He gestured to the yard, where a freshly painted white gazebo held a small intimate table for two. A dozen white candles in glass holders lit up the newly screened-in interior.

"It's exquisite!" she cried and covered her mouth

with her hand. "However did you repair the poor thing so quickly?"

"Gus and Joe with a crew worked on it over the last few days." He grabbed her hand and pulled her back into the kitchen. "Lulu wanted to stay and serve us, but I decided we could easily handle our own plates. Tonight it's all about us. The wine is uncorked and chilling in the gazebo. Why don't you go out and pour us a glass while I bring a tray with our plates?"

Minutes later, once they were seated, Torrie gently touched the four white roses in a brass vase on the table. "Four?" she asked. "You picked four roses? For the four weeks we've known each other?"

He smiled. "I'm told the Chinese believe the number four is sometimes considered unlucky like our number thirteen, but the Buddhists think it represents the four greatest powers of our planet: earth, wind, water and fire. For me, it's an auspicious number. We met on June 4th. We went out to dinner four days later. It's been four weeks since our first encounter. And let's not forget there are four people I want to make into a family."

"How sweet. Elsa insisted you were a romantic at heart!"

"Speaking of Elsa," Rich removed a letter from his inside coat pocket. "Here's a sealed letter from the Forresters. I have no idea what it says."

"How did you get this?" Torrie eyed him cautiously, her eyes flitting from his face to the letter.

"I sent Lars and Elsa to upstate New York to hammer them with irrefutable evidence and, with a little bit of persuasion, to convince them Iris is their granddaughter."

"So that's where Elsa and Lars disappeared to?" Her lips curved downward into a frown. "You sent them without asking me?"

He interrupted, before her temper reached a full boil, "Admit it, Torrie, you would have said no, and this hang-up with Daniel's parents is a wedge we have to remove before you can go on with your life and forward with me. It's eating at your very soul, and it's hanging over everyone's heads like a thick black cloud. Open the letter and let's see what they have to say."

With much apprehension, she slipped her fingernail under the seal and removed a sheet of paper. It was a handwritten note. Silence surrounded them as she read it, and finally looked up at him with a startled expression. "They say they know I'm hurt and angry with them, and after talking to Lars and Elsa, they want me to meet with them at my own convenience. I can choose the day, time, and place...and if I wish, I can bring Iris with me. They understand my trepidation and are willing to give me all the time I need to come to terms with their reckless and cruel behavior." She waved the letter at him "How did you do this?"

"I didn't do it. Your sister is quite a formidable force. And let's not forget your brother is a car salesman."

"Unbelievable. This is the best present I could ever have. For six years it's eaten half my heart away thinking they actually believed Iris wasn't their grandchild and I'd cheated on Daniel." Tears in her eyes, she pushed her chair back from the table and rounded it to take his face in her hands. She kissed him tenderly on the mouth. "I love you, I really do. Thank you."

He pulled her down onto his lap, reached into his coat pocket again, and pulled out a velvet ring box. "I love you, too. I want you to marry me. I'd get down on one knee, but this is so much cozier." He squeezed her gently. "Don't cry. Please don't cry. I want you to marry me. I want you to raise as many white Austrian vintage roses as your heart desires. I want to have more kids with you. I want to be part of your crazy family with all your lunatic brothers. I want you to be my wife. I want us to live here in Hickory Valley." He flipped open the ring box and a huge square diamond, surrounded by twelve small round ones, glittered in the candlelight. "What do you say, Torrie Jane Larson?"

"Yes. Yes!" she squealed, swiping the tears from her cheeks. She pulled his face toward her and kissed him passionately on the lips again. "I say, yes!"

Grinning, he removed the diamond and placed it on her ring finger.

"You know, to be honest, I'm not really hungry," she admitted sheepishly. She slid off his lap and stood. "For food." Her aqua gaze pierced the distance between them and shone with a glint of expectation. She held out her hand. "Unless you are."

"What I'm starved for isn't on this table." He rose. "This can all be rewarmed." He grabbed her hand and pulled her up the yard and onto the porch.

"Wait!" she said, turning. "I want to see the gazebo all lit up one more time. The candles might be out when we come back later. I can't believe you restored it. It's exquisite. We're going to have many meals out there, just like your grandmother and grandfather did. And I want to get married out there by the gazebo and the roses. With only family and close friends in attendance."

"Anything you want," he agreed.

"And I want our girls dressed in frothy pink dresses."

"I'm sure they'd love that idea."

"And I want Lulu Smith to work for us."

"I'm certain she wouldn't have it any other way." His mouth quirked with humor. "But we have to wean her from those Redman points before I go broke."

Together they stood on the lighted porch and looked out into the night. After a few minutes, Torrie turned and placed her hands around Rich's neck. She sighed and gave him a stunning, but happy smile. "Everything is beautiful. Thank you for such a perfect night."

"No, you're beautiful," he whispered and drew her into a warm hug, his arms wrapped around her, his cheek resting on the side of her face. "And the night is still full of pleasant surprises," he whispered near her ear. He hungrily kissed her like a drowning man needing to replenish himself with oxygen.

Around them a warm breeze kicked up and swept in from somewhere by the side of the porch where the rocking chairs stood. It seemed to surround them, embracing them in a warm cocoon of swirling wind, caressing and circling them for a brief moment before sweeping away into the yard, over the gazebo, and into the star-filled sky above.

Pulling away, Torrie looked around with a bewildered expression. "Heavens, I don't know what just happened, but it was delightfully unexpected and surprising."

From the corner of his eye, Rich took a peek at the

last rocker on the porch, but it stood rock still. "Oh, darling, you have no idea how surprising it could have been," he said. "No idea at all."

A word about the author...

Judy Ann Davis began her career in writing as a copy and continuity writer for radio and television in Scranton, PA. She holds a degree in Journalism and Communications and has written for industry and education throughout her career.

Over a dozen of her short stories have appeared in various literary and small magazines and anthologies, and have received numerous awards.

When Judy Ann is not behind a computer, you can find her looking for anything humorous to make her laugh or swinging a golf club where the chuckles are few.

She is a member of Pennwriters, Inc. and Romance Writers of America, and divides her time between Central Pennsylvania and New Smyrna Beach, Florida.

Visit her on:

Her blog: www.judyanndavis.blogspot.com

The web: www.judyanndavis.com

Facebook: Judy Ann Davis Author

Twitter: JudyAnnDavis4

Pinterest: www.pinterest.com/judyanndavis44/

Author Page:

https://www.amazon.com/Judy-Ann-Davis/e/B006GXN502/

Goodreads:

https://www.goodreads.com/author/show/4353662.Judy_Ann_Davis